Return to Death

A Mortician Murder Mystery-Book 1

A. E. Howe

Books in the
Mortician Murder Mystery Series
(in order):

Return to Death
Gambling on Death

ISBN-13: 978-1-7346541-5-8

CHAPTER ONE

Kay Lamberton slammed the stick into gear as she accelerated out of Gainesville. *Why am I doing this?* she asked herself before reaching down and turning up the volume on the cassette player. The Doors competed with the engine for audio dominance. Kay was grateful that she didn't have to listen to the radio. All that had been on for the past week were reports about the attempted assassination of President Reagan.

When she passed the sign informing her that she'd entered Melon County, even the music couldn't drown out the anger and the questions running through her head. In only fifteen miles she'd have to deal with a lot of crap that she thought she'd left behind.

The small town of Lang, Florida was warm and sleepy on this Tuesday afternoon in early April. The limbs of live oak trees stretched over the streets, hung with Spanish moss that dangled low enough for children to reach up and touch. Kay felt a stab of painful nostalgia as she entered the town. She'd been born in Gainesville at Alachua General Hospital, but the neighborhoods of Lang, where she'd been the mortician's daughter, were home.

The old grey Victorian that she'd grown up in was

courted on all sides by live oaks and magnolias, which in turn were attended by a retinue of azaleas. Immediately, Kay noticed that the grass was unevenly cut and the south side of the house was badly in need of a pressure washing. She wasn't surprised. Wasn't that why she was there? Not to mow the yard and clean the house, but to fix it. Fix the mess that her father had left behind. She had to remind herself that it wasn't his fault. He certainly hadn't expected to die of pneumonia before he turned fifty-five.

She parked around back beside the old hearse, which was cloaked in enough dust that she could have written her name on the rear windshield. It was amazing that some smart-ass kid hadn't already scrawled *Help! Let me out!* on the glass.

Sighing, she got out of the car, leaving her luggage behind. She'd have to make more than one trip anyway, and she wanted to get the dreaded confrontation with her little brother over with. Not calling ahead had been the right thing to do, but it meant that the conversation would probably start with him accusing her of crashing his little party.

The back door was unlocked. Also not a surprise.

"Hello!" she shouted, walking into the house. Lee could have been anywhere.

"Coming!" Kay heard a man answer. She kept on walking through the embalming room. There were no bodies, she noted.

"What are you doing back there?" A tall, thin man with long and lanky dark hair, who couldn't have been more than twenty, stood in the doorway, frowning at Kay.

"Who are you?" Kay asked, looking him up and down. He was dressed in a black jacket, tie and black pants. The jacket was unbuttoned and Kay could see a couple of stains on his white shirt.

"I work here. Who are *you*?" he said, looking more perturbed.

"I'm Lee's sister and half-owner of this funeral home," Kay said, and was pleased to see the startled look on the man's face.

"Oh."

"So?" Kay said, narrowing her eyes for emphasis.

"I'm Lester Andrews. I work here." He turned his head and yelled, "Lee! Your sister's here!"

"What?" came a reply from upstairs.

Kay shook her head when Lester started to answer. "I'll take care of this," she told him as she brushed past him.

She was mildly satisfied that the foyer, and what she could see of the casket room and the viewing room, weren't in a complete state of disrepair. *How much could the place have gone to wrack and ruin in three months?* she asked herself, and then remembered that she was talking about the destructive force of her little brother.

"Lee!" she thundered, facing up the six-foot-wide staircase.

In seconds, her half-dressed brother stood at the top of the stairs, running his hand through his brown hair and looking down at her with a stunned expression on his face.

"You didn't call," was all he managed to say.

Kay looked at him, taking in his five-foot-ten frame that was carrying a few extra pounds, but was still in the type of shape that a twenty-six-year-old could maintain without much effort. He was wearing black dress pants, a white T-shirt, socks and no shoes.

"Crazy me, I thought I could just drop in, seeing as I own half the business."

"Yeah, right, of course." Lee started down the stairs, half tripping in his socks. "I'm just surprised."

"Who is he?" Kay pointed to Lester, who had followed her into the hallway.

"That's Lester."

"He *told* me his name. I mean what is he doing here?"

"He's… he's helping out. You know, wants to be a funeral director," Lee said as he reached the bottom step.

"You can't afford any full-time employees. You've got Jerome if you need a hand with a funeral."

"Well, things come up. Jerome has his regular job." Lee stopped talking when he saw the look on Kay's face, then added brightly, "We had a funeral today."

"How many have you had this week?"

"It's been kind of slow."

"How many?"

"The one today. But we had the viewing yesterday."

"How many last month?"

"Like I said, it's been…"

"How many?"

"Total?"

"*Yes.*" Kay felt her blood rising. She'd tried to prepare herself for this, but there was a big difference between suspecting it and seeing lifetimes of work by her grandfather and father going down the drain.

"Three burials."

Kay winced. It was worse than she thought. "Dad said that you need to bury two people a week to stay afloat. Three to make a decent profit. You're not even managing one a week."

"That's not fair. There were slow times when Dad… was alive."

Kay saw his jaw clench. She knew that their father's death had been harder for Lee than for her. Harder for him for the very same reason he couldn't be trusted to run the funeral home. Lee had always been the baby of the family.

"I'm going to be here for one week so we can get this all cleared up." Kay turned and headed back out to the car to bring in her stuff.

"What do you mean 'cleared up?' What do we need to clear up?" There was an edge of desperation in Lee's voice as he followed her out of the house.

"I told you on the phone last month. You can't run the funeral home."

"No, wait, we haven't talked this over." The desperation was now mixed with anger.

"How many clients have you lost?"

"What do you mean?"

Kay stopped, slapped her hand against one of the carport columns, then looked him square in the eyes. "How many deaths around here do you know of that have gone to other funeral homes?"

"A few."

"No. The number."

"Since when?" Lee muttered, looking anywhere but into her eyes. She knew he was stalling.

"Since three months ago when Dad died."

After a long pause, Lee said very quietly, "Fifteen."

"See."

"But we've taken care of ten people who passed away," he pleaded.

"You can't lose more than half your business. You're operating at a loss. Dad barely kept this place afloat as it was."

"I may not be the best salesman," Lee admitted.

"It's not even about that. Those fifteen families would have come here when Dad was alive. He didn't have to sell himself. You're twenty-six. Too young. People just don't feel comfortable with a funeral director who's young. Even Dad worked for several years under his own father."

"We had ten funerals," Lee repeated defiantly.

"In three months." She turned away.

"I'm good at this. I don't want to work for someone

else," he said as Kay opened the hatchback of her car.

"Lee, you're an artist when it comes to embalming someone. But that's not good enough to keep this place running."

"Hi, dear!" came a loud, clear voice from the window of the apartment over the carport. Kay didn't need to look up to know that it was Ruby Bowen. Her father had hired the eccentric older woman as a housekeeper over a year ago, the latest in a long line of similar hires since their mother had died.

"Are you going to tell Ruby that we're closing?" Lee said in a hoarse whisper.

"Eventually." That was one job she wasn't looking forward to.

"Let's talk this out. We can come up with a solution," Lee begged.

"We can talk, but it's not going to make any difference. When we were in the lawyer's office after Dad's funeral, I knew this was where we'd end up." She took pity on her younger brother. "Dad never expected to die when he was only fifty-four. If he'd lived to be sixty-five or seventy, then you'd have been ready to take over the business. In that case, I'd have sold you my half and everything would be great. But not like this. You couldn't buy my half if you wanted to. Even if you had the money, I wouldn't sell it to you knowing that in a year or two you'd be broke and the place would be sold to whichever funeral home in Gainesville could come up with the money to pay its debts and take it over."

"So you'll just sell it to them now?" Lee asked as they heard the slow and steady steps of Ruby coming down the stairs from her apartment.

"We don't have any choice." Kay lifted her suitcase and duffel bag from the car.

"We? Do I have any say in this?"

"If there aren't any choices, then what good is it to have a say?"

"What's all this shouting about?" Ruby asked as she joined them and reached for Kay's bags. "Let me help you with those."

"I've got them. Thanks." Kay wondered what would have happened if she'd handed over either one of the bags. Both of them weighed at least forty pounds. At only five feet tall and one hundred and thirty pounds, Ruby was squat and sturdy, but how much could she carry at her age?

"Then you have to let me fix you a snack." Ruby was already heading for the kitchen door.

Kay knew there was no way she'd get out of this without eating something. "*Just* a snack. I had a big lunch."

"We've got some wonderful strawberries. The last of the season."

"*You're* going to tell her she's losing her job… and her home," Lee told Kay.

"Later." Kay was already exhausted. Closing the funeral home was going to be worse than she'd imagined. *I was delusional to think that Lee might be reasonable.*

"It's not just Ruby. You have to fire Jerome too."

"Jerome is only part-time. He's got his full-time job as a deputy. You can fire Lester."

"I don't want to fire anyone," Lee said defensively. "We just need some time…" They were still talking in gruff whispers to keep from being overheard.

"Enough," Kay said when they reached the stairs. "Carry this."

Kay tossed the duffel bag at Lee and he almost fell over backward catching it. For a moment he looked like he was going to toss it back or just let it drop, but instead he started up the stairs.

"I'm not going to give up without a fight," he grumbled

just loud enough for Kay to hear him.

"Fight all you want." She followed him up the stairs, carrying the suitcase.

Ten minutes later, everyone gathered in the small kitchen as Ruby fried up cheese sandwiches. Kay and Lee exchanged looks over the table, but they both kept silent about her plans to sell the home. Neither wanted to be the one to give Ruby and Lester the bad news.

After Kay escaped upstairs to her room, she grabbed a change of clothes from the duffel bag, then headed to the bathroom for a shower. Stripped down to her bra and underwear, she looked at herself in the full-length mirror on the inside of the door and frowned. Her shoulder-length brown hair was boring. A few times when she was younger, she'd tried covering it with peroxide and ended up with a straw-colored mess. It was worth a laugh, but not a long-term solution.

She looked at her shoulders, flexing right and left. *Too broad for a woman's figure*, she thought, frowning some more. Then she remembered how well that upper-body strength had served her when she'd enlisted in the Army as a nurse.

She'd arrived in Vietnam one month before the Battle of Hamburger Hill. In two months, she'd gone from a child to a woman who could drag wounded soldiers from tent to tent, or pack up a temporary aid station for deployment or evac in an hour. She'd had a hard time at first, with the soldiers thinking she was more a sister or a girlfriend than a nurse. Then, one night while she was getting some much-needed sleep, a mortar round had gone off outside her tent. The piece of shrapnel wasn't very large, but it had left a small scar on the soft curve where her neck met her shoulder.

In the mirror, she watched her fingers lightly stroke the scar tissue. She hadn't told her patients, but word had eventually gotten around that she had a Purple Heart and the scar to go with it. She'd done a number of brave and stupid things before that moment to help save lives, but somehow the fact that she'd been touched by the searing hot metal of a Vietnamese mortar shell had made her one of them in the eyes of the other soldiers. That acceptance made her proud. Proud of the scar, and proud of the soldiers and civilians she'd helped during her two tours of duty.

Kay took one last look in the mirror. Her body might not have been the type to grab the eye of every man on the street, but that had never bothered her. She just wished it was a little more attractive to some of the men that she *did* want to notice her. She climbed into the clawfoot tub, then drew the curtain and let the almost-too-hot water wash away the miles and the years since she'd last spent much time in this house.

Back in her room she walked around, looking at the trinkets from her childhood. Since she'd left the funeral home for good fifteen years earlier, her room had been used only for the occasional overnight guest. Her father, widowed when Kay was only fourteen, had never brought himself to change anything.

Am I right to force Lee to sell the funeral home? Our home? she asked herself.

Lee couldn't run it alone. That much was clear, and she'd known it from the day that their father had died. Lee wasn't mature enough to handle running the business, and there wasn't enough money to hire someone to help him. There was no other choice but to sell.

Kay ran her hand over the pine bookcase where her mother had painted vines running up and around each shelf. Her fingers lingered next to the five Parker Family mystery books that her parents had given her for Christmas when she was twelve years old. The stories revolved around a brother and sister, Joey and Ellie Parker, who solved mysteries in their small town. At the time, Kay had been sure that the books were a none-too-subtle attempt by her parents to encourage her to play nice with her brother, and Kay had pretended not to care much for the books. In truth, though, she'd loved them and had checked out the other ten books in the series from the library. The parents in the books, a high school science teacher father and a nurse mother, played a role in each mystery, and Kay had to admit that the mother's profession had influenced her choice of a career.

After flipping through the books, she turned to the other items on the bookcase. She picked up a ceramic horse, one of a dozen that were lined up on a shelf. It was black with three white legs, and its mane and tail were made of black hair. Her mother had gotten it for her on a trip to Kentucky. Where was she going to put all of these memories? She couldn't throw them away. Pack them up? Put them in storage until she discovered what the rest of her life was going to bring?

After two enlistments in the Army, she'd been traveling throughout the Southeast as a freelance nurse. Her latest stop had been Huntsville, Alabama, but she'd never stayed anywhere more than a year. *When am I going to settle down?* she wondered.

As soon as her mind started down the *what-am-I going-to-do-with-my-life?* trail, she put the horse back on the shelf with the others and tried to shut down her thoughts. She had too many other things to worry about. Besides, she'd ridden over that road enough to know that the answers wouldn't be found when she was alone in her bedroom at night.

CHAPTER TWO

Lee wasn't asleep when the phone rang after midnight. He'd been lying wide awake, trying to formulate a plan for talking his sister into giving him some time to turn the business around.

"Lamberton Funeral Home," he answered the phone by the bed.

"Lee? This is Jerome. We got a body over here on Church Street. It's Rick Bruhn."

"Seriously?" Lee sat up in bed.

"No, this is a big joke. *Yes*, I'm serious, you fool. A neighbor saw him at the bottom of the pool."

"We can pick up the body?"

"Doc Porter's signed off on the cause of death."

"Okay. Give me half an hour. Will you help load him up?"

"Yeah, you get here fast enough. My shift should have ended at eleven, but then this came up. I've been out here freezing for three hours."

"On my way."

Lee climbed out of bed, not worried about making himself look presentable. Pants, a shirt and shoes were all that was required to pick up a waterlogged body in the middle of the night.

His stomach grumbled a bit as he walked out to the carport, having long digested the grilled cheese sandwiches that Ruby had made in honor of the prodigal daughter. *Bet she wouldn't have fed Kay if she'd known that the Judas is working to put us all out on the street*, Lee thought.

He bypassed the new Cadillac hearse that his father had bought just over a year ago and that Lee now saved for paying funerals. Instead he climbed into the old, dusty Lincoln model and said a little prayer that the engine would turn over. *Needs a new battery or maybe an alternator. Probably both.*

"Good girl, Bertha," he told the hearse as the motor grumbled to life. "Warm up fast." He regretted not grabbing a coat on his way out of the house.

The address Jerome had given him was on the north side of town, in a small neighborhood of upper-middle-class homes that had been built in the early sixties. Anyone with money who wasn't a farmer or who didn't live in the historic neighborhood around the town square lived there.

The neighborhood streets were curvy and a few were dead ends, so Lee took his time in the dark. After a sharp left turn, it was clear which house was his destination. A police car and two patrol cars from the sheriff's office were parked in front, lights flashing.

Lee backed into the driveway with the help of Deputy Jerome Carter, who waved him in like he was parking a 747.

"The meat wagon's here. Time for me to go back to work," said the cop, stepping on a cigarette butt that he'd tossed in the driveway.

Lee recognized him from previous pick-ups. "Stockton."

"Lamberton." Stockton gave him a curt nod and headed toward his car. The two deputies shook their heads as they watched the cop's bowlegged gait.

"That man should be riding a horse," Jerome said, the dark skin around his eyes crinkling with laughter. He indicated the other deputy standing beside him. "Lee, you know Linnie?"

"Sure. I picked up a body at an accident he was working a couple of years ago."

"That was a nasty one." Linnie shook his head. "Y'all got this? I should get to that burglary they just called in."

"I'm done after this. See you tomorrow," Jerome said, waving him on.

"The body in back?" Lee asked, looking toward the house.

"I'll show you." Jerome walked to a gate that led to the side yard.

Lee couldn't see much, but the ranch-style house looked like it sat on a large lot of at least two acres. He could see the houses on either side, though they were distant and dark. There was a concrete path leading through the side yard to the back where the pool was bathed in a green glow from its underwater lights. Around the pool were several lawn chairs and a couple of inflatable rafts.

"Chilly night for a swim," Lee said, shivering a little in his flannel shirt.

"He probably went in the water around eight."

"Still would have been dark. Seventy degrees at the most."

The body lay on the concrete deck of the pool, sightless eyes staring up at the night sky. Bruhn had been wearing a pair of green, boxer-style swim trunks with black stripes down each side. A puddle of water surrounded the body.

"You sure we don't need to take him to the morgue in Gainesville?" Lee asked.

"Nah. The sheriff and Dr. Porter are satisfied." Jerome saw the expression on Lee's face and explained, "Porter pushed water out of his lungs and said it smelled like pool water. You know, chlorinated. And we talked to the neighbors, who said Bruhn was staying here while his parents are away. One guy said he heard Bruhn swimming at night at least twice this week."

"If he was a regular swimmer, then why did he drown?"

"Don't ask me," Jerome said defensively. "You want the body or not?"

"Absolutely." Even if he didn't get the funeral, Lee would at least get paid for pickup and storage. He looked around, trying to judge the best way to get the body out to the hearse. The path they'd used had been too narrow for the stretcher and the grass to the side was thick and deep.

"Guess we can carry it out to the hearse." Jerome had helped Lee move enough bodies that he'd known immediately what the mortician had been thinking.

Lee started to bend toward the body, then stopped and asked, "Where are his folks?"

"They're in Europe. According to the neighbors, he sent them on a trip to France and Italy for their fortieth anniversary."

"He rich?"

"Yep. A big-time exec for an insurance company in Atlanta. Looks like his folks have some money too. The dad's a lawyer."

"I met them once," Lee said, causing Jerome to stare at him. "He dated Kay in high school."

"Your sister dated the dead guy?" Jerome asked, his eyebrows raised.

"Yeah. They were pretty serious." Until that moment, Lee hadn't thought about how Kay was going to take this. He didn't even know if she and Rick Bruhn had stayed in touch over the years. "I met his parents at Kay's graduation."

"That's crazy."

"Hey, it's a small town. I'm used to picking up people I know."

This was certainly the truth. When Lee was a kid, it had fascinated him when the people he'd seen in town would end up in his dad's embalming room being prepared for burial. When he was thirteen, he'd finally been allowed to help. By the time he was in high school, his dad had taken to supervising as Lee did some of the restoration. He'd heard his father talking about it one day with Buck Watson, the man who did most of the backhoe work for burials. Buck had asked if it was legal to let Lee work on the bodies. His dad had said no, and that he wouldn't have done it if the boy wasn't so damn good at it. The words had caused Lee to swell with pride and made him determined to go to school to become a funeral director like his father.

"Nobody knows where his parents are," Jerome grumbled, interrupting Lee's memories. "Sheriff Pratt did get the name of the travel agent. He'll try to track them down tomorrow."

"Did he hit his head?"

"Who? Pratt?"

"No, not the sheriff. Did Bruhn hit his head on the bottom of the pool?" Lee asked as they both leaned over to pick up the body.

"Dr. Porter didn't say anything about that."

"I'm still wondering how a man who was a good swimmer managed to drown in his own childhood pool."

"Does it matter? 'Cause the sheriff and the doc have made up their minds," Jerome argued.

Lee just shrugged.

Jerome and Lee had worked together for four years, so they were quick and efficient. In less than fifteen minutes, they were rolling the body into the back of Bertha.

"You need me to follow you to the house?" Jerome asked as he closed the door.

"Ride with me. I'll bring you back after we unload him."

"Guess I don't have to call shotgun."

As the hearse cruised through the dark and deserted streets of Lang, Lee looked over at Jerome as he settled back in the seat. "Kay's home."

"When?" Jerome sat up straight and looked at Lee, who was satisfied that he'd surprised the deputy.

"Today. She's going to try to close down the funeral home."

"She can't do that. You own half the business."

"Only half. She can force the issue."

"Folks just got to get used to your father being gone. 'Sides, you're pretty young for a funeral director."

"All true. But what can I do? Kay thinks we're headed into bankruptcy."

"Are you?"

"How would I know? I never was good at all that business stuff. I do know that we're letting too many funerals go to Gainesville."

"You're the best embalmer in this part of the state."

"Doesn't do me any good if I don't get any bodies to embalm."

"Hire someone to front the place."

"What, like some old guy to be a kind of figurehead?"

"Yeah, maybe. Someone who can help with the business side of things too."

"Who could I find that wouldn't take all the remaining profit? I know enough about business to know you have to pay the people who work for you. Dad was barely making enough as it was. Even with a front guy, it might take months for us to get more business. Kay is never going to speculate on us making good in the long run." Lee snapped his fingers. "Hey, maybe *you* could do it. Folks already associate you with the home. And you've told me you're tired of working for the sheriff."

"You know better than that. The Hamilton Funeral Home is the black funeral home in town. Maybe you haven't noticed, but I'm a rich dark mocha color. You'd lose all your remaining white business."

"That seems stupid."

"Maybe, but I don't think all the laws in the world will ever integrate churches, barbershops or funeral homes. Now, I could ask Mr. Hamilton if he needs a good embalmer."

Lee sighed. "Hopefully it won't come to that."

"Man, I'm going to miss the extra cash."

Lee parked the hearse and they rolled the stretcher into the cooler attached to the embalming room, where they transferred it onto a metal gurney. The refrigerated storage area was large enough that two gurneys would fit side by side, plus there were additional shelves if they needed to store more bodies. The room was large enough to hold six, but Lee was glad to have even one inside it.

After taking Jerome back to his patrol car, Lee returned to bed, hoping that he could convince his sister to keep the funeral home open long enough for him to come up with a plan to save it.

CHAPTER THREE

Kay got up early. Her mind was filled with all the tough conversations she needed to have with people she cared about. She wanted to get cleaned up and have a little breakfast before the arguing started. Just because she was right about this didn't mean it was going to be easy to convince everyone else that it was time to sell up and move on with their lives.

Downstairs in the kitchen, she found Ruby cooking eggs and bacon while Lester leafed through the *Gainesville Sun*.

"Do you live here?" Kay asked Lester, her voice still groggy with sleep.

"I try to get here early in case Lee needs me," Lester said with a grin.

"He gets here early for breakfast," Ruby said without animosity, holding her skillet and spatula and looking expectantly at Kay. "Now what would you like?"

"Eggs and toast will be fine. And coffee." Guilt tugged at her. Letting someone make her breakfast when she was planning to kick them out of their job and home seemed low.

"Over easy or scrambled?"

"Scrambled," Kay said, following her nose to the coffee pot.

Everything in the house was the same as it had been when she'd come down for her father's funeral. The pain from his unexpected death was still raw, and made even worse because they'd never had the chance to breach the emotional gap created by her sudden departure from the family fifteen years earlier. Kay could barely recall the emotions and turmoil she'd felt when she'd been a teenager. Those feelings seemed like they'd happened to someone else. *They did*, she told herself. She was no longer the same person. Too many events, including her enlistment, two tours in Vietnam and her father's death, had molded her into a person her younger self would not have recognized.

"I left some of my bacon for Yin and Yang," Lester said, getting up and putting the extra bacon on a napkin before he left the kitchen.

"They'll love you for that." Ruby smiled at him.

Kay remembered meeting the woman's two portly cats when she'd been there three months earlier. The only difference between the two mackerel tabbies was that one had green eyes while the other had yellow. Kay couldn't remember which was which.

"They're brothers, you know." Ruby was looking at Kay as though she knew that Kay had been thinking about the cats.

Kay nodded. "You told me that the last time I was here."

"That's right. Yin was comforting you out on the porch. He's very thoughtful."

"Yin has green eyes?" Kay had spent a long afternoon on the small back porch avoiding the mourners who had come to pay their respects to her dad. She had appreciated their thoughtfulness, but it was all too emotionally overwhelming. The green-eyed cat had sprawled across her lap, encouraging her to pet him while giving off a slow, steady purr.

"He does. I find those green eyes calming. He has the most relaxing purr." Again Ruby seemed to have read Kay's mind. "Yang, on the other hand, is the one I go to when I need to come up with a plan. His yellow eyes inspire me to action."

Another pang of guilt hit Kay when she realized that she would be making the two cats homeless too. *Am I prepared to fire her and kick them all out of their apartment?* she asked herself. *Of course, if the business fails then that will happen anyway.* If she took care of things now, in an orderly fashion, then at least the funeral home could afford to give Ruby severance pay and let her and the cats live there for a while until they could find somewhere else to go. *I know I'm right*, Kay told herself sternly.

"Who's in the cooler? If we're going to keep him, I'll clean him up." Lester came back to the kitchen, looking at Ruby and Kay with raised eyebrows.

"I heard Bertha leave late last night and come back a couple of hours later, but I don't know who Lee picked up," Ruby said.

"He's lying in the cooler. Nothing on but a swimsuit," Lester told them.

"Lee didn't call you to help?" Kay asked.

"Nah. If it's that late at night, it's probably a call from the cops. One of them or one of the ambulance guys can help him load up."

"I remember when your dad ran the ambulance service," Ruby said to Kay.

"That was steady income." Kay remembered her dad picking up accident or heart attack victims and taking them to one of the hospitals in Gainesville. Looking back on it, though, she realized how jarring it must have been for them to be picked up in a hearse.

Upstairs, Lee was jolted awake by a burst of music from his clock radio. With a groan, he slapped around on his nightstand until he found the "off" button. He wanted nothing more than to sleep for another couple of hours, but then he remembered Kay and why she was there.

I need every minute I can get to derail this train, he thought as he rolled out of bed.

Dressed, he headed downstairs where he found everyone still in the kitchen. Kay had just finished her eggs and turned to look at him as he walked through the door.

"Who's the body in the cooler?" Lester asked before she could.

"A drowning victim. The sheriff's office called for us to pick him up. We don't know if he's going to be ours or not." Lee avoided the question of the man's identity. Knowing that Kay was likely to take the news hard, he didn't want to blurt out the name in front of everyone. Though Lee had been fairly young at the time, he remembered that Kay's relationship with Rick Bruhn had been pretty serious.

"I'll leave him then," Lester said.

"The sheriff's office will contact the next of kin. If we haven't heard anything by four o'clock, I'll call over there and see what's going on."

Kay got up and put her plate in the sink. Holding her cup of coffee, she headed for the back porch.

"What do you want for breakfast?" Ruby asked Lee.

"Nothing right now," he said over his shoulder as he followed his sister onto the porch.

"There's something I need to tell you," he said when they

were out of earshot of the others.

"I'm not ready for an argument. We'll hash everything out later. Let me wake up first."

"Not about the home. It's about the guy we picked up last night."

Kay put her coffee down on the wicker table. "Even if you get the funeral, one funeral isn't going to turn your finances around."

"This isn't about any of that," Lee said in frustration. "The body from last night. It's Rick Bruhn."

Kay stared at him for a moment as though she hadn't heard him, then she said softly, "What?"

"He drowned last night at his parents' house."

"Rick?" Kay was stunned. Even though she knew that Rick had moved to Atlanta years ago, every time she'd come home to Lang she couldn't help thinking about him, always with a mix of nostalgia and loss. "I want to see him."

"That's probably not a good idea."

"I don't really care what you think." The words weren't spoken in anger; they were simply how she felt.

"That's just who the sheriff said it was," Lee said, backpedaling. Now that he thought about it, he hadn't seen any identification. Could it have been a mistaken identity? Odds were that the deputies had just assumed it was Rick since the neighbors said he'd been watching the house for his parents. Maybe no one had confirmed it.

"I'm going to look." Kay brushed past him, her coffee forgotten.

"Wait! I'll bring him out," Lee said, following her toward the embalming room.

Kay stopped before she reached the stainless steel door to the cooler. When he was sure that she wouldn't follow him, Lee opened the door. He pulled the sheet back to reveal Rick Bruhn's head and shoulders. The face was cold and grey. Without more time, Lee couldn't think of any way to make the body more presentable, so he pushed the gurney out of the cooler and into the embalming room.

At first, Kay didn't recognize the face that stared up from its stainless steel bed. Then slowly the features melded with her memories until it was her former boyfriend staring back at her, his eyes frozen in death. Kay's heart began to break.

"That's Rick," she managed to say before turning and walking quickly out of the room.

Control was slipping away from her as she ran upstairs. No sooner had she closed the door of her bedroom than the enormity of what she'd seen crashed into her. Her hand went to her mouth as she stifled a cry of pain. Kay lay down on the bed and buried her face in a pillow to hide the sounds of her sobbing. It was as though the death of Rick had wiped away the last vestiges of her childhood and whatever small bubble of optimism and innocence she still possessed.

Why does this hurt so much? Kay wondered. *I haven't seen him in years.* The idea that there'd ever been any chance of getting back together with him was ludicrous. But she realized that deep inside her there had always been a romantic ember that imagined them meeting again, talking about their time together and maybe even laughing at how young and naïve they had been.

After a long while, her crying stopped and she regained control of her breathing. She went down the hall to the bathroom, washed the tears off her cheeks and headed back downstairs.

"I'm sorry." Lee was waiting for her, looking anxious.

"I'm fine. It just took me by surprise seeing him… like that." She had to fight back the image of his face as she said it.

"Of course. I knew you all dated, but I was kind of off in my own world back then."

"You were eleven when I graduated. Kids don't pay much attention to anything that doesn't involve them. I used to think I'd marry Rick one day. But that didn't work out…" Kay's voice trailed off as her mind poked at memories she thought she'd left buried.

"I always wondered why you wound up in the Army. Dad was… touchy about it. I thought it was just 'cause he thought it was a dumb idea."

Kay sighed. "That was part of it. My relationship with Rick had fallen apart in senior year and there were a lot of reasons I left, but I know my leaving upset Dad."

"All I cared about then was Little League. I didn't realize you were having a hard time."

"Of course you didn't. You were just a pain-in-the-ass kid." Kay gave Lee a small smile.

"I know Dad worried about you. He stopped watching the six o'clock news when you were over there. It sounds stupid, but I thought it was kinda cool that you were in Vietnam. Do you remember that first Christmas when you came home?"

"Do you remember how awkward it was?" she countered

"Yeah. You weren't… I don't know, interested in decorating or anything. I guess I can understand that now. The guys I've known that were over there talk about how strange it was coming back to a world that was… normal after being in that other, crazy place."

"It took me a long time to adjust. Funny, when I was over there I thought about Rick and his friends finishing up college, and I'd get angry looking around at the men who were sacrificing so much for so little." She shook the thoughts away. "Where are Rick's parents?"

"Europe on an anniversary trip. Does he have any other relatives?"

"I met an aunt and uncle once. They were down here

from Alabama, I think. There were a couple of kids with them too, but that's about all I remember."

"The sheriff's office will find someone." Lee was hoping for the funeral, but he didn't want to sound ghoulish when Kay's emotions were involved.

"Wish you could do something now. It seems awful to just leave him in the cooler."

"You know better," Lee admonished. "We can't touch the body until we have permission from the next of kin."

"I know." She looked at Lee and softened. It was clear that he was concerned both about her and the closing of the funeral home. She was sure there wasn't any way to salvage the business, but she decided to listen to whatever he had to say. "Look, I know what you think about selling the funeral home. I'll give you a chance to show me any plans you have for saving it. Just remember, the business plan needs to be thought out, not just a bunch of stuff about how much Dad would have wanted us to keep it going."

"You know who would buy it if we sell." Lee was unable to keep a slight growl out of his voice.

"The Garlands."

"Exactly. How could you even think about selling out to them? Scott Garland did everything he could to undermine Dad when he was alive. And during the last three months, guess who has stolen most of our business?"

"He *is* a businessman."

"More a businessman than a funeral director. He does all kinds of shady crap." Lee let his dislike of Garland and his practices boil to the top. "I'd rather burn the place down than sell it to him."

Kay sighed. "That doesn't make sense. As soon as Lamberton's closed, he'd scoop up all the business anyway. We may as well recover what assets we can from it."

"We could at least keep the house," Lee said in a small

voice, feeling like he'd already lost the fight. *Haven't I?* he asked himself. *How can I come up with a plan to save this place?*

"Don't be silly. Look at it. How much have you spent in the last couple of months on maintenance?"

Lee thought about the pipes that the plumber had replaced a month ago, the patches in the roof and the fuse box that needed work. "Some."

"And if you live here, where are *you* going to work? Not for Garland, I assume."

"Hadn't really thought about it. There are other funeral homes."

"For you, Hamilton's probably isn't an option. Besides, they're a small operation like we are and just hire extra help on occasion."

"I don't need you to tell me about the funeral business around here!" Lee yelled at her, unable to contain his anger at the thought of losing the funeral home. He was about to say something that he would no doubt regret, but was saved by the phone jangling on the wall in the kitchen.

Both of them turned and looked toward the door as the ringing stopped. They could hear Ruby talking to whoever was on the other end.

"For you, Lee," she eventually called out.

Kay and Lee looked at each other, acknowledging their unfinished business before Lee headed for the kitchen.

"Lee Lamberton," he answered.

"Mr. Lamberton, I'm Todd Bruhn, Rick Bruhn's uncle. I got a call…" His voice broke. "I, um, got a call from the sheriff's office that my nephew has drowned. They told me you have the body."

"That's right. I would be glad to discuss the arrangements for his burial."

"We're still trying to get ahold of my brother and his wife. I don't know what this is going to do to them."

"I understand that they're in Europe?" Lee said gently.

"That's right. We don't have their itinerary, so we can't be sure whether they're in France or Italy, let alone what hotel they're in. I'm going to drive down there just as soon as I can make some arrangements here."

"Would you like me to go over to the house with a deputy and see if we can find a copy of their itinerary? Maybe Rick kept one," Lee offered.

"Could you? I've still got a while before I can get away. From here in Montgomery, it'll take me over five hours to get there. I just… The sooner we tell my brother, the sooner they can get on a plane and head back home."

"Give me an hour, then I'll call you back. What's a good number where you can be reached?" After Bruhn gave him the number, Lee took a deep breath and pushed forward. "I was wondering if you'd like us to begin preparing Rick's body?"

"Preparing? I don't know." The man seemed confused by the question.

"We would just clean him and have him ready either to embalm or to transfer him wherever his parents wish." Lee's voice had taken on the calming tones he'd learned from his father.

"Yes, of course, that makes sense."

Lee assured him that he'd call him back in an hour, then hung up.

"You're going over to his parents' house?" Kay's question startled Lee, who'd almost forgotten that she was right behind him.

"I need to call Jerome so he can go with me."

"I want to come too," Kay said in a firm voice that didn't offer any other options.

Lee quickly called Jerome. The deputy tossed out a few polite curse words about being woken up after a long night before promising to meet them at the house in thirty minutes.

CHAPTER FOUR

Lee and Kay got to the Bruhn house just before Jerome pulled up on his Kawasaki motorcycle.

"You can get us in?" Kay asked as Jerome walked up to them.

"No problem. The sliding back door will be a breeze."

They followed him around the side of the house and then past the swimming pool to the glass doors.

"This lock is worthless," Jerome said, putting his shoulder gently against the door and pushing and lifting until he managed to slide the door open.

"What's the sense of having a lock?" Lee shook his head. "You got to put a bar down to keep someone out."

"Okay, enough with the crime prevention class," Kay said, feeling like a criminal. She reminded herself that they were only doing this to help the family.

"If they left an itinerary, it'd probably be in the kitchen or by one of the phones," Lee said. "I'll look in the kitchen."

"I'll take the bedrooms." Jerome was already moving

toward the back of the house.

Lee had just entered the kitchen when there was a ferocious scream that caused him to stumble back out of the kitchen. His heart raced as a high-pitched voice, wavering slightly, yelled that it wanted breakfast.

Kay and Jerome hurried to Lee's side and the three of them looked cautiously through the doorway into the kitchen. Next to a bay window they could see a large object on a stand and covered by a black cloth.

"What the ever-loving hell is that?" Lee asked.

"Ha!" Jerome laughed and pushed past him. "It's a bird. Must have been asleep last night when we were walking around the house." He pulled the drape aside to reveal a cockatoo dancing back and forth on its perch.

"Get the food! Lazy! Hungry now!" the bird said loudly.

"I got a cousin who has a bird like this. They can raise quite a ruckus," Jerome said with a grin.

Ignoring the bird, Lee headed to the phone near a counter. "Found it!" he declared, holding up a piece of paper while scanning a long list of dates and hotels. He glanced quickly at the calendar hanging over the phone and added, "They should be in Rome at the Palazzo Coliseum or something like that. Here's the number."

"That's going to be cheap," Kay muttered.

"Not our phone. Besides, I don't have to call them, I just have to call the brother." Lee picked up the phone while reaching into his pocket for a piece of paper with the brother's number written on it.

The bird was still screaming for its food.

"Will one of you feed that bird? Here, there's instructions at the bottom of this list." Lee handed Jerome the typed sheet.

Jerome looked at the paper. "His name is Beretta. Like the TV show."

Todd Bruhn answered on the first ring. There was gratitude in his voice when Lee gave him the information. "I'll call right now. If they aren't in their room, I'll leave a message for them to call my house. My son will be here. I hate to leave it to him to break the news, but I feel like I need to come down there as soon as possible."

"Is there anything else that we can do for you?" Lee asked.

"You've been very kind. I'll come by and… I'll let you know what his parents decide."

"I'm going to look around a bit," Jerome said when Lee hung up the phone. He had finished feeding Beretta and was juggling a set of keys he'd found on the counter.

"Why?" Kay touched his arm.

"I've got a feeling about last night." Jerome was frowning.

"What kind of feeling?"

"Like the sheriff should have looked at this a lot closer."

"What are you looking for?"

"Anything that don't look right. Like this." Jerome reached down and picked up an empty bourbon bottle from out of the trash can. "They did draw some of his blood last night. It will be interesting to see what his blood alcohol level was."

"We can help," Lee said cheerfully. He'd do anything to keep Kay's mind off of closing the funeral home.

"You take the living room. I'm going to the garage to check out his car," Jerome said, holding up the keys. "When I get back, we'll go to the bedrooms."

"These folks don't live my life," Lee mumbled, looking at the living room. It was neat as a pin, with royal blue carpet and white furniture that didn't look like it had ever been used. The only exception was a spot on the couch in front of the wardrobe-size cabinet TV where a few magazines and a two-day-old newspaper suggested that Rick had spent some time there. Lee scanned the one bookcase in the room, which held a mix of motivational books and bestselling novels from the past ten years.

"That was interesting." Jerome strode into the living room. "There are three suitcases in the trunk of Rick's car."

"Why's that so interesting?" Lee was still looking at the books.

"If this was his destination, you'd think he'd bring his luggage inside. Why does a guy pack a bunch of suitcases for a trip and then leave them in the car when he gets where he's going?"

"Maybe he was planning on going somewhere after his parents got back," Kay suggested.

"That's what I thought." Jerome pointed at Kay and nodded. "So I opened them up. Guess what? No snorkel and mask or bathing suit. No dinner coat or golf outfit. Just clothes, books and, get this, family pictures."

Lee and Kay were both paying attention now.

"Like he was moving," Lee said.

"That man gets a gold star." Jerome clapped his hands.

"Guess it's possible," Kay allowed.

"Let's check out the bedrooms and see what he decided to bring into the house," Jerome suggested.

The bedroom where Rick had been sleeping still had mementos from his childhood, including several plaques for scholarship from Melon County High School. Next to those, Lee saw a few small trophies for baseball and track.

Kay let out a gasp when she saw a picture of her with Rick at their high school prom. It felt like a hundred years ago since she had held onto his arm as they posed in front of the school's logo. Her smile was broad and genuine while Rick looked happy, though perhaps a bit embarrassed. Or maybe his expression was the result of the bottle of rum that their friends had brought and passed around.

How long after the photo was taken had she caught him kissing Millie Jessup? An hour, maybe less? Kay's eyes welled up at the memories. She wiped at them angrily, then started opening dresser drawers while Lee rummaged in the closet and Jerome looked around the bed and nightstand.

"Ha! He seemed to be a bit concerned for his health." Kay and Lee turned to see what Jerome was talking about. He held up a dark object that he had pulled from under the bed.

"That's a gun." Kay stated the obvious when she saw the gleaming blue steel weapon in Jerome's hand.

"A very nice Colt 1911, National Match." Jerome sniffed the barrel. "Hasn't been fired since it's been cleaned." He pushed the release and a full magazine dropped to the bed. Then he racked the slide and a round flipped out of the chamber and fell next to the magazine. "Loaded for bear."

"An unloaded gun isn't good for much," Kay said, repeating an expression she'd heard dozens of times when she was an Army nurse.

"You got that right. But why'd he feel the need to go around armed?" Jerome asked. "In my neighborhood you're a fool not to, but here?"

"He *was* staying here by himself," Lee said.

Jerome shrugged, then looked at Kay. "You knew him. Was he a gun guy?"

"I don't know. Back in high school he went hunting a few times, but he wasn't one of the kids that had a rifle rack in their pickup. In fact, he drove an old Bug. I guess he was kind of a country hippie."

"Hippie around here? What did he have, two inches of hair instead of a buzz cut?" Jerome joked.

"I said kind of." Kay didn't know what was annoying her more—having to defend someone she felt had wronged her, or her grief over losing the chance of meeting him again and putting their past to bed. *To bed?* she thought. *Is that what I really wanted?*

Reluctantly, Jerome reloaded the gun and placed it back under the bed.

"You'd think he'd have an address book or a date book," Lee said as he finished looking through the suitcase he'd found in the closet.

"You're right about that. Nothing over here," Jerome said as he got up from the floor by the nightstand.

"A big-time executive should have notebooks and maybe a briefcase." Lee shook his head.

"In school he always kept the best notes," Kay agreed. "There wasn't a briefcase or anything in his car?" she asked Jerome.

"Nothing but a bunch of clothes and books that he shouldn't have had along on a trip like this," Jerome said with narrowed eyes. "I'm thinking, but it's not making much sense."

"You think someone *took* his briefcase and papers?" Lee asked.

"Hold on, Captain Kangaroo, you're hopping to some pretty big conclusions. This ain't right, but there could be all kinds of explanations for it."

"Like?" Lee asked.

"Like he'd quit his job or been fired. Or maybe he needed a real break from work. Hell, I don't know. I just think it's too soon to be bringing in mysterious bad guys to steal stuff we don't even know he had with him."

"But there's something wrong." Kay was surprised how strongly she felt.

"Yeah, I'd agree with that." Jerome didn't sound happy admitting it. "But it might not have anything to do with his death. Could just be a coincidence."

"I thought you cops don't believe in coincidences." Lee gave him a crooked smile.

"I've seen so many crazy coincidences, it'd blow your mind."

They were halfway to the back door when they saw a man with a revolver pointed at them.

"Jerome! What in the ever-lovin' 'possum are you doing here?" the deputy asked without lowering the gun. Both Lee and Jerome recognized him.

"We came over to get Bruhn's parents' itinerary for his uncle," Jerome said. "Now put that gun down, Henry."

"Oh, sorry," Deputy Henry Booker said, lowering the gun. "The neighbor reported a suspicious car. Wouldn't be the first time a burglar heard about a death and robbed the house."

"You're right there," Jerome agreed.

"Hey, pretty lady." Henry looked at Kay as he put his revolver back in its holster.

Kay gave him an appraising look. The deputy was almost six feet tall with black hair and a few too many pulled pork sandwiches around his waist. His eyes were bright blue with a little sparkle.

"I'm Kay, Lee's sister." She gave him a polite smile.

"Oh!" Henry glanced at Lee to see if he'd stepped on his own tongue. "Lee and I went to school together. Though I was a year ahead." He nodded to Lee, who gave him a nod and a smile in return.

"I've been out of town for a while," Kay said.

"Henry Booker," he said, sticking out his hand awkwardly. Kay shook it.

"Heard the guy drowned," Henry said, turning to Jerome.

"That's what they say." Jerome nodded as he walked past Henry toward the front door, Lee and Kay on his heels.

"Hey, now. What am I going to report?"

"That everything was fine," Jerome told him.

"But shouldn't I mention that you were here?"

Jerome stopped at the door. "How'd *you* get in?"

"I stopped at the neighbor's first. He gave me a key."

"Then you better lock up."

"How'd you get in here?"

"Back door was unlocked," Jerome lied.

"Like Jerome said, we were asked by Bruhn's uncle to come by and look for information on how to contact the parents," Lee said.

"He's right," Kay seconded.

"Fine, I'm not sayin' nothin'." Henry held up his hands in surrender. "Just want to make sure our stories are straight."

"Anyone asks, just say that you checked it out and everything was fine. You don't need to write a damn report about it," Jerome said.

Once they were outside and Henry had left to return the key to the neighbor, Kay asked, "Why don't you want anyone to know we were here?"

"Maybe…" Jerome said, heading for his motorcycle. "…Maybe I smell trouble and don't want any part of it."

Lee and Kay drove back to the funeral home in silence.

"I'm going to clean up the body," Lee said as they got out of the car. Then he saw the look on Kay's face. "I mean Rick."

Kay sighed. "In truth, I prefer to think of it as a body. The thought that Rick Bruhn is lying in our cooler is… strange."

Lee turned to his sister. "You must have known other people that Dad worked on over the years."

"People, yeah. A teacher from elementary school and a friend of Mom's. This is different. I really *knew* Rick. We were the same age and… I don't know, there's just something wrong about all of this."

"Death only seems right for the elderly."

"That's part of it… but not all. I knew young men who were killed in the war, but I met them over there and we all knew the risks." Kay bit her lip. She didn't know how to explain her gut feeling that Rick shouldn't have been on that stainless steel gurney waiting for burial, and not just because of his age.

"Do you want me to handle everything when his family gets here?"

"No. I want to talk to them." Kay had no idea what she would say, but she wanted closure.

"I'll let you know when the uncle arrives," Lee told her, then headed for the embalming room.

Kay wandered into the kitchen, where she found Lester sitting at the table with a copy of Stephen King's *The Stand.* "Have you been sitting here since breakfast?" she asked.

Lester lowered the book. "Nope. I met with a client when y'all were off playing Hardy Boys."

"Someone came in?" The thought of Lester talking to potential clients was frightening.

"Don't get that look. I didn't scare them away. The lady has already talked to Lee. All she needed was a couple of casket brochures. And I swear I pushed the top-of-the-line Batesville models. She's already leaning that way."

"You should let me or Lee talk with the clients."

"What's it matter if you're just going to sell us out?" Lester looked at her with a steady gaze.

"The more pre-sales we have on the books, the more money we're worth," Kay said, staring back at him.

"You're cold, man." He shook his head.

"Practical. Which is what's needed around here. Why Lee thinks it's a good idea to just let the place sink into debt rather than get out while the getting is good is beyond me."

"I don't want him to get out."

"I can understand that. It's not every job where you can sit around reading books all day."

Lester stood up. "I know when I'm being abused. I'm going to help Lee." He picked up his book and walked out of the kitchen, his nose in the air.

"He never did tell you who he was giving those brochures to."

Startled, Kay turned to see Ruby coming out of the pantry with two mason jars of peaches in her hands.

Seeing the look on Kay's face, Ruby smiled. "I was eavesdropping." There was no apology in her voice.

"You just surprised me."

"Like in a Hitchcock film. I love movies. I saw my first one when I was ten. It was at the Tampa Theatre. Did you know that they've renovated it?" Ruby jumped from subject to subject like she was performing a high-wire act at the circus.

"No," Kay said, a bit unsure which question she was answering.

"You're making a mistake."

"What?" She was lost again in Ruby's twists and turns of subjects.

"Selling the funeral home would be a big mistake. Not that you *are* going to sell it."

"What? Why?"

"I'm making peach cobbler. It's really a summer dessert, but I like to have it when it's cool as a reminder that summer will come again," Ruby said with a wistful air.

"Why did you say I'm not going to sell the home?" Kay asked again.

"Mrs. Caster."

"Who?"

"That's who Lester gave the brochures to. Mrs. Caster. Your father buried her husband two years ago. She's been dithering about her own funeral ever since."

"What's that got to do with me selling the home?" Kay tried to get Ruby to focus.

"You're not going to."

"It's really not your decision," Kay said, feeling both annoyed and exasperated with the self-assured woman.

"Not yours either. I'm not telling you *not* to. I'm telling you that you won't."

Kay didn't remember Ruby being this… dense after her father's funeral. That had been the longest time that Kay had ever spent with the woman, and she'd mostly stayed quietly in the background, preparing food and taking care of visitors. But now she seemed deranged.

"I don't want to discuss this with you."

"Nothing to discuss," Ruby said as though it was a known fact, like two plus two equals four.

"Really?"

Ruby just nodded.

Even though she knew she should just walk away from the conversation, Kay asked, "Why do you think I'm not going to sell?"

"I get these… Well, I'd call them premonitions, but they're more than that. Sometimes I just know things."

Kay was sorry she'd asked. "When did you start working for Dad?"

"A little over a year ago. It was almost two months after I moved into the apartment that Yin and Yang showed up."

Kay tried to keep up with Ruby's constantly shifting train of thought. "Your cats?"

"No one owns cats," she said as though schooling a child. "I'm very blessed to have them living with me."

Kay was beginning to feel a little bad about her plans to

sell the funeral home and put this poor, deluded woman back out into the job market. Who would possibly hire her?

CHAPTER FIVE

In the embalming room, Lee rolled the gurney bearing Rick Bruhn's body out of the cooler and over to the sink where he could wash it down. Pulling back the sheet, he looked at the grey body under the stark white fluorescent lights. The eyes were open and staring blindly at the ceiling.

Lee had always thought that there was an odd peace and sadness in the corpses he prepared for burial. The ratio of peace to sadness was on a sliding scale that was directly proportional to the age of the deceased. Today he saw little peace.

Lee was rinsing Rick's hair when Lester came into the room, putting on an apron and latex gloves as he approached the table. Lester sometimes had issues with concentration, but Lee knew that he was serious about learning the work.

"I've washed his front. I just need to do a few other things before we turn him over."

Not all morticians thoroughly cleaned a body before beginning the embalming process, but Lee felt that it was a sign of respect—a harkening back to the days when bodies had been cleaned and dressed by family members before being laid out for the community to pay their respects.

Lee donned a headlamp, then leaned over to open Rick's mouth to check for any objects that might be lodged in the throat. It wasn't a necessary procedure, but over the years he'd learned that it was a good idea to check each body thoroughly. When he peered down Rick's throat, he noticed a discoloration.

"That's odd," he muttered.

"What?"

"Here, look down at the roof of his mouth and the back of his throat," Lee said, waving Lester forward. Lester looked in as Lee held the mouth open, canting his head so that the light from his headlamp shown clearly on the area.

"Something scratched the hell out of the inside of his mouth and throat," Lester said.

"Yep." Lee released Rick's jaw, then looked closely at the dead man's face. "Do you see anything around his mouth and nose?"

Again Lester bent over Rick's face. "Maybe a little red here?" he said, pointing to the edge of the mouth.

"We need to call Jerome."

Lester's expression turned grave as he realized what Lee meant. "You think he was killed?"

"Yes." Lee took off his gloves and dropped them into the trashcan before picking up the receiver from the phone on the wall.

Jerome answered after the fourth ring, sounding distracted. "What?"

"It's Lee. Rick Bruhn was murdered."

"What leads you to that conclusion, Detective Lamberton?" Jerome asked with a full measure of sarcasm.

"I'll tell you if you quit being a snot."

"Well, excuuuuuse me," Jerome said in his best John Belushi impression. "Do tell?"

"There are abrasions in his mouth and throat and some odd blotching on his face."

There was silence on the other end of the telephone as Jerome pondered this information. Finally he said, "And you just *had* to tell me this?"

"I thought you were the one who thought the death looked hinky."

"Thinking it was hinky didn't mean I had to do anything. Now you tell me something I might have to stick my neck out over. Well, shit! I'm headed your way. Best I look at it before I commit to anything," he grumbled and hung up before Lee could say another word.

As he set the receiver back on the hook, Lee thought about Kay. How was she going to react to this development? *Best let Jerome take a look first*, he thought, turning back to the body.

"Go get me the Polaroid camera," he told Lester, who'd been listening to the phone conversation. "It's in the office."

Lester came back quickly, giving Lee time to take a few pictures of Rick's injuries before Jerome knocked on the back door.

"I took pictures," Lee said after Lester led the deputy into the embalming room.

"Guess that's why you're holding a camera," Jerome said, shaking his head.

"Guess that's why you're a detective." Lee held up the camera and flashed a bulb in Jerome's face.

"Jerk."

"Off."

Jerome and Lee exchanged mock angry looks as they went over to the body.

"Can you see the discoloration around the mouth?" Lee

asked. Jerome didn't feel the need to answer.

"He was probably smothered," Lee said, pressing the issue.

"Big man to be smothered like that. Especially without any defensive wounds." Jerome's voice was grim.

Lee opened Rick's mouth and pointed a flashlight into the dry cavity. There were clear signs that something had scraped the top and back of Rick's mouth and throat.

"You'll have to tell the sheriff," Lee said.

Jerome straightened up and looked at Lee. "Do you know what the Melon County clearance rate for murders is?"

"No, not really." Lee wondered what the question had to do with this particular corpse.

"A hundred percent. Pretty good, right? We must be regular wizards of law enforcement down there at the sheriff's office."

"What are you saying?"

Jerome sighed. "You know how the sheriff manages to solve every murder in the county?"

Lee and Lester shook their heads in unison.

"Simple. If a murder has a ready-made suspect with blood dripping off his fingers and a dozen witnesses who saw him holding the murder weapon with his fingerprints all over it, then that's great. That's clearly a murder. But if there's a dead body with a knife sticking out of its back and no suspects in sight… well, that must be a bizarre accident or an unusual suicide."

Lee and Lester both gave him puzzled looks.

"Don't you get it?" Jerome asked. "If it can be easily solved, then it's a murder. But if not, then it's not a murder. It's that simple. They just come up with an explanation that won't screw up those perfect stats."

Lee saw the implications now that Jerome had drawn it out for him. Feeling at a loss, he asked, "So what do we do with Rick?"

"How the hell should I know?" Jerome's voice was loud and angry.

"We can't just bury him."

"I'm telling you, if I go to anyone at the sheriff's office and try to convince them that this is a murder, the next job I'll have with the county will be riding on the back of a garbage truck."

"That's crazy!" Lester sputtered.

"We can go around them. Go to the State Attorney or the Florida Department of Law Enforcement," Lee suggested.

"That's not the way things work. No one at the state level is going to want to step on a sheriff's toes unless he's doing something illegal like taking bribes or dealing drugs."

"What are you all yelling about?"

Everyone turned to see Kay standing at the door.

"I… I…" Lee stuttered. He looked to Jerome and Lester for help, but they were both busy examining their feet.

"What?" Kay tried not to look at Rick's body.

"We're pretty sure that Rick was murdered," Lee said abruptly, giving up the thought of trying to hide it from her.

"How… How do you know?" Kay asked hesitantly.

"Do you really want me to tell you?"

She took a deep breath. "Yes."

Lee waved her closer to the stainless steel table and pointed at Rick's body.

"See this discoloration around his mouth and nose? Something rubbed against his face while he was dying."

"Like someone was holding a pillow over his mouth and he was fighting it?" Kay said slowly, like a child answering a difficult math question.

"Exactly," Lee said. "And there are scratches on the roof of his mouth and the back of his throat."

"The killer forced something down his throat?"

"And into his lungs," Jerome said quietly. "Like I said, I saw the EMTs force water out of him. That was one of the reasons Doc Porter called it an accident."

Kay looked at the three men. "Has anyone called the sheriff's office?"

"That's what we were discussing," Lee said.

"What's there to discuss?" Kay asked.

With a heavy sigh, Jerome explained the situation.

Kay's first inclination was to tell them that they were crazy and demand that they get on the phone with the sheriff right now. However, she'd spent enough time in the Army to know that Jerome was telling the truth. She'd seen more than one officer who was willing to do the unthinkable if it made the stats look better for him. And as far as going to the state went, she'd seen plenty of brass who wouldn't interfere unless there was criminal activity that they couldn't ignore.

"So where does that leave us?" she asked, giving them all hard looks.

"See, that's what we were *discussing*," Lee said snarkily.

"We can't let the asshole get away with it," Kay said, looking down at Rick's dead eyes while fighting to hold back her emotions.

"If the sheriff's office isn't going to do anything, then I guess *we're* going to have to find out who did this," Lee said, not sounding very sure of himself.

Jerome stared at him, shaking his head. "You know that's not easy, even when you have the authority to do it."

"We've got you," Lee pointed out.

"You gone crazy?"

"What's the worst that can happen? You get fired? All you do is complain about working there anyway."

"Like *you* pay me enough to support my family." Lee knew that Jerome helped out his divorced sister and her two kids whenever he could.

"It's not like you'd have to do much," Kay said.

"Don't jive me. Five minutes into this *Brady Bunch* investigation, you're going to have me running tags and background checks. I can't do that stuff just 'cause I want to."

"This could be cool. Like *Scooby-Doo* only without the dog," Lester said, causing everyone else to glare at him.

"Jerome, if we come up with evidence and a suspect, will the sheriff do his job?" Kay asked.

"If we had evidence and a suspect, I could take it to Lieutenant Wilkins. He's all right," Jerome said with an admission of grudging respect.

"We don't know anything about investigating a murder," Lee said, then turned to Lester. "And watching *Scooby-Doo* while stoned doesn't count."

"Hey, I resemble that remark," Lester said.

"I dated an MP in Japan for two months," Kay said with a frown. "We just ask lots of questions and look for mistakes in alibis. You've already found evidence on Rick's body."

"I took pictures too," Lee admitted. "Do we tell his uncle or parents?"

"No," Jerome said with a hard edge to his voice. "You tell the family and they're going straight to the sheriff. They do that and he doubles down on accidental death, then he'll never budge, even *with* a suspect and evidence."

"He's probably right," Kay said, having seen her share of egotists react when confronted. "We'll just start talking to people and see what happens."

"Do we have to cut our hands and do some weird blood oath?" Jerome asked, shaking his head. "Oh man, I know I'm gonna regret this."

"Have you ever investigated a murder?" Kay asked him.

"You kidding? I'm lucky they let me write tickets." He

paused and turned serious. "I've run down a few burglars and crooks in Casstown. That was easy; I just asked around. People there know who the bad guys are. 'Course, I'm the right color so they pointed me in the right direction." Casstown was the predominately black section of town south of the railroad tracks.

"Someone must have information about this murder. We just have to get them to talk to us," Kay said with a grim nod toward Rick's body.

"One person knows *all* about the murder. The murderer," Lester chimed in, sounding a little less excited.

"You really *are* going to play Shaggy, aren't you?" Lee frowned at him.

"He's right." Jerome looked at each of them in turn. "This ain't no joke. The person who did this is a ruthless bastard. He's not going to just throw his hands up and say, Okay, you got me.'"

"You're right, of course." Kay nodded. "We need to be careful, try not to raise too many suspicions."

"Rick's uncle ought to be in town in a couple of hours," Lee said with a glance at his watch. "I'll talk to him. Maybe he knows why Rick had the gun with him."

"Some people just like to have protection," Kay said with the knowledge that she had a Colt 1911 holstered inside her purse.

"There was also that empty bottle of bourbon in the wastebasket," Lee said.

"Some people like to have a drink… or two." Lester grinned.

"We could go back to the house before the uncle gets here." Kay looked at Jerome.

"I'm off duty," Jerome said, then shrugged. "Sure. We can go back. This time we'll check in with the neighbors first so they don't call it in. 'Sides, that will give us a chance to ask them a few questions about last night."

"What can I do?" Lester asked with way too much enthusiasm.

"Help me get Rick's body ready for embalming," Lee said, bringing Lester back to earth. "Hopefully the family will let us prepare him for burial."

CHAPTER SIX

An hour later, Kay met Jerome at the Bruhn house.

"You look official," she said. Jerome had gone home and changed into his deputy's uniform.

"I thought the green might offset the color of my skin when we're talking to the neighbors," he said with an ironic grin as he got off his motorcycle.

They decided to start with the neighbor who had called in the report about Rick's body.

"He told us the story of how he found the body last night, but no one was asking him about strangers hanging around or anything like that."

"What's the guy's name?" Kay asked as they walked down to the curb and around to the craftsman-style house next door.

"Louie D'Angelo, better known as Loopy Louie. He owns a big discount appliance store in Gainesville."

"No kidding? I remember him. He always ran his Loopy Louie ads during the Terror TV show on Saturday afternoons."

"Still does."

They walked up the steps to Louie's front door. Kay shifted behind Jerome, not sure how they were going to explain her reason for being there. Jerome was in his uniform and no one was going to question his right to ask questions, but who was she?

The doorbell chimes played a synthesized version of The O'Jays' "For the Love of Money," which went on for at least a minute before the door opened.

"Sorry, I always got to hear my song before I open the door. Hey, if you like the doorbell, I've been sellin' 'em down at the store. Forty percent off this week, plus you'll get your regular ten percent law enforcement discount." Louie said all of this before really looking at Jerome. "Guess you aren't here to buy a doorbell. Come on in." He backed away from the door.

Kay recognized the signature cigar and wild hair of the man—although, not surprisingly, he looked considerably older than he had on television fifteen years ago.

"Come into the living room. Excuse the mess, but I just chased off the third wife. I used to think it was cheaper to have a wife than a housekeeper and a prostitute. The ignorance of youth," he said offhand as they followed him into the living room. Despite his comments, it was neat and orderly except for a box from Momma's Best Pizza sitting on the coffee table.

"Sit wherever," Louie said before dropping heavily down on the couch. His short, pudgy body hit the cushions with a small creak from the wood frame.

"We'd like to talk to you about the death of Rick Bruhn," Jerome explained.

"Yeah, I figured. The neighbor's kid." Louie shook his head sadly. "They're going to be torn up over that. Always showing me pictures of their son the successful insurance guy."

"Did you ever meet him?" Jerome asked.

"A couple of times. You know, across the fence. Neighborly like. He'd already moved away from home by the time I bought this place. He seemed like a nice guy. I thought he might come down and buy a stereo for his car. Fancy car, but it still has a factory sound system. That's no good, I told him. You want something that will impress the girls."

"Did he say anything about a girlfriend?"

"Nah, and I know 'cause I listen for that stuff. If they got a wife or a girlfriend, that's a soft spot. Opens up a whole new market of goods you can sell 'em." Louie looked thoughtful for a second. "Come to think of it, he was kind of quiet. I thought the first time I saw him, knowing what he did for a living, that he'd try and sell me insurance. I thought, boy, this is going to be something, two salesmen going head to head. But he never once mentioned his job."

"Did you see anyone else over at the house while he was there?"

"Hey, it's not like I'm some nosy neighbor hanging over the fence. I got a business to run." He paused again. "Maybe there was a car in the driveway a coupla times. I noticed 'cause I knew that the Bruhns were out of town. Even with the son there, I've been kind of keeping an eye on the place. I like the Bruhns. Good neighbors. No parties, always keep their place looking nice. Not like some people these days. Hey, what you asking all these questions for?" A hint of suspicion entered his voice.

"Paperwork. You know what government is like. My boss told me to get out here and fill in all the questions left unanswered on the reports." Jerome made this speech in a smooth, country-boy tone that was easy and disarming. Kay could tell that he'd anticipated Louie's question.

"I understand that. The IRS is always riding my butt. Paperwork." He waved his hand as if swatting at an annoying fly.

"Just a few more questions," Jerome told him. "Any strange noises, loud voices or that sort of thing coming from next door in the last week or so?"

"He was quiet as a church mouse. I was worried when Pearl told me her son was going to be staying at their house while they're gone. I thought, oh boy, big-time executive, maybe he'll have wild parties or something. Nah, nothing."

"Can you tell me again about seeing the body?"

"Gives me the creeps to think about it. See, I can see their pool from my bedroom window. No big deal. I never give it a thought. But last night I got up to take a leak." He paused and turned to Kay. "Sorry, I should watch what I say, but I guess you're a police lady, you probably hear it all."

"I've heard worse," Kay said without addressing his assumption that she was a deputy.

"Anyhoo, I was coming back to bed and saw the green glow from the pool. Struck me as unusual. Thinking back on it, the Bruhns almost never turned the light on, so when I saw it I did a double-take. I was still half asleep." He stopped and looked embarrassed. "I tell you something, you won't tell nobody else?"

"If you want it off the record, it's off the record." Jerome smiled encouragingly.

"See, I've been watching this show, *In Search of*, with that guy who's got the pointy ears. They had an episode on there about UFOs and, being half asleep, I thought, whoa, there's one landing in the side yard. I felt stupid when I looked out the window and saw it was just the glow from the pool light. I could see the guy in the pool. I watched for a minute and he was just floating there under the water. Like, my mind couldn't make sense of it for a coupla minutes. Then I was like, damn, he's been underwater for a while. That's when I woke up quick and called the cops."

"Good for you," Kay said. "When did you go to bed?"

Jerome gave her a brief glance, trying not to look too surprised that she had asked a question. Louie didn't notice.

"I go to bed early. Nine-thirty or ten. I get up at four so I can get into the store and have a few hours to go over inventory and mark down the deals of the day. Always a few hot deals to bring in the customers."

"And you didn't notice the pool light on then?" Kay asked.

"Nope. I would have too. The wife smashed the bedside lamp when she was packing, so I got to turn the light on and off using the switch by the door. She busted it on purpose 'cause I bought it for her. Tiffany, five-hundred-dollar lamp. I would have replaced it except my blood pressure goes up every time I think about it."

"And you didn't hear anything between the time you went to bed and the time you got up to… take a leak?" Kay asked, trying to keep him on track.

"I sleep the sleep of the just. Never cheated no one that wasn't trying to cheat me. That includes my ex-wives."

Jerome looked over at Kay. "I don't think we have any more questions for now," he said, taking a card out of his pocket. "If you think of anything you might have forgotten, give me a call."

"Come on down to the store," Louie said, putting Jerome's card in his pocket as they all stood up. "I'll cut you a deal on anything you want."

Jerome started to leave the room before turning back. "I'm surprised you aren't at the store now."

"I went in this morning and got the sales set, but I never got back to sleep last night, so I came home early. I'm not going to be one of those guys that works himself into the grave just so his family can enjoy his money."

After they'd walked away from the house, Jerome asked, "What'd you think of Loopy Louie?"

"Seems like a nicer guy than I would have expected."

"Got to admit, I kind of liked him too. Still, he's slick." Jerome didn't explain his comment.

"The other neighbor now?"

"And after that, the one across the street. They're the ones with the best view of the driveway."

The house on the other side of the Bruhn house was a two-story white clapboard farmhouse with an almost new C10 Chevy pickup parked in the driveway.

Jerome pressed the doorbell. When they didn't hear any movement from inside the house, he rapped on the door. After a minute, they thought they heard someone walking inside, but still the door remained closed. Exasperated, Jerome knocked again.

"Hello?" he called. Nothing. "We want to talk to you about the death of your neighbor last night," he said loudly enough to be heard inside. For good measure, he added: "We know you're in there."

"My parents aren't home!" a teenaged voice yelled from the other side of the door.

"We'd like to talk to you."

"I don't know."

"I'm holding my badge up to the peephole. Are you tall enough to see it?"

"Yeah." The voice sounded both scared and irritated. Slowly the door opened, revealing a young man on the cusp of adulthood who was looking suspicious.

"Can we come in?" Jerome asked.

"We can talk out here. My parents told me not to let anyone inside when they aren't here." This sounded preposterous coming from someone who had to be all of sixteen or seventeen.

"Out here will work." Jerome smiled in a way that was meant to be reassuring, but could have also been described as predatory. Kay suddenly had an overwhelming desire to know what the boy was hiding in the house.

"What's your name?" Kay asked as the boy came out and pulled the door shut behind him.

"Terrance Reeves. Who are you?" He had dropped the little boy act.

"I'm Ms. Lamberton." Kay was determined to maintain the upper hand.

"Where are your parents?" Jerome asked.

"They went up to the mountains. We've got a cabin up in Tennessee and they go there every spring."

"So they weren't here last night?"

"No. Like I said, they went to Tennessee." His voice had gone from suspicious to condescending.

"Were you here last night?"

Kay could see the calculations going on behind the boy's eyes as Jerome asked the question.

"When?" Terrance asked.

"I guess you were out part of the night, so why don't you just tell me when you got back here?" Jerome leaned forward and his voice had assumed a confrontational tone to match the boy's attitude.

Terrance hesitated.

"Son, I don't care what you were doing last night if it didn't involve the death of the man staying next door. Just tell me when you came home and what you saw."

"I heard the guy had an accident." The boy evaded Jerome's questions.

"Where'd you hear that from?"

"A friend called and said he'd heard a guy in my

neighborhood had an accident. That's all." The boy's posture and tone were becoming even more defensive.

"So when did you get home?" Kay was tired of the dancing around.

"It was after midnight." Terrance's eyes shifted to Kay when he answered.

"How *long* after?" Jerome pushed, causing the boy to look back at him.

"Fine, I got in just after two o'clock." He wasn't happy to admit it.

"I guess your parents don't want you staying out that late," Kay sympathized.

"I'm not supposed to stay out past ten." He ground his teeth. "I wasn't doing nothing wrong. I took my girlfriend into Gainesville to the movies. That's all."

"What'd you see?" Jerome wanted to know if the kid was lying.

"*The Howling*." Terrance didn't miss a beat.

"That's a horror movie, right?" Kay asked.

"Yeah, werewolves and stuff, but it's sort of funny too."

"What time did the movie start?" Jerome asked.

"Hey, what is this?"

"If you're telling the truth, then your parents don't need to know. Just tell me when the movie started."

"It was at the Oaks Mall and I think it started at ten-thirty, something like that. I bought popcorn, she got a box of Snowcaps and we both had a Coke. You happy?"

"Yep. So you got home after two. Did you see anyone in the driveway next door?" Jerome asked, knowing that the boy had gotten home too late to be of any help, but enjoying jerking his chain.

"No."

"Did you hear anything from the house?"

Terrance looked thoughtful for the first time. "No, no

sounds. I wasn't too worried since the Bruhns are out of town. I didn't think their son would rat me out for coming home late."

"Did you ever talk to Rick Bruhn?" Jerome asked.

"I was looking at his car a couple of days ago. Nice. Not my thing, but I can appreciate a nice machine. He came out and talked to me when he saw me looking at it."

"What'd you all talk about?"

"Just cars. He was into luxury cars while I'm more about 4x4s and race cars." There was a brief pause before he added, "I liked him okay."

"Did he say anything that didn't have to do with cars?" Jerome pressed.

"I thought he had an accident. You know, drowned."

"We're just being thorough," Jerome said.

"Only thing he said other than talking about cars was that he would be staying here until his parents came back. Then he was going to hit the road."

"That's what he said, hit the road?"

"Yeah."

Kay and Jerome asked a few more questions, but the boy didn't have anything else to add.

"What do you think about Terrance?" Kay asked Jerome as they headed across the street to a yellow brick, ranch-style home that looked straight off the cover of a 1955 *House Beautiful* magazine.

"He's what I call Little Trouble. He'll sneak out of the house or shoplift a quart of beer, but he's not going to steal a car or assault someone. Once we shook him down, he told us what he knew."

"Which wasn't much."

"Every yard down field gets you closer to the goal posts."

"That's a very methodical outlook."

"Man, I'm not all action. There's a thinking machine up

here." Jerome tapped his head as they crossed the yard of the house.

"I don't doubt it. I think Sherlock Holmes pointed out that the dog who doesn't bark tells you as much as the one that does."

"Exactly," Jerome said, grinning at her.

They reached the polished wood door and were about to knock when the door opened to reveal Aunt Bea, or at least a woman who would have been perfect casting for the matronly aunt from Mayberry.

"I saw you all coming from across the road. Is it about the poor Bruhn boy?" Her hands were rubbing each other nervously and her forehead was wrinkled with concern.

"We'd like to ask you a few question," Jerome told her with a polite smile.

"Oh, of course, come in." The woman backed away from the door. "I don't know what we can tell you. Would you like some coffee? We can sit in the kitchen."

Kay and Jerome followed her through the living room, which was liberally sprinkled with doilies and porcelain figurines.

"Dennis!" the woman yelled with the volume of a construction worker yelling up to the riveters.

"You don't have to shout!" came an answer from the back of the house.

"The police are here and want to talk to us about the death of that poor boy across the street," she answered, only slightly lowering the volume. "He thinks he can hear," she said in a normal voice to Jerome and Kay. "I'm Marge, by the way."

She directed them to sit at the kitchen table while she fussed with a pot of coffee and brought over a plate of cookies.

Dennis came in wearing pastel shorts and a Florida

Gators football polo. He appeared to be in his late sixties or early seventies and walked stiffly, but with a straight back.

"Don't know why y'all want to talk to us," he said gruffly, easing himself into an empty chair at the table.

"We just have a few questions for you," Jerome assured him.

"Don't I know you?" Dennis was looking hard at Kay.

She squirmed under his gaze. She'd been wondering the same thing since she'd seen him enter the kitchen. Then everything clicked into place. The name Corfield on the mailbox should have warned her.

"I graduated from Melon County High School in 1966," Kay admitted. Dennis Corfield had been the assistant principal and had taught a couple of English classes. She'd been in his class and had just managed to squeak out a C+.

"Lamberton. I remember you. Smart, but you took too many days off. I think you were…" Dennis paused. "You were always skipping school with Rick Bruhn." His eyes were wide. "And now he's dead and here you are. But you aren't a cop. Your family runs the funeral home," he stated, sounding just like the disciplinarian that he'd been at the school.

"She's helping us out as we go around talking to folks," Jerome said, trying to gloss over the issue.

Dennis Corfield didn't look like he was buying it, but just as he opened his mouth to say something else, his wife came over with the coffee and started pouring cups for everyone.

"Milk and sugar?" Marge was either oblivious to what they'd been talking about or wasn't about to get involved.

"Sugar, please," Jerome said quickly, appreciating her intervention. "You can go ahead and have a seat. We'd like to talk to both of you."

Marge smiled and took the seat next to her husband, who was still looking like he wanted to ask more questions.

"Have either of you seen anyone hanging around the Bruhns' house since they left? Other than their son, of course," Jerome asked.

"We aren't nosy parkers getting into other people's business." Dennis frowned.

"We just thought you might have noticed a strange car or person. Not that we think you would be purposefully looking, but just in passing," Jerome said, taking a neighborly sip of coffee as he tried to disarm the man's suspicions. All Jerome needed was for someone like Dennis Corfield to call up the sheriff's office and demand to know why a deputy was questioning them about Rick Bruhn's death. *Then the shit would really hit the fan*, he thought.

"Car? Did you see anything, Marge?" Dennis asked his wife.

"I did notice a few cars coming and going. I was only looking 'cause I knew that the Bruhns were out of town."

"When was this?" Jerome and Kay leaned forward as one.

"The Bruhns left for their trip a week ago Sunday. That's when we met Rick. I went over to see if they needed anything for their trip. Of course, I remembered him from when he was in high school. The Bruhns moved here when he entered the ninth grade. Isn't that right, Dennis?"

"Rick was okay. Always thought he was smarter than he was, but he didn't get into too much trouble. More when he was going out with *you*."

Kay smiled thinly as Dennis gave her a hard look. She remembered Rick having a bit of a wild side, though it was really more that he had a habit of taking chances. There was just a bit of the adrenaline junky in his genes. Kay had to admit that she'd found it appealing when she was young and immature. But it hadn't taken her long in a war zone to decide that taking risks should be reserved for only the most dire situations.

"So about the cars?" Jerome attempted to put Marge back on track.

"That's right, the cars. There was a tan station wagon in the driveway on Monday afternoon. I didn't see anyone around the house, just the car. Then on Thursday the station wagon was back and there was a fancy little sports car. I didn't see any other cars. Oh, and on Thursday I saw a woman near the house. Good looking, well dressed. I couldn't quite tell how old she was. Not too old or too young, I'd say." Marge leaned back in her chair, looking very satisfied with herself.

"Did you see or hear anything unusual last night?" Kay asked.

"I know that you're just filling in the forms, but y'all sure are asking a lot of questions," Dennis said.

"You're right. We haven't been completely honest with you," Kay said, causing Jerome to look at her and, ever so slightly, shake his head no. Kay ignored him. "My brother picked up Rick's body and brought it to our funeral home. As Lee was cleaning the body, he noticed several… irregularities. He showed them to me." Kay shrugged. "From what I saw and from what Lee explained, I think there's something odd about the way Rick died."

"This is an official investigation?" Dennis's eyes were mere slits. Kay could tell that, even at his age, Dennis was no fool. She glanced at Jerome, who looked like he wanted to slide out of the chair and right on out of the house.

"No," Kay admitted. "I… begged Jerome to look into it, even though he explained that the evidence we have isn't enough to cause the sheriff to open an investigation."

"That doesn't make a lot of sense. I'm sure that the sheriff would want to look into any apparent evidence," Dennis argued.

"Honey, remember what you said last November."

"What?"

"You said that you couldn't decide if the sheriff was more stupid than stubborn, or the other way around," Marge reminded him.

"Yep, I guess I did say that." Dennis looked thoughtful.

"I thought it would be best if I just looked into it with Miss Lamberton before we bother the sheriff with it," Jerome jumped in, having seen a glimmer of light at the end of the tunnel.

"I can see that. If he's still anything like the Tommy Pratt I had in class, I guess the sheriff would be a pain in the… you-know-what to work for. I had him my first year teaching English. He would have failed if I hadn't given him some dumbed-down extra credit work."

"About last night… Did you see or hear anything unusual?" Jerome said, getting the conversation back on track and away from speculations about the intelligence of his boss.

"There might have been a car over there around ten o'clock," Dennis said.

"You didn't tell me." Marge sounded hurt.

"I can't say for sure, but at night when I'm sitting on the couch, if a car turns into the driveway across the street, the lights sometimes hit their front windows and reflect into our house. The angles are just right, and if we have the curtains open, the light flashes across the wall." He sounded like a physicist explaining his latest discovery.

"I never noticed that," Marge muttered. Dennis looked like he was about to say something, but thought better of it.

"You didn't look out the window?" Jerome asked.

"I thought about it since I knew the Bruhns were out of town. And I would have if I hadn't known that Rick was over there."

They asked a few more questions without learning anything new, then thanked the Corfields for their assistance. Marge showed them to the door and gave them each a bag of oatmeal chocolate chip cookies to take with them.

"I'm going to talk to some of our high school friends," Kay said as they walked back to their vehicles. "I can't imagine Rick being in town without getting in touch with some of them."

Jerome stopped and turned to her. "This isn't a game. If Bruhn was murdered, then someone in this town is dangerous. Us talking to neighbors is one thing. You going around questioning his friends is another. Odds are, if he was killed then it was by someone he knew."

"I can take care of myself. Besides, I'm not stupid. I can talk to our friends about Rick without sounding like Columbo. A mutual friend is dead. The most natural thing in the world is to want to talk about him, including the last time any of us saw him." Kay was standing with her shoulders square and her jaw set.

Jerome shrugged and turned back toward his motorcycle. "You get yourself into a mess, don't be begging me to bail you out," he said over his shoulder.

"Wouldn't dream of it!" Kay shouted back.

As she got into her car, Jerome wheeled his motorcycle alongside and said, "Be careful." Then he started the powerful motor, made a tight turn and roared off down the street.

Kay watched him leave and found herself feeling more alone than she had in a long time. She shook off the feeling and started the car, then headed off to find Zach Terrill, Rick's best friend for most of high school.

CHAPTER SEVEN

The doorbell rang as Lee and Lester were rolling Rick's body back into the cooler. Lee pulled off his gloves and was heading to the front to see who it was when he heard Ruby talking to the visitor.

"I'm sure that Mr. Lamberton will answer all of your questions, if you'll just wait here. You're a Scorpio, aren't you?"

"What the hell does that have to do with the time of day?" a gruff male voice grumbled.

"Scorpios are fierce but calm. You have fire in your eyes."

"I want to speak to the owner now." Then he huffed out a tight: "Please."

"I'm Lee Lamberton," Lee said, coming into the hall and approaching the man.

"You own this place?" The man seemed doubtful.

I need to look older, Lee thought for the hundredth time since his father had passed away. "How can I help you?" he asked in his best funeral director voice.

"I'm Chester Madison. I understand that you have the body of Rick Bruhn here." He paused for only a second. "I want to see him."

"I don't understand. Are you family?" Lee frowned.

"Not exactly."

"Then what is your relationship to Mr. Bruhn?"

The tall man moved a step closer to Lee. He was in his mid-fifties and over six feet tall, with slicked-back hair showing grey at the temples. He wore a tailored, three-piece suit. Lee refused to be intimidated by him.

"I am the president of Granite Insurance Company. Rick Bruhn was our chief operating officer."

"So you're his employer?" Lee said, still very fuzzy on why the man wanted to see Rick's body.

"Crudely put, but yes, he worked for me. Rick was an important asset to our company. More than a week ago he took off without telling anyone where he was going. I've had people hunting him since last Wednesday. This morning I was told that he's dead. I'd like to see for myself." Madison made it sound like it was the most natural thing in the world for someone to drive more than five hours in order to see the body of one of his employees.

"Why do you need to see his body?" Lee was also wondering how the man had found out so quickly that Rick was dead. Did he have an informant in the sheriff's office?

"Our company relies on its reputation. Our records and the policies that we write are highly sensitive and demand the highest level of integrity. Not just from a personal and professional standpoint, but from a legal one. To have one of the most important members of our team disappear is… upsetting. I'm in the process of having our books and policies audited and now I want to make sure that this isn't some sort of scam or dodge."

"Was Rick the type of man to run a scam or dodge?"

"Don't be stupid! If I thought that, do you think I would have let him run the company? Honestly, I didn't think he was the type of person to run off and die either." Madison was clearly bothered by Rick's behavior.

Lee had a moment when he wondered if it was actually Rick Bruhn in his cooler, but then he reminded himself that Kay had no doubts.

"His uncle is on his way here as we speak. He will formally identify the body, though it has already been seen by a close friend and his ID confirmed from his driver's license by a doctor and the sheriff's office. You may speak to his uncle when he arrives," Lee said with all the authority he could muster.

"It will only take a second for me to know if it's him or not."

"I already told you that—"

"I don't care about everyone else. *I* want to see the body. Other people could be in on the scheme." Madison's voice was becoming a bit shrill.

"Please, this is a funeral home," Lee reprimanded him. Of course, there wasn't anyone else in the house except for Lester and Ruby, but the officious jerk didn't know that.

"How much do you want?" Madison lowered his voice as he shifted tactics.

"It would be improper for me to show you the body without permission from the family," Lee said, though it was only partly true. People came and went from the embalming room all the time, though it was usually someone who worked there or who was delivering something. Still, Lee thought there was something fishy about the guy. "How do I know you're who you say you are?"

Clearly seething, the man pulled his wallet from his pocket and showed Lee his business card and driver's license. Lee decided that now wasn't the best time to point out that both items could be faked.

"Okay, I accept that you are who you say you are. But I can't show you Rick's body until his uncle gets here and says it's okay."

"Call him."

"He's on the road. He should be here late this afternoon."

From the look on the man's face, Lee could tell that he was trying to make up his mind about something. Finally he said, "I'm asking you to take liberties with your professional ethics, so I guess it's only right that I should be willing to do the same."

"I'm listening." Lee thought about telling him that ethics didn't work that way, but he wanted to hear what the man had to say. *I guess that shows which side my ethics are buttered on*, he thought ruefully.

"There is a million-dollar life insurance policy on Rick Bruhn. The policy includes a double-indemnity clause."

Lee whistled. "I guess you really *do* have a good reason for wanting to know if that's really Rick Bruhn who's lying in my cooler. Who benefits?"

"I'd rather not tell you that."

"And I'd rather not show you his body."

The man clenched his hand several times while his eyes scanned the foyer. "Okay, it's a deal."

"What?"

"You show me the body and I'll tell you who the beneficiary of the insurance policy is."

Lee frowned. Had he been tricked? Maybe, but the bottom line was that he really wanted to know who would benefit to the tune of over a million, or maybe two million, from Rick's death.

"It's a deal," he said. He started to turn toward the

embalming room, but stopped and looked back at Chester Madison. "We never tell anyone about this visit or this conversation."

"My thoughts exactly."

Lee led the way, making sure that Lester wasn't inside before letting Madison come into the embalming room.

"You can wait here. I'll pull him out of the cooler."

Lee wondered if the man would notice the marks on Bruhn's face. He decided that he wouldn't mention them if Madison didn't remark on them.

When the gurney was in front of Madison, Lee pulled the sheet down to Rick's torso.

"He was found in his parents' swimming pool," Madison stated as he bent over the body.

"Where did you get all your information?" Lee asked, but he was ignored.

Madison bent his face down close to Rick's and began to scan the body, starting at his forehead. "I'd like a pair of gloves," he ordered.

"What's the magic word?" Lee asked and received a nasty glare in return. "They're on the counter behind you," he said, pointing. He certainly wasn't going to fetch them.

Madison grabbed two gloves and snapped them on, then he lifted Rick's eyelids and looked closely at his cold, dry eyes. Next he checked the body's nose and felt the back of the head. Lee didn't need to be told that this wasn't the first corpse the man had examined.

Without asking, Madison looked around and picked up a pen light from the counter. The discoloration had faded a bit, but from the way Madison shone the light and looked closely at the face, Lee knew that he'd noticed it.

"Why isn't this body at the coroner's office?" he snapped.

"They determined it was an accident, drew blood and told us we could take it," Lee said.

"An autopsy should be performed."

"You're preaching to the choir."

"I'll need to use your phone."

"Who is the beneficiary?" Lee asked, reminding the man of their deal.

Madison sighed. "His parents. Specifically, his father and then his mother."

Lee pointed to the wall. "The phone is over there. Remember, mum's the word about our little agreement."

As Madison moved toward the phone, Lee thought about the fact that Rick's parents would receive two million dollars if the death was declared an accident. Would his parents have killed him for the money? Lee had never met them, but stranger things had happened. Two million dollars could sever any number of family ties. Still, it took cold blooded to another level.

"Yes, I want to speak with the sheriff," Madison said into the phone. "I'm Chester Madison of Granite Insurance… I want to talk to him about the death of Rick Bruhn… Yes, I'll wait." After a long pause, he introduced himself to the sheriff. "I expect there to be an autopsy. Our company holds a multi-million-dollar policy on Rick Bruhn… It's going to be *your* problem too if I have to get other authorities involved in this investigation."

There was more conversation back and forth, but Madison still looked irritated when he hung up the phone.

"Get anywhere?"

"He's agreed to an autopsy," Madison said.

No sooner were the words out of his mouth, than the phone rang. Lee answered it.

"Yes, of course. I'll have it ready to go," he said when the sheriff informed him that the coroner's office would be sending someone over to pick up Rick Bruhn's body. He hung up and turned to Chester Madison. "You've got more pull than we do, I'll give you that."

"It will still be up to the sheriff whether to open an investigation or not. My company doesn't want this to drag out." He was talking to himself as much as to Lee, who noticed that every word was accompanied by a frown.

"The marks are superficial. They might suggest some alternatives to accidental death, but they aren't definitive by any means," Lee reminded him.

"You saw this evidence and didn't inform the sheriff?"

"I think you'll find that there will be plenty of foot-dragging."

"I see. You didn't want to get on the wrong side of the sheriff's office, so you were just going to let this slide." Madison was working himself up into a fit of self-righteous anger.

"You're half right. There wasn't any point in poking the sheriff when he'd just stonewall us. But we weren't going to ignore it. In fact, we were going to look into the murder ourselves," Lee said.

"We?"

"My sister and… a friend." Lee didn't want to get Jerome in trouble. If Madison had any more run-ins with the sheriff, he might let Jerome's name drop if things got out of hand.

"You're crazy. Rick's death needs to be properly investigated."

"What needs to happen and what does happen are sometimes two different things," Lee pointed out to Madison, who was now red-faced and puffing.

"I am not going to pay out two million dollars for an accident when the man was murdered."

"You'll still have to pay a million, right?"

"If the beneficiaries weren't involved in the murder."

"Still, you save a million dollars, which is not chump change. On the other hand, you're going to open up an investigation into the murder of your chief operating officer. Are you sure that no one in your company is involved? 'Cause I wouldn't think a scandal like that would be good for the bottom line."

"Why would you even suggest that?" Chester Madison's expression had changed from indignation to caution.

"You're the one who said he left Atlanta under mysterious circumstances."

"I said he left without telling anyone."

"And was that normal for him?"

"No," Madison admitted very softly.

"You might even say he ran off."

"We don't know why he left."

"But he obviously didn't want anyone at Granite Insurance to know where he went."

"Apparently. So why do you want it swept under the rug?" Madison asked.

"I told you, we don't. We're going to find out who did this to Rick. After some discussion, we decided that it might be easier if we didn't spend a lot of time trying to push the sheriff to do work he wasn't going to do anyway."

"I see your point, though it seems short-sighted. Finding the killer does you no good if you can't prosecute them."

"We've got a plan… of sorts."

"And it involves what, exactly?"

"I'm not going to say. It might compromise one of our… little band of brothers and sisters." Lee smiled gamely, but Madison still frowned at him.

"I think I'll stick with an official inquiry. Having said that, I'll let you all go about your business without informing the sheriff."

"Thanks. Can I ask a couple of questions about Rick?"

"Like what?"

"How'd he get his job?"

Madison looked thoughtful. "We can make this an exchange. I've got a few questions myself."

"Fair enough. So how did he start working for Granite Insurance?"

"I'm surprised you don't know. It was during his sophomore year at Harvard. He was in the business program with my son. They became friends, and when Jerry found out that Rick was struggling to pay his bills, he offered to get him a summer job selling insurance for us."

"Why are you surprised I didn't know that?"

"Because he came down here and sold life insurance policies for several summers. Very successfully. We carry several hundred policies on people who live in the five surrounding counties. All of them were sold by Rick when he was off from school."

"I guess that's pretty impressive. I was too young to have paid much attention to what he was doing during the summer."

"Wasn't your sister dating him?"

Lee had to hide his surprise that the man was aware of the relationship between Kay and Rick. "They broke up before they graduated."

"That answers one of my questions."

"So he was a great salesman?"

"It's not that hard to sell policies. We have a plethora of agents that do a great job with sales. What was impressive was that Rick sold policies to people who would *keep* those policies. We have an average cancellation and default rate of fifty-three percent on new contracts. Rick's rate was closer to twenty-one percent. Remarkable. When he graduated, we hired him."

"Being a friend of your son didn't hurt."

"Hurt? No. But help? Not really. My son isn't interested in insurance. Thinks it's dull. Now he's a talent agent out in

Hollywood." There was more than a little derision in his tone when he mentioned his son's current occupation. "Rick and my son remained friends while Rick and I became partners in the company."

"He was that good?"

"Great is the word. Until this past week, he was the most dependable man I had ever worked with. Really cared about the company and the customers. Same as the way he handled sales when he was in college, making sure that the policy was what the customer needed and could afford. That was the type of integrity he carried forward into the management of our operations."

"Then he just suddenly packed up his bags and left?"

Madison shook his head. "I want that mystery solved as much as I want to catch the person who killed him."

"Did he have any enemies at the company?"

Madison shrugged. "More than I did? More than the chief financial officer? Or the head of human resources? No. If you're in business, you make enemies. But people don't kill each other over business disagreements." He frowned. "Well, not usually."

"Exactly. Not usually." Lee thought about the way that Chester Madison had talked about his son's career choices. Did he favor Rick Bruhn over his son? Could his son be jealous or fearful of losing his inheritance?

"Why did your sister and Rick break up?" Madison asked suddenly.

"Did he talk much about my sister?" Lee countered with his own question.

"On more than one occasion. From the way he talked, I always felt that his feelings for your sister were the reason that he never settled down with any of the women he dated in Atlanta. Answer my question. Why did they break up?"

"Does anyone outside a relationship really know why a

couple breaks up?" Lee said, then quickly threw his hand up to stop Madison from objecting to his second deflection. "All I know is that there was a moment at a high school dance when Kay thought Rick was cheating on her. I don't have any of the details, but you can't think that has anything to do with the murder."

"Look at it from my point of view. Rick talked about his relationship with your sister with more real emotion than I ever heard him talk about anything. One day, completely out of character, he disappears. Where do I find him? Here in Melon County, just when I understand your sister happens to be home for the first time in months." Madison stated his case and, again, Lee wondered where he was getting his information.

"Kay didn't get here until…" It dawned on Lee that she'd arrived just hours before Rick's death.

"You begin to see my point."

"There's no point to see," Lee stammered, sounding unconvincing even to his own ears. "My sister was shocked when she learned that Rick was dead."

Chester Madison nodded to himself. "I accept that. But for now, I think we'll each go our own way. Perhaps when we meet again, we'll find that our paths are better aligned with each other." He turned and left the room without waiting for Lee's response.

Lee followed him, trying to think of how to answer the man's odd comment. A sharp retort? A witty parting comment? Nothing came to mind as he watched the man walk out the front door.

"Who was that?" Lester came out of the kitchen holding a half-eaten ham sandwich.

"A friend or an enemy. It's hard to say." Lee turned to Lester. "The coroner is coming to get Bruhn's body."

"What?" Lester looked confused and Lee explained the

situation. "Isn't that going to be a little hard to explain to Rick's uncle?"

"You'll think of something to tell him," Lee said and received some satisfaction from the baffled look on Lester's face. "I'm kidding. That will fall on my head. It's not going to be much better when I tell Jerome and Kay what's happened."

CHAPTER EIGHT

Kay didn't know where to start to look for Zach Terrill, so she went to his parents' house, the one he'd lived in when they were all in high school. Zach's mother had taught English there when Kay and Zach were students, before becoming a guidance counselor.

"Zach? He moved out years ago. Do I know you?" his mother asked when she opened the door. She was wearing a spandex exercise outfit that Kay found embarrassing to look at. The woman had bulges in both the right places and the wrong places.

"I'm Kay Lamberton. We went to school together."

Mrs. Terrill's mouth fell open and her eyes went wide. "Of course! Were you ever in my class?" she asked and then answered her own question. "No, but I remember that Zach couldn't talk about anyone else! Come on in!"

"I really need to talk to Zach." Kay didn't want to get drawn into half a day of reminiscing about high school.

"Of course! He lives over on River Street. He's got

himself a nice little house, but he's not married. Dated quite a… one or two girls, but nothing serious." She gave Kay an up-and-down look like a horse trader sizing up a brood mare.

"What's the address?" Kay asked quickly. River Street was back in a quiet, residential area not far from the town square.

"He has a great job with the county. Works in the courthouse."

"The address?"

"Zach won't be home now. What have you been doing all these years?" Mrs. Terrill seemed reluctant to let Kay go on her way.

"Where can I find him?" Kay was equally anxious to get out from under the woman's microscope.

Kay wasn't sure if Mrs. Terrill actually sighed or if she just looked like she did. "He's playing baseball over at the city field."

"Thank you so much." Kay turned quickly and headed back toward her car.

Mrs. Terrill called out louder than necessary, "You must come by for dinner! Zach would love that."

Kay gave a brief wave over her shoulder in acknowledgement, then escaped into her car.

There was a decent crowd at the baseball field. The team up to bat was wearing red jerseys with *Melon County* stitched across the front while the team in the outfield sported blue jerseys reading: *City of Lang*. The teams were made up of people aged anywhere from twenty to sixty and everyone seemed focused on the game.

Kay searched the dugout for Zach, wondering if she'd recognize him. *How much can he have changed?* she wondered. Her eyes fell on a player sitting on the bench and rubbing down a wooden bat while occasionally looking up at the action on the field.

The answer was that Zach hadn't changed much at all. His hair was cut a little longer than she remembered, but it remained dark and straight. He was frowning as he sanded the bat. Kay knew that he would have heard about Rick's death. The county's grapevine was finely tuned.

She walked over to the fence that ran behind the dugout. One of the county's players was warming up with a bat on the other side.

"Excuse me," Kay said, flashing a smile and waving to get his attention. He smiled back and came closer. "Could you ask Zach to come over here for a moment?"

"We're in the middle of a game," he said, stating the obvious.

"Please."

"Okay, sure. Who are you?"

"Kay Lamberton."

He nodded and went down in the dugout. A moment later, Zach came out with a huge smile on his face.

"Wow! I can't believe this." A second after the words were out of his mouth, the smile fell from his face. "I guess you heard about Rick."

"I did. He's at our funeral home."

"Oh, wow." There was a cheer from half the crowd and Zach turned to look at the field. The batter had struck out and the city players were coming in from the outfield. "I've got to go. We have two more innings. Can you wait for me?" His eyes were pleading.

"Of course."

"As soon as we're done, I'll meet you by my car. It's the blue Blazer over there." He pointed as he backpedaled onto the field. Kay nodded and went over to the stands to find a seat. The air was cool and the sun was warm, making it a perfect day for watching the game. Everyone in the stands seemed in a good mood, eating, drinking and shouting at the players and each other.

Kay enjoyed watching Zach play more than she would have thought. He still had a touch of youth in his movements, a memory of a time when he could run and throw without a thought for what it would mean the next day. The next two innings went fast with the pitchers aggressively challenging each batter and the fielders making a minimum of mistakes. When she saw Zach coming in from the field for the last time, she climbed down from the stands and headed toward the Chevy Blazer he'd pointed out.

"I'm glad to see you," he said, wiping sweat from his forehead. "I need to get cleaned up. Do you have a car?"

"Over there," she said with a nod toward her car.

Several players from the county team stopped to ask if Zach wanted to join them at the Sudsy Dog for a beer, but he waved them off.

"Can you follow me over to the house?" he said to Kay.

She followed him through town and parked behind him in the driveway of a modest Cape-Cod-style house, painted grey with white shutters. Inside Zach poured her a glass of iced tea before excusing himself to get a shower.

Kay wandered around the living room, browsing the titles in the three bookcases. The first was filled with books on American history, with an emphasis on military conflicts. The second boasted an impressive collection of horror novels from authors including Saul, King, Lovecraft, Poe, Layman and a dozen more. The last bookcase held dozens of books on municipal planning and zoning, many of which looked like college textbooks.

When Zach came back into the living room, they settled on opposite ends of the couch. Zach whirled the ice in his own glass of tea thoughtfully.

"After I heard about Rick's death, I didn't want to play

today, but this was the big county-city matchup and the team was counting on me. Rick was always the big sports guy in high school. I guess he would have understood me supporting my team."

"Did you see him this week?" Kay asked.

"I didn't even know that he was in town. We lost touch when he went to college." Zach paused. "No, that's not true. We lost touch when we entered the twelfth grade." Kay thought she detected a hint of bitterness in his tone.

"I don't remember…" Kay was trying to think back. Had Rick changed when they started their senior year? *Teenagers are so self-absorbed*, she thought. *I don't remember much that didn't directly involve me.*

"Y'all were the special ones," Zach said, and this time there was no doubt about the edge of spite.

"Who?"

"Come on! You have to remember. Millie Jessup, Vince Edwards, Burton Sedgewick, Clint Peters, Rick and you. All of you in the honors classes and all bound for college. Not that any of you were *that* smart. I never understood why everyone thought you were so special."

"You're including *me* in this group?" Kay asked, shocked.

Zach got a chagrined look on his face. "Not really you. Even back then I saw you in a different light. I guess you proved me right when you headed for nursing school, then joined the Army."

"I proved something."

"You slugged Millie and Rick at the prom."

"It was more of a slap with Rick. Millie, I just pushed."

Kay could still see them huddled in a dark corner of the lunchroom, Rick with his hand on Millie's chest and both of them trying to suck the other's tongue out. The smell of cheap wine and paint hung in the air as Kay came up to them and began slapping Rick while shoving Millie away. In the end, she'd stormed out of the prom, crying and screaming. She'd skipped the next couple of days of school until she could bring herself to see them again. The last month of her senior year had been one painful experience after another. There had been too many classes and moments in the hall when she saw them together, or when she could hear the whispers, imagined or real, from all the other students.

"I was an idiot in those days," Zach admitted. "All I wanted was to talk to you. Did you know that? You hitting Rick just made you more of a goddess in my eyes."

"Goddess?" Kay laughed harder than she had in months. "You can't be serious." She saw the hurt look on his face and knew that he had been. "Hey, look…"

Zach raised his hand. "You're right. I had a crazy crush on you."

"When was the last time you talked to Rick?" Kay asked, trying to steer the conversation in a less awkward direction.

"I hadn't seen him in years, not until the funeral last October. Maybe I'd seen him around town a few times when he was visiting his folks. We'd wave, say hi. Nothing more."

"But you used to be close, right?"

"Thick as thieves in middle school and most of high school. Something… maybe it was ambition… got ahold of Rick those last couple of years in high school. He started talking about going to an Ivy League college. Me, I was happy listening to records and reading books. Guess I did a lot of thinking about girls too, though I couldn't seem to manage to do more than *think* about them. I guess that was something else that separated us. Rick was able to get the girls he wanted."

"His ambition *was* one of the things I found attractive about him," Kay said, admitting something she hadn't fully realized at the time.

"Now I can understand that." Zach looked hard into her eyes. "Did you ever notice that I had a thing for you?"

"Do you want the truth?" Kay asked. He smiled and gave her a slight nod. "No. I was all about Rick until I caught him cheating."

"Life is so strange. Rick's dead and now here you are, in my living room." Zach shook his head as though trying to make sense of the world's odd twists of fate.

Something he'd said earlier came back to Kay. "You mentioned that you saw him at a funeral last fall. Whose?"

"I thought you would have heard. Clint Peters."

"Clint's dead?" Clint had been a bit of a know-it-all, but nice enough.

"Cut his wrists."

Kay was stunned. Another one of her classmates was dead. She felt her gut tighten. Could there be a connection? All of a sudden, the focus of her visit changed. Half of her mind told her that coincidences happened, but the other half insisted that if two of her high school friends had suffered violent deaths within six months of each other, then it couldn't be a coincidence.

"Tell me about it," she encouraged.

"I avoided the details once I heard that it was kind of… gruesome. His wife found him in the master bath, half submerged in the tub."

"Were they sure it was suicide?"

"What kind of question is that? You think he accidently slit his wrists while shaving in the tub?" A second after Zach said it, his eyes opened wide. "No way someone murdered him. That's crazy!"

"You just said that you don't really know anything about his death, so how can you so easily dismiss the possibility that it was murder?"

"I heard that he slit his wrists. I mean, people don't get

murdered like that." Zach didn't sound very sure.

"You'd be surprised what can happen."

"Wait a minute, what is this all about? You look me up to ask questions about Rick, who just died, and now you're insinuating that Clint's suicide might have been murder?"

Kay studied Zach. Thinking back to high school, she had to admit that she couldn't remember much about him. If she'd been asked about him two days ago, all she would have been able to say was that he was kind of a nerdy guy who'd been friends with Rick. Could he be trusted? He'd already figured out that there was more to her visit and questions than just a concern for old friends, so did she have a choice but to trust him?

"I told you, my brother has Rick's body at our funeral home. There are some… indications on the body that there might be more to his death than just an accident."

"You're kidding me!" Zach looked shaken by the suggestion.

"I'm telling you what I've actually seen."

"That's… But why? I mean, I haven't spent time with him in years, so I don't know much about his personal or professional life…" When Zach realized what he'd said, he stopped and thought for a moment. "I guess that's right. I *don't* know what he's been up to in the last decade. People change. Still, murder? You'd have to have a strong reason to kill someone."

"That's what I'm looking into."

"Wait, you're not with the police. Why are you looking into the murder?"

"Because the sheriff's office already declared that his death was an accident. Do you think they're going to admit they've made a mistake?"

"Sheriff Pratt is a prat. He's never admitted to a mistake in his life."

"My point."

"But *you*?"

"If not me, then who?"

"Now you sound like a PSA," Zach said with a frown.

"Who could I talk to about Clint's death?"

"The *Gainesville Sun* covered the story. Not much, just a blurb really. Clint and his wife were living in Gainesville at the time, so the Gainesville Police Department would have been the ones investigating. Of course, you could talk to Tracy, his wife."

"Tracy? Do I know her?"

"Maybe. She's four years younger than us. Her father had a farm out on the west side of the county. Grew watermelons."

"You seem to know her pretty well."

"I dated her sister for a couple of years after high school. Sadly, their dad died of a heart attack a year later, so they sold the farm and moved to Jacksonville. That's where Tracy met Clint."

"They hadn't known each other before?"

Zach shrugged. "You'd have to ask her."

"Where's she living now?"

"Right here in the county. After Clint died, she bought the Ra Resort. They've done a lot of updates."

"That place still exists?" Kay felt herself blushing. Named after the Egyptian sun god, the resort had been little more than a hippie commune of naturists started by University of Florida drop-outs in the late sixties.

"Booming business," Zach said with a grin, then cleared his throat guiltily. "At least, that's what I hear."

"Have you been there?"

"I had to approve some of the renovations as part of my job with the county," he said, skirting the question.

"Where does she live?"

"Oh, out there on the property. She lives in the old Boxer house, which was part of the farm before the hippies bought it."

Kay cringed as she asked the next question. "I wouldn't have to… you know… go nude if I just go out there to talk with her, would I?"

"Her house is on the edge of the resort. And even if you went into the main park, they don't require that you go nude… though most of them are," Zach said, amused by her discomfort.

"That's reassuring, I guess." Kay's shyness about nudity annoyed her. She'd found it a complication while in the military, where such niceties couldn't always be accommodated. This foible of hers confused her too. She had no problem getting naked with a man that she was dating and had feelings for, but in front of strangers or acquaintances, it made her feel squirmy inside.

They talked a while longer about growing up in the rural county when life had seemed much simpler. Finally, Zach asked, "Are you moving back to Lang?"

Kay heard an unfamiliar inflection in his voice and was startled to realize that it was interest. Specifically, interest in her. While in the Army, she'd gotten used to being an object of desire. She'd known that the real reason for the soldiers' lust had been the lack of any other targets. Once she figured that out, their advances weren't very flattering. This was different.

"I'm just here to take care of some business with my brother."

"And to solve Rick's murder." Zach gave her a soft smile. "Maybe we could get together for dinner before you finish all your business and run out of town again."

"I'd better go." Kay stood up and headed for the door, but before she left she turned back and said, "Dinner sounds like fun."

"I'll call you," Zach said as she closed the door behind her.

CHAPTER NINE

Onward to the nudist colony, Kay said to herself as she backed out of the drive and headed east out of town. She remembered the general location of the resort and Zach had filled in a few turns and landmarks that she'd forgotten. He also mentioned that there were discreet signs pointing the way.

Kay thought about finding a payphone to call Lee and let him know where she was going, but she didn't want to take the time. *Besides*, she thought, *half the phones on this side of town are always out of order.* She'd waste half an hour just trying to find one that worked.

She turned left onto a dirt road marked by a sign reading simply "Ra Resort – 1 Half Mile" with an arrow pointing the way. A chain-link fence marked the boundary of the naturist resort and, at the entrance, a sign informed visitors exactly what to expect if they went past the farm gate and onto the grounds—nudity. Kay took a deep breath and drove in.

For another quarter of a mile, she drove through piney

uplands with no signs of habitation nor a nude bottom in sight. Then she came to a second gate with a small shed manned by a stout guard. He was over six feet tall, stocky and not wearing a stitch of clothing. His legs were propped up on a stool and he was readying a copy of James Michener's *Covenant.*

Kay had her window rolled down already, so when the man put down the book and came over to her car, she had to keep her eyes focused on the windshield or she would have been looking almost directly at his personal equipage.

"Now you don't look like a member," he said in a slow, Tennessee country drawl.

"No. I was hoping to see Tracy Peters. Do you know if she's home?" she asked, trying to be polite even if she couldn't look at him.

"I can tell you aren't used to the naturist lifestyle," the man said with a kindness that almost relaxed her. Almost.

"Aren't you cold?" She couldn't help herself. It was a warm spring day with the temperature in the upper seventies, but there was a cool breeze.

"It's nice here in the sun." He smiled. "Just relax and we won't take offense if you look down at your feet a whole bunch," he said, chuckling. "You'd be surprised how quickly you can get used to being free of the bindings that society wraps you up in. Kind of nice to be around others that can be unburdened too. Oh, listen to me givin' you a sales pitch. I was a salesman for almost ten years. You'll get a kick out of this. I sold men's clothes. Ain't that a hoot! I'm Jeb, by the way. I'll need your name before I can point you on your way. Miz Tracy is here at the resort, but I can't tell you if she's at her house or at the resort proper. Stop at the office and Myra can call around and find out where she is."

"I'm Kay Lamberton," she told him, feeling like she wasn't at all prepared for what was to come.

"Fine, Miz Lamberton." He wrote her name down on a clipboard. "Miz Tracy's house is the first road to the left, but like I said, if you go straight for a couple hundred yards past that turn up there, you'll come to the resort's office and Myra will get you headed in the right direction, which could save you time. Truth is, during the day Miz Tracy spends most of her time keeping an eye on things down by the lake."

Kay didn't want to have an eye on *anything* down by the lake. Should she go straight to the house and hope for some luck, or just submit and put herself at the mercy of Myra?

"Thank you." She gave a slight wave as she drove down the well-traveled dirt road, undecided which course she was going to take until she came to the cut-off to the house and turned onto it. *I can always go to the office if Tracy isn't home*, she told herself.

The house appeared around the first turn. Like a prim and proper farm woman, the sturdy two-story country house stood watch over the property. It was surrounded by half a dozen live oak trees that looked like they could have been seedlings when Ponce de Leon named the land *La Florida.*

Kay blinked in shock as a woman, firm and fit and naked as the day God made her (except for a pair of slip-on shoes), walked out of the house.

The woman looked at the approaching car with an open expression, as though she wanted to wave but not without knowing who she was waving at. Kay saw a vintage VW Bug in almost mint condition parked next to the house and, without looking at the nude woman, parked her car beside it.

As soon as Kay put her car in park, she saw the shadow of the woman at her window.

"May I help you?" The woman smiled in the window at Kay, who wished she'd back up so she could get out of the car without being uncomfortably close to the woman's…

parts.

"I'm a friend of Rick Bruhn and I was hoping to talk to Tracy Peters." Kay had no choice but to look at the woman.

She put her hand up to her mouth and her eyes softened. "I heard about that on the radio. I'm Tracy. I thought you were a visitor who made a wrong turn. Happens a lot. I really should put up better signage. Come on up to the house."

"I'm Kay Lamberton."

"Kay. I don't remember Clint or Rick mentioning you. Wait. Lamberton? Are you related to the Lambertons that own the funeral home?"

"I'm Lee's sister," Kay said, following Tracy toward the house.

"I really appreciate what your father did for us when Clint… died. I was sorry to hear that he had passed as well. I'm so sorry," Tracy said, sounding sincere.

As they walked up the steps to the porch, Kay admired Tracy's long, black hair that reached almost to her… Kay averted her eyes and took in the two rocking chairs and small table that occupied the porch.

"Can I get you something to drink?" Tracy asked.

"I'm fine. I just have a few questions."

"Then let's sit out here. Though it's a little cool… I think I'll go get a coat."

Kay was relieved that Tracy was going to put on some clothes and she wondered if the woman was doing it simply to make her feel more comfortable.

"Now, what kind of questions could you have for me?" Tracy asked when she came back out of the house wearing a light windbreaker.

"I'm sorry to come here unannounced like this." Kay thought that she needed to pave the ground with an apology before diving into a bunch of questions about Tracy's husband's suicide.

"No need to apologize. I'm glad you're here. I've been wanting to talk to someone since I heard about Rick's accident. But why do you want to talk to me?"

"That's the other part I want to apologize for. I'd like to ask about your husband's death."

For the first time, Tracy's expression closed up. Her eyes became hooded and her mouth clamped tight until there was little more than a sharp hard line where an open smile had been just moments earlier.

"I don't want to talk about that." Her words were clipped and hard.

"I understand your reluctance…" Kay started and, as soon as she saw Tracy's face turn red, she knew that she'd said the wrong thing.

"You understand? I doubt that." Tracy stood up.

"Wait. I should know better than to say something that stupid." Kay wasn't just saying that. After growing up with a family whose business was grief, she should have learned some things. *Apparently not*, she chastised herself.

"Just hear me out." Kay knew that she only had one chance to gain Tracy's confidence. "I… We think there's something wrong about Rick's death," she hurriedly explained, knowing that Tracy was close to telling her to leave.

Her words had the desired effect. Tracy stopped and looked at Kay, who wished she knew what the woman was thinking. Whatever it was, Tracy decided to hear Kay out.

"The radio didn't give any details. I think the words they used were tragic accident."

"They found Rick in his parents' swimming pool last night. The sheriff and coroner decided that he'd drowned."

"You have a different opinion?" Tracy sounded skeptical.

"We do."

"Who's we?"

"My brother and… a friend." If Tracy went to the sheriff and complained, Kay didn't want to get Jerome in trouble.

Tracy eased back down into the rocker. "When Clint died, I didn't believe it was suicide. Denial is one of the stages of grief."

"We have more concrete proof." Kay didn't want to say anything else. She didn't know if she could fully trust this woman.

"What kind of proof?"

"I'd rather not say right now."

"If you have evidence, then you better go to the police."

"They've made up their minds and aren't going to listen to us." Kay was already tired of explaining that the sheriff's office wasn't going to do their duty where Rick was concerned.

Tracy seemed to consider all of this for a moment. "Even if I accept what you're telling me, what does this have to do with my husband's death?"

"I don't know. When I heard that a friend of Rick's had died just six months before he did…" Kay shrugged. "I just wondered if there could be a link."

"That seems like a stretch." Tracy paused and looked past Kay for a moment before continuing. "However, I can see why you might jump to conclusions. You have to understand, Clint's death was the worst thing that has ever happened to me. If losing him wasn't bad enough, I was the one who found his body." Tracy dropped her eyes to the ground

"Zach mentioned that."

"We lived in Gainesville. Clint had started his own law office and had big plans to expand it. Not just locally, but to other towns across the country."

"He was a lawyer?" Kay was embarrassed that she'd come here knowing nothing about Clint.

"You went to school with him, right?"

"Yes. He was friends with Rick. Clint was one of the smart kids. I guess they'd call them gifted today. Rick kind of aspired to be seen that way." Kay hesitated before saying the next part. "I didn't really see myself as part of their group. I, well, I liked being in the band." She shrugged.

Tracy gave her just a hint of a smile. "I was a band girl too."

"How did you meet Clint?"

"I met him in Jacksonville. He was just out of Yale and was working for a firm there while he prepared for the bar exam. There was a bonfire on the nudist beach south of St. Augustine. I looked over at him and the fire reflected in his eyes… then I fell in love. Later we learned we were both from Lang, which seemed to confirm that our meeting was kismet."

"And you eventually moved to Gainesville?"

"In a roundabout way. Clint didn't like working for a big firm, so he was kind of flailing around, searching for a place where he could make his mark. One day he got a call from a friend of his who was working his way up the ladder at the University of Florida. You might know him, Vince Edwards. He was a member of Clint's clique in high school. Vince had some legal problem that he wanted Clint to help him with. One thing led to another and Clint decided that there were a lot of university folk who needed good lawyers.

"It was a good idea," Tracy continued. "So good that Clint had started looking at other small communities with large universities. If the community is small, then there's a limited number of lawyers who aren't connected with the schools. And the small-town lawyers usually aren't used to handling cases that can be international in scope. So Clint wanted to create a chain of law offices that cater to the needs of university professionals and students. He had already dealt with cases as diverse as immigration, discrimination, patent and copyright law."

"Clint sounds focused. I… don't know quite how to ask this next question." Kay was working hard at treading softly. If she got kicked off the property now, would she ever get another chance to talk to Tracy?

"One of the benefits of being a nudist is that you learn not to hold things back," Tracy said encouragingly.

"My question is about the resort. Did you own it before Clint died?"

"No. I managed it."

"That's my question. Didn't Clint find it awkward having a wife that worked… here?"

"Actually, I think it was an asset. When people found out where I worked, they were curious about us. It set us apart. Made us more interesting."

"Now you own it?"

"It's sort of funny. Not ha-ha funny, but strange funny. I wouldn't be able to own this place if it hadn't been for Rick. He sold me and Clint life insurance policies years ago. When the insurance company paid out, I had an opportunity to buy the resort and took it. Clint and I had spent some time here. Times when he was happy. *We* were happy. I thought it would be a proper way to use the money."

"But he committed suicide. I didn't think insurance companies pay if their beneficiaries kill themselves."

"I didn't either. Turns out that it's not uncommon for that stipulation to apply only in the first year of the policy. That was the case with Clint's policy."

Does this mean anything? Kay thought. *The woman benefited from her husband's death and, on top of that, the man who sold them the insurance policy died under unusual circumstances, was maybe even murdered. There* has *to be a connection.*

"I was a nurse in the military," Kay said. "I saw a number

of suicides. The causes are always a complex weave of reasons and emotions. If Clint's death was suicide…"

Kay watched as Tracy put her head in her hands. "Please stop! Don't do this. I just reached the point where I've accepted that it was suicide. I can't start thinking it was otherwise."

"Just tell me what you think happened." Kay felt uncomfortable watching Tracy struggle with her grief. Was she being sincere, or was she putting on a display to convince Kay that she had loved her husband? Kay couldn't tell. She'd known plenty of people who were convincing liars.

"I don't know why he killed himself. What I do know is that Clint had been acting… distant the last few months before it happened. I just thought he was working hard. Distracted. When I'd ask him if anything was bothering him, he'd just say that he was tired. Which made sense at the time. He was working twelve hours a day most of the time. The guilt of knowing that he was hiding some… secret pain and that I didn't take the time to find out what it was… It just crushes me if I think about it."

"Can you tell me about his death?" Kay kept her voice low and soft, having already made up her mind that if Tracy didn't want to talk about it, then she wouldn't push her.

"I had been here all day—not in this house of course; I mean working at the resort. I got home just after six. It was the first really nice fall day that we'd had, so I wasn't too surprised when I saw Clint's car in the driveway. As hard as he worked, he would sometimes take off early from the office if the weather was really nice. Our house had a Florida room in the back with a desk and typewriter where he could work if he wanted to. I half expected to hear the clacking of the typewriter, or him talking on the telephone when I opened the back door. Instead, the house was quiet. I think I knew something was wrong as soon as I stepped over the threshold. I had a bag of groceries and instead of putting them up, I just dropped the bag on the kitchen table and started calling for Clint."

"Was the door unlocked?"

"We never locked the back door if we were home. I did look into the Florida room, even though I knew he wasn't there. Clint wasn't a quiet man. He was always working on something and never seemed to do anything quietly. I got scared when I didn't find him downstairs. I imagined him sick in bed or… or… I don't know what I thought. All I know is that I never once thought that he would be lying in the bathtub with his wrists slit."

Tracy was managing to hold herself together as she talked, which surprised Kay. From the way she told the story, she'd obviously been over it more than once, with the police, with family, maybe even with a psychologist.

"I'm so sorry," Kay said, wanting to reach out and touch the woman's arm to comfort her, yet uncomfortable making the gesture. No small part of that had to do with Tracy's nudity. "If this is too much…"

"No. I think saying it out loud is good for me, and I've had to tell it before. It's not like the images don't play through my head every day." Tracy paused for a moment, then said, "There was a note on the bed that I didn't notice before I went into the bathroom. The note just said: 'I'm sorry. Remember that I have always loved you.'"

"How long had he been dead?"

"His skin was white and cold when I touched him. The police said that he had to have been dead for at least two hours. Later I learned that he'd left his office around three."

"Did his colleagues notice anything odd about his behavior?"

"No. They learned that he'd met with his lawyer a week

earlier and had written up a new will, including instructions for how to divide up the business and a twenty-page business plan if they chose to stay together and move forward with the firm." Tracy wiped at tears that had managed to escape her eyes.

"Was anything disturbed in the house?"

"I tried to find something out of place. Some sign that another person had done this. I even hired a private detective to follow behind the police, just to make sure they were doing everything they should. I… there was nothing to suggest that it was anything other than suicide. I couldn't look through all of his papers because of lawyer-client confidentiality, but his partners went through them for me and assured me there wasn't anything in them that was out of place or unusual for the work he was doing."

Kay sighed and leaned back in the rocker. She was trying to think of something else to ask or another avenue to pursue, but there didn't seem to be anything left to say.

"I appreciate you talking with me."

"I just can't imagine how Clint's death could be related to Rick's," Tracy said earnestly.

"Had they stayed in touch?"

"They were good friends. I think Rick might have been Clint's best friend. We didn't see much of him, though. At least I didn't. Clint went up to Atlanta a couple of times a year on business. They'd always get together then. Sometimes Clint would even stay with Rick."

"I dated Rick in high school," Kay admitted. *Why did I tell her that?* she thought.

Tracy really looked at her for the first time since they'd met. "You're *that* Kay. I should have recognized the name when you told me. Now I remember Rick and Clint talking about you."

"Really? I can't imagine what they could have said." Kay

was taken aback at the fact that Rick had given her a second thought.

"Nothing bad. In fact, Clint thought that Rick shouldn't have let you get away." Tracy's eyes got big and she smiled. "That's right, there was something about Millie. Rick kissed her and you punched Millie." Tracy put her hand to her mouth and stifled a laugh. "I would have loved to see that. Millie is so full of herself." Now she did laugh and shook her head.

"I didn't really punch her." Kay couldn't help smiling too. "How well do you know Millie Jessup?"

"Too well. Clint did some work for her. Copyright infringement, something to do with her second book. A screenplay with the same plot was being talked about in *Variety* and Millie was all outraged. As if her books aren't just retellings of a hundred other books. Still, I guess they're bestsellers for a reason."

"Let me guess, you don't like her much."

"The first time I met her was at a party we held after Clint passed the bar. She took me aside and asked me if I thought I was good enough for Clint. She was more than a bit drunk, but I could tell that every word she spoke came from her heart."

"Why did she care?"

"About me and Clint? I get the impression that she takes more than a little interest in the men around her. I wouldn't doubt that she purposefully let you see her and Rick. And it went both ways. Millie seemed to have a hold over the guys, even years later. Clint, Rick, Vince and Burton… like she owned them."

"She *was* pretty."

"Still is," Tracy admitted grudgingly.

"I know that back in high school, the four guys often followed her around like puppies. Looking back, I was probably envious of her long before the incident at the prom. She was prettier and smarter than me. The worst part was, I could see that Rick thought she was too."

"I think there was a small part of Clint that still pined away for her. He'd never have admitted it, but when she called I could see a sparkle in his eye. I tried not to let it bother me. We all have our first crush. I'm sure that's what she was to him. Who knows about the others."

"She's married, isn't she?"

"Married, divorced and married again."

"Where is she living now?"

"North Carolina, Chapel Hill. She's a guest lecturer at the university. She's always had a… thing for Thomas Wolfe. Very literary. Have you read any of her books?"

"I'm more a horror and fantasy fan, but I've flipped through a couple of her novels. Never saw what the fuss was all about." Kay shrugged.

"Pretentious would be my one-word review of all five of her books. I'd just nod when Clint would gush over them. I'll tell you this: she wouldn't have gotten any of them published if she didn't have that Columbia University diploma and hadn't spent every waking moment hobnobbing with only the very best publishers."

"Is hobnobbing a euphemism?" Kay asked, one eyebrow raised.

"Sounds rather obscene, doesn't it?" Tracy smiled. "All I know is that she always did more than a little flirting anytime I was around. At any party, she knew who was the most influential person in the room."

The jangle of the telephone sounded from somewhere in the house. Tracy excused herself and went to answer it.

"They need me at the office," she told Kay when she came back onto the porch.

"Thank you for talking with me." Kay stood up.

"I liked Rick. On top of that, I owe him for this." She spread her arms. "Clint and I never would have bought insurance without him…" She frowned. "It's odd. I never considered the possibility that the insurance might have contributed to Clint taking his life."

"How's that?"

"I don't think he would have done it if he'd thought he'd be leaving me without a net of some sort to catch me." Tracy's voice and eyes were distant. "All the things you think of when you really don't have any answers." She walked down the steps.

"If you think of anything else, you can reach me at the funeral home," Kay told her as she followed her out to her car.

"I'll be at Rick's funeral," Tracy assured her.

CHAPTER TEN

As luck would have it, the two attendants had just loaded Rick's body into the back of the morgue's station wagon and driven away when Todd Bruhn pulled up to the funeral home.

"The county took the body?" Bruhn looked exhausted from his drive.

"Chester Madison was here. He insisted," Lee said.

"Rick's boss?"

"Seems there was a large policy on your nephew's life."

"That's not surprising since he worked for an insurance agency. Worked his way through college selling life insurance."

"Can I get you something to drink?" Lee had brought Bruhn into his office and steered him toward the couch in the corner, fearing the man might collapse from exhaustion.

"The drive was rough. My days of driving nonstop are coming to a close." Lee judged Todd to be in his late fifties, possibly older considering how the man looked as he slouched on the couch. "If you have something with a little punch to it, that would be great."

"Gin, bourbon, brandy or something else?" Lee's father had kept a well-stocked bar in the office. *A stiff whiskey can help a widower quicker than kind words and sympathy*, his father had told him on several occasions.

"Brandy," Bruhn said, unbuttoning his coat.

After he'd downed half a glass, he sighed and pursed his lips. "I was surprised that the body hadn't gone directly to the hospital. Aren't autopsies standard operating procedure when someone young like Rick dies suddenly?"

"Most of the time," Lee agreed. "Unfortunately, we have a sheriff who cares more about the numbers than the truth."

Bruhn grunted. "Is there any question that it was an accident?"

Lee had been trying to decide what he would tell Bruhn if that question came up. He'd settled on winging it. "It's hard to say for sure. There are some odd features I noticed on the body." He didn't want to say anything else. It wouldn't help to have the Bruhns badgering the sheriff too… at least not yet.

"What type of features?"

"I don't think I'm qualified to say. I just noticed some anomalies. I think you should wait for the official determinations from the autopsy"

"And if they don't agree with your assessment?"

"I'm a mortician, not a doctor," Lee emphasized, "but if you want to hear my opinion after you get the autopsy findings, I'll be glad to tell you what I saw."

"At that point it won't mean much."

"My opinion doesn't mean much now."

"You own this place?" Bruhn waved his now-empty glass around. The combination of the drive and drinking on an empty stomach was loosening him up.

"My sister and I do."

"Young, aren't you?"

Lee explained about his father's death. Todd nodded.

"My father died young. Killed in the South Pacific. Never should have been there; he was forty years old. Captured in Bataan. You ever heard about the Bataan Death March? Everyone talks about the Nazis, but the bloody Imperial Japanese were just as sadistic. Twenty years ago, one of his comrades got drunk and told my brother and me what happened. Our dad got his head cut off by a Japanese soldier because he tripped and fell against an officer's leg. I can't get that damn image out of my head." He looked at the glass as though he was surprised that it was empty. "My brother lives with it too. Now he's lost his only son. Shit."

For a moment, Lee thought that Todd Bruhn was going to slump over on the couch. Instead the man rallied.

"I got to get as much of this…" He waved his hands at his surroundings. "…finished as I can. My brother and his wife are pretty tough, but I don't know how they're going to cope with… Rick meant everything to them.

"My mother was tough too, but I'd still catch her sometimes, crying and hugging Dad's picture. That picture never had any dust on it." He looked at the empty glass again. "Don't think another drink would be a good idea. Not unless you want me to take a nap here on your couch." He gave Lee a small smile.

"If you need to rest, we have a guest room upstairs. The bed's already made up," Lee offered.

"I need to get checked in to a motel."

"The Howard Johnson's at the interstate is decent and they have a restaurant."

"Yeah, the big orange roof. That will do." Bruhn stood up. Lee was surprised that he didn't wobble.

"If it was murder, do you have any idea who could have

done it?" Lee asked him suddenly.

"Murder? It's strange to think about someone hating Rick enough to kill him." The man looked like he was going to sit back down, but instead he put his hand out and steadied himself against the wall. "I can't think of anyone. Murder?" He shook his head as though trying to dislodge the word before it settled in his brain like the image of his father's beheading, unwanted yet forever with him.

"I'll walk you to your car. We can talk more tomorrow." Lee didn't have the heart to ask the man any more questions.

"Tomorrow. Sure, there's still time before Edgar and Pearl get here."

After seeing the man off, Lee wandered around to the back of the building. Lester was washing down the new hearse. He'd turned the radio on in one of the family cars and the cloying lyrics of that song about piña coladas competed with the noise of the water spraying off the hearse's hood. Ruby was nearby, feeding her two big tiger-striped cats at the bottom of the stairs that led up to her apartment. Lee received curious glances from the two cats before they went back to gobbling down the pieces of fish that Ruby was doling out.

"Do you think she's going to back down?" Lee asked Ruby. He knew he didn't have to give a context for the question.

"Don't you worry. She's not going to shut the funeral home down," Ruby said with so much assurance that Lee could almost believe it. He knew that Lester was half convinced Ruby could see into the future.

"I hope you're right."

"She didn't drive all the way here to sell the home. Look at you, big kitty," she said to one of the cats.

"Is that Yin or Yang?"

"Yang. See the darker stripe behind his ear? He's the

smarter of the two. You're right to pursue this murder." Ruby switched topics with her usual random fashion.

"You know something about Rick's murder?"

"Yin does." She pointed to the other cat, who was sprawled on his back, licking his expansive stomach.

"I don't understand," Lee said, which was the normal state of affairs when Ruby made one of her odder statements.

"The direction in which he licks his stomach indicates the level of disturbance he detects in the spiritual realm," she explained as naturally as she would have announced the current weather conditions.

"The spiritual realm?"

"Both of my dears can feel the vibrations. If the spirits were upset that you're looking into this man's death, they would be agitated."

"These spirits care about Rick's murder?" Lee's father had used to chastise him for teasing Ruby, but he couldn't resist. Even though Lee never meant to make fun of her, he just couldn't let some of her wilder statements go unchallenged.

"Murder causes a great disturbance in the spirit realm. That is why it often leaves a ghostly presence behind as spirits who hunger for justice." Her voice was serious and full of undertones.

"And the cats are tuned in to the spirits?"

For a moment, Lee thought he'd gone too far. Ruby turned and gave him a hard look, her unnaturally black hair blowing in the breeze as though spirits were wafting around her head.

"Cats embody the ancient essence of Bastet. They are close to the void and able to cross through the veil that separates the two realms. We're going to have fried chicken for dinner. Which would you prefer, creamed corn or lima beans?"

Lee let the spirit world go. "Lima beans would be great. Are you making homemade biscuits?"

"Of course, silly. I know how much you and Lester love them." Ruby turned and headed for the house, leaving Lee and the two satiated cats in her wake.

Lee petted Yin, who allowed the attention for a few strokes before reaching up to clean the parts of his body that Lee had touched. When Lee reached over to pet Yang, the cat got up, climbed the stairs to Ruby's apartment and squeezed his ample self through the cat door.

"My labor provides the money that feeds you," Lee reminded them.

"Is Ruby crazy or some kind of mystic Mary Poppins?" Lester asked, walking past Lee to turn off the faucet.

"Jury's still out. Half the time I think she's crazy, but the other half of the time she's hitting every nail on the head."

"So does she think your sister is going to throw us all out on the street?" Lester pulled a crumpled box of Winstons from his pocket and took out a cigarette that he had to bend back into shape before lighting.

"Currently the vibes say no."

"What's the deal? Could she really force you to sell the place? That doesn't seem right. Your dad left it to you."

"I told you. He left it to both of us. I think he had some notion that it would cause us to be like best friends. Brother and sister working together to keep the old business going."

"Any chance of that?"

"None whatsoever. We've never been close. She picked on me when I was a kid. Probably resented me coming along after having Mom and Dad to herself for seven years."

"So what options do you have?"

"I could buy her out if I had enough money."

"How much?"

"You going to loan it to me?" Lee said with a humorless laugh.

"Just asking."

"The will says either of us can buy the other out. We just have to pay for the value of any material property."

"What's that mean?"

"Means I wouldn't have to pay her for the value of the name or any projected earnings. Just half of what the house, cars and equipment are worth."

"The house is pretty old," Lester said, looking up at the eaves of the house where the paint was peeling.

"The house is worth maybe seventy. Cars about thirty. I wish Dad hadn't bought the new hearse. Spent most of his savings to pay cash for that. I guess the equipment is worth another ten. So a hundred-and-ten divided in half. All I need is fifty-five thousand dollars."

"Don't have it?"

"There was twenty thousand in the bank when Dad died. I've spent half of that to pay for operating expenses. Ten thousand left and half that is Kay's."

"Go to a bank for a loan," Lester said with a shrug, tapping the ash from his cigarette.

"I…" Lee hated to admit to Lester that he hadn't even thought about it. Could he get a loan to buy Kay out? "Maybe… Hey, you missed a spot on the Cadillac."

Lester groaned. "Can I save the family car for tomorrow?"

"Might want to do it now. I think there's a cold front moving through tomorrow."

Lester looked disappointed, but Lee had a point. Lester turned off the radio in the family car and rolled up the windows, then did the reverse on the hearse. This time the radio played the mellow strains of Christopher Cross's "Sailing."

Lee wandered back to his office to take another look at the books. He wondered if a loan would be a good idea, and he thought of the farmers he knew who had been driven out of business thanks to banks pushing big equipment loans that they couldn't afford. Lee was afraid that by asking for a loan, he might be digging his own grave.

CHAPTER ELEVEN

Kay knocked on the doorframe of the office a little while later. Startled, Lee looked up.

"You're hard at work," Kay said.

"I know you don't think so, but I do take the business side of things seriously," Lee answered, feeling the need to defend himself.

"I'm sure you do. The trouble is, the town isn't willing to take *you* seriously."

"Which is why I need more time."

Kay came over to the desk and dropped into one of the two wingback chairs in front of it.

"I want to find out who killed Rick. I don't think arguing about our family business is going to help us find his murderer. That conversation can wait." She wanted to tell Lee that there was no point talking about it anyway since she'd made up her mind, but that would just drive a deeper wedge between them at a time when they needed to pull together.

"We might *not* have to play junior detectives." Lee went on to tell her about Rick's boss calling the sheriff and the resulting removal of the body to the morgue.

"Is there a chance the sheriff's department will take it seriously now?" Even as she asked the question, Kay felt confident they wouldn't.

"Probably not," Lee said, confirming her thoughts. "Jerome can test the waters. Maybe it will make a difference." He shrugged.

"But the coroner isn't going to fake the results."

"No, he's competent and honest. However, I still don't think there will be anything that is determinant."

"So what? Then the cause of death will be undetermined."

"The cause will be lack of oxygen," Lee snapped. "Whether he drowned or suffocated, I don't know if the coroner can determine that. But he's not likely to put murder as the cause. And when the results come back, Pratt can spin it any way he wants. Maybe he'll put in a little leg work before closing it out, again, as an accident."

"There's more than one possible murder," Kay tossed out.

"What!" Lee sat up and leaned forward. "Who?"

Kay told him what she'd found out about Clint Peters's death.

Lee was dubious. "So Rick's friend Clint died six months ago. But the Gainesville police declared it a suicide. If he'd drowned in the tub, I could see a direct connection. But slit wrists?"

"There's something odd about his death coming six months before Rick's." Kay knew she was deep in the nebulous territory of hunches and intuition.

"The Gainesville police probably did a thorough job. They aren't as self-serving as our sheriff."

"Clint's widow inherited a million dollars."

Lee whistled. "That's a heck of a motive. Which gives even more credence to my belief that the GPD probably did a deep dive on his death."

"Jerome might have a contact over in Gainesville. We ought to at least look into it a bit. No one else is going to tie these deaths together," Kay insisted.

"For good reason. One's a suicide and the other is… something else."

"I thought you were sure that Rick was murdered."

"Would I swear to it in a court of law? There's evidence that something rubbed across his face and scratched his throat. More than that…" Lee shook his head.

"Don't wimp out on me now. There's also the fact that a million-dollar life insurance policy was at stake in both cases." The more Kay went over it in her mind, the more convinced she was that there was something fishy here. She just wasn't sure if she was convincing Lee.

"I'm trying to be practical. We aren't cops. We don't even play cops on TV." Lee gave her a small smile that wasn't returned. "I stick by what I said."

Lee found himself wishing that he'd just done his job and kept his mouth shut. How was stirring up the sheriff going to help him save the funeral home? And was getting on his sister's good side by solving her old boyfriend's possible murder worth the effort?

"The deaths are connected," Kay said emphatically. "Both of them had an insurance policy for a million dollars from the same company."

"Which is why the president of said company was trying to ramrod an investigation."

"Did he mention Clint's death?"

"Don't you think I would have told you?"

"You weren't the smartest of Mom's kids," Kay said in a

childish way that reminded him of their many fights.

"Why did you always pick on me?" he asked.

"Because you could always get away with anything," Kay tossed it off easily, but there was a truthful bitterness in her words.

"That's ridiculous," Lee said, stung. "You were the one who could do anything you wanted."

Her face turned red. "Are you kidding? Dad was never happy with anything I did. You, on the other hand, were his pride."

Lee wanted to throw more hot words at her. The only thing that stopped him was the thought that if he burned this bridge, there would be no rebuilding it for a long time… way past the chance of saving the funeral home. He took a deep breath and held his tongue until his emotions were under control.

"You're right about the insurance," he finally said, bringing the conversation back to the subject at hand. "Do you think that this is some type of Hitchcock-crisscross-*Strangers-on-a-Train*-thing where Clint's wife switched murders with Rick's parents?"

"No, that's ridiculous. But maybe someone profited from both deaths who isn't obvious."

"Like the insurance company," Lee said, intrigued. "But the company is going to lose money."

"Don't they have underwriters or something?" Kay asked. "Insurance for the insurance company?"

"I don't have a clue. But maybe. I see your point. That might explain why Rick was running away. He could have discovered that the company was involved in some underhanded money scheme."

"Exactly."

"I'll give you this much. That angle is worth looking into."

"What did you learn from Rick's uncle?" Kay pushed.

"Nothing really," Lee said. "He was exhausted, both emotionally and physically. He seemed shocked that Rick might have been murdered."

"Maybe *he's* involved somehow."

"Chester Madison said it's Rick's parents who are the beneficiaries of the insurance."

"And we haven't met them yet." Kay frowned.

"Didn't you meet them when you were dating Rick?" Lee asked.

"A couple of times," Kay admitted. "But it's hard to think back. And we were kids. We didn't hang out with his parents any more than we had to." Kay closed her eyes. "Let me think. Mr. Bruhn seemed… distant, maybe? Rick's mother… She was okay, but I always got the feeling she had higher hopes for her son."

"You weren't good enough?" Lee couldn't help needling his sister.

"*We* weren't good enough. Some folks don't want undertakers in the family."

"It's not like I play with dead things," Lee said defensively.

"*Working* with the dead isn't much better."

"Those damn *Living Dead* movies haven't helped."

Kay sighed. "Honestly, I think there was more to it than just the funeral home stuff. Rick's mom was really pushing him to go to an Ivy League college."

"I don't really remember much about what happened. When did y'all break up?"

"Prom. I'm not surprised that you don't remember. You were too busy being a spoiled brat," Kay said with only a wee bit of venom. Lee ignored the cut.

"Is that when you started thinking about the Army?"

"Yeah, though I vacillated about it a bit while I was in

nursing school. But once a recruiter came and talked to us, I knew it was something I had to do. He talked half a dozen of us into enlisting and they paid for our last year of school."

"Strangely, I *do* remember the night you told Dad that you were enlisting."

"He wasn't happy."

"I was watching the *Wild Wild West* in the den when I heard y'all arguing. I turned the old black-and-white down so I could figure out if it was a full-fledged fight or just an argument. That's when I heard Dad storming up the stairs."

"I can still hear the door slamming."

"He was mad for a week."

"Then two months later he called and told me that he loved me, even if I made stupid decisions." Kay smiled at the memory.

"He sure was glad when I was rated 4-F."

"Yeah, how'd you manage that?"

"I have a spot on my lungs from that bout with pneumonia when I was seven. The doc stamped me 4-F and sent me on my way."

"As much as you're a pain in my ass, I'm glad you didn't have to go over there," Kay said darkly as unwanted memories began to surface.

Lee looked away and changed the subject. "We need to figure out what Rick was doing here. His suitcases left in the trunk of his car, leaving work without telling anyone where he was going and the gun tucked under the mattress all suggest that he wasn't just babysitting his parents' house."

Kay nodded. "We also need to find out who he talked to while he was here. Tracy and Zach hadn't seen him…"

"They say they didn't talk to him," Lee corrected her.

Kay looked pensive for a moment before nodding her head. "Right. I have to stop taking people at their word. I will say that they both seemed credible. So who else could

Rick have met with? One of the neighbors saw a station wagon, a sports car and a woman at different times, so he definitely had some visitors. I'll check out the rest of his friends that I know."

Even as she said it, Kay cringed. She didn't want to play high-school reunion. Her original plan had been to get in, settle the business with her brother and then get the hell back out of town as quickly as possible. She gritted her teeth and told herself that she'd do whatever she could to find out what happened to Rick.

"I can't get the insurance money out of my head," Lee said. "Two million dollars. That's the elephant in the room. *Could* it have been suicide?"

"How could he smother himself and then pump water into his own lungs?" Kay asked doubtfully.

"He could have made the marks on his face and ran something down his throat before drowning himself, just to throw the investigators off," Lee suggested.

"But *why* would he kill himself? More to the point, why make it look like an accident? His parents would get paid whether it was suicide or not."

"The gun and sneaking away from work with no warning suggest that he was in some kind of trouble. He might have planned on running, but then decided not to."

"So he kills himself and makes it look like murder?"

"To muddy the waters, just in case the cops didn't think it was an accident. Remember the end game—to get insurance money for his parents."

Kay shook her head. "I can believe that Rick wouldn't want to leave his parents without anything, but I don't think he would have done it in their pool. That's heartless."

Lee sighed. "You've got a point. Still, desperate people do desperate things."

"None of this makes much sense. The trouble is, no one

seems to know what was bothering Rick."

"Yeah, we're back to trying to find someone he talked to during the past week."

"I'll look up some of our old friends," Kay said, resigning herself to a prolonged trip down memory lane.

Lester came into the office looking excited.

"Customers," he whispered, pointing toward the front of the house. "Two old people. They came by while I was washing the family car. I put them in the parlor."

Lee went out into the parlor where a man, stoop-shouldered and wearing a pastel pullover and polyester slacks, was nodding to his wife, a plump woman in a floral-print blouse and too much jewelry. She was telling him to sit down and stop pacing. Both appeared to be in their late seventies.

"I'm Lee Lamberton," he said, holding out his hand to the old man, who gave it a couple of quick shakes.

"Ben Hallston. This is my wife, Lillian. We were hoping to speak with your father."

"I'm sorry, but my father passed away three months ago."

Hallston looked confused. "I didn't know that." He gave his wife a significant look.

"I'll be glad to help you in any way I can," Lee said, using his most professional voice.

"I'm sorry to hear about your dad. He and I were friends years ago." Hallston cocked his head to the side. "Oh yeah, I remember you. Just knee-high when we moved."

"Sorry, I don't remember…"

"Of course you wouldn't. I ran the print shop here in town. Sold out and we moved up to Virginia. We just wanted to stop by and say hi." He glanced at his wife again, who frowned.

"Are you sure there isn't something else?" Lee could tell

that they had come to the funeral home with a purpose beyond seeing his dad.

"We've moved back to Florida," Lillian said and flipped her husband a hard look.

"That's true," Hallston admitted with a longing glance at the door. "Okay, we're interested in your… prearranged plans, I guess you call them."

"I'd be glad to explain the options. If you'll come into the office, I have brochures and samples to show you." Lee made a point of standing between Hallston and the front door, while pointing the way to the office.

Reluctantly, Hallston moved toward the office as Lee herded the man and his wife out of the parlor.

CHAPTER TWELVE

Kay half-listened from the kitchen as Lee talked with the Hallstons. Part of her felt sorry for him, while another part believed that he was hopeless and that she needed to push the sale of the funeral home before there were no assets left to sell.

But for now the mystery surrounding Rick's death took priority for her. Closing or selling the business would mean that they would lose any rationale for talking to Rick's family and friends. If they handled Rick's funeral, though, there would be ample opportunity to discuss his life.

Kay went upstairs and rummaged around until she found her old senior yearbook. On the cover was a rampant tiger above the words: *Melon County High School.* The year, 1966, was stamped in large gold numbers across the bottom. Her dad had insisted that she buy one. At seventeen, Kay had been horrified at the candid shots of her that had landed in the *Ledger*, and even more uncomfortable with her formal senior portrait.

Opening the book now, she was more amused than horrified at the pictures she saw. She had been in several clubs, including the science club and band. She'd joined the science club because she had already been thinking about nursing and thought it would look good on her college applications.

She had to admit that most of the reason she'd been in the band had been because of Rick. He'd been a drummer and was quite good at it. Kay, on the other hand, had been a decent enough clarinet player, but she'd gotten into more than one argument with Mr. Stevens, the band director, over her mediocre talent and lack of commitment. Each time, she'd practice extra hard for about week, then slack off again. The real benefit of the band to her had been the long bus rides to games at other schools, when she and Rick could sit together, holding hands and whispering small jokes and promises.

With her brain full of memories, Kay wiped tears from her cheeks as she went through the yearbook and made a list of several of Rick's friends and a few teachers he had liked. Then she started making phone calls.

"Hi, this is Kay Lamberton. You probably don't remember me."

"Of course I do! I heard you were in town. We just *have* to get together!"

Catherine Ritter had been a cheerleader and not one of Kay's close friends, but she'd known everyone in school, so that put her at the top of the list of folks Kay wanted to talk to.

"That would be great. Would you have time tomorrow?"

"Sure! Why not! Let's get lunch. My treat. I divorced Sammy Guthrie last year—you know, Guthrie Motors—and he's paying dearly for the years we were together. I'd love to spend some of his money on you. Not that there's anywhere in this ol' town to get a decent meal. I know! Let's go to the Brown Derby in Gainesville." Catherine said all of this at typewriter speeds that left Kay feeling whiplashed.

"That'd be great. I want to hear all about our friends from school."

"I was devastated to hear about Rick. Is that why you're in town? I couldn't believe it when I heard. You know Clint Peters died last year? Oh, and your father. I *am* sorry." Magnolia blossoms seemed to drip off the woman's tongue as she spoke and, even while she recounted the recent deaths, she still sounded chipper.

"It's been a tough year," Kay admitted, not seeing any reason to explain that she had made plans to come back to Lang long before Rick's death.

They agreed to meet at noon the next day, though Kay didn't know how she'd get through a whole lunch with the woman. She felt worn down after less than ten minutes on the phone with her. It had been the same way in high school. Catherine had been a social butterfly with a calculated focus on boys that had frequently included a few discreet whispers about her sexual skills. Kay wondered if Sammy Guthrie had been her first divorce.

"Dinner!" Lee called from downstairs.

As soon as Kay heard the shout, her nostrils picked up the scent of Ruby's fried chicken. She followed the aroma to the kitchen and found Lee, Lester and Ruby filling plates and glasses.

"Did you sell them a plan?" Lester asked Lee.

"I got a brochure in their hands and the wife said that they'd be back in touch."

"Ouch," Lester groaned.

"I think she meant it."

"Fingers crossed 'cause…" Lester looked at Kay as though he wasn't sure if he should continue but, being

Lester, he did. "Things haven't been as busy as they could be."

"They'll pick up," Lee said firmly, also sparing Kay a glance.

"Darn right it'll pick up," Ruby said. "There are baked potatoes in the oven, one for each of you, with an extra one for Lester."

Lester looked like a kid who'd just received a gold star from his teacher. "He carried my garbage to the curb," a smiling Ruby explained to Lee and Kay. Kay tried not to roll her eyes.

There was a knock at the kitchen door and Jerome, wearing his green uniform, walked in.

"Aren't you on duty?" Lee asked.

"I get thirty minutes for food. Sometimes." His radio crackled with calls and he turned it down to a muted whisper.

"I forgot to mention that Jerome stopped by earlier and I told him to come around for dinner," Ruby said as she got him a plate.

"He can't have my extra baked potato." Lester gave Jerome a hard look.

"Keep your damn potato, son. You're a few potatoes short of a sack anyway." Jerome took the plate from Ruby and sat down at the table next to Lester. The two of them started eating like they were competing to see who could clean their plate the fastest.

"We've got a few leads," Lee told Jerome after the deputy had finally slowed down.

"I heard about that insurance guy stirring the pot and getting the body taken to the morgue for an autopsy. The sheriff bit the head off of anyone who came near him the rest of the day."

"And there was another death," Kay said.

"What?" Jerome looked up with narrowed eyes.

"A friend of Rick's was found dead in his bathtub, six months ago in Gainesville," she said flatly. "They say it was suicide."

"They? You mean the Gainesville police?" Jerome asked.

"That's what his wife said. She owns the Ra Resort."

Jerome chuckled. "We call it the raw resort, r-a-w. Those folks don't have no shame." Then he turned thoughtful. "Does seem a bit of a stretch that two young guys would die like that so close together."

"Stranger things have happened," Lee said, not sure about having one investigation turn into two.

"You're right about that. Still… I got a friend on the GPD violent crimes squad. He's been there for years, so he could give us the goods." Jerome stuffed the last of his meal into his mouth and stood up. He took a long drink of sweet tea, then said, "Let me use your phone. I'll give him a call, see when he can meet me. What's the other dead guy's name?" He was already moving toward the phone on the wall.

"Clint Peters. It would have been sometime mid-October last year," Kay said.

Five minutes later, Jerome hung up the phone. "Milton's on call eleven to seven. We're to meet him at Skeeter's around eight."

"In the morning?" Lee wasn't a morning person.

"Think you can get up that early?" Kay asked.

"I'll be up," Lee grumbled.

"Morning is the best part of the day." Ruby smiled at all of them. "Don't you leave this house without a piece of my upside-down cake," she said to Jerome as he picked up his plate and headed for the sink.

"No, ma'am, wouldn't dream of it." Jerome had a fondness for sweets like other men did for alcohol. Only his nervous energy kept the pounds off.

Ruby wrapped up a piece of cake in a napkin as Jerome radioed dispatch that he was back in service. An awkward silence fell over the table after he left the kitchen.

"Y'all need to talk it out. Cake?" Ruby asked as she put slices on plates.

"I want to know what we're getting ourselves into. We're a funeral home, not a detective agency," Lee said with a hard look at Kay.

"We're in this now." Kay shrugged.

"Can I have a bigger piece?" Lester said when Ruby handed him a slice.

"Murder doesn't wait for the right person to solve it. You two are in the right place at the right time now. I think it's your responsibility." Ruby sliced off a yeoman's piece of cake and handed it to Lester.

"I know why you're so hungry," Kay said to Lester, who looked up with innocent eyes. "I can smell it on you."

"What?" Lester said, feigning innocence.

"So the boy smokes a little weed. Wouldn't hurt you to try it," Ruby said and handed Kay a slice of cake.

Kay stared at her.

"And don't give me that look. I was a mature hippie, but a hippie all the same."

"*You* were a hippie?" Lee couldn't keep the smile from his voice. Though now that he thought about it, it explained a lot about Ruby.

"I hung out with the Beach Boys and even met that nasty little man and his family of deluded halfwits. I added a little bit of cinnamon to the pineapple."

"Wait, are you saying that you met Charles Manson?" Kay asked, thinking that Ruby was nothing if not interesting.

"Certainly. I went out to that ranch. Filthy. Not hippie-dirty either. Filthy deep down. You could literally smell the evil." She pointed her spatula around the table. "I pick up on bad vibes. I felt them when your friend was here, before they took him off to the morgue. I wish we had some ice cream. A bit of vanilla would be perfect. I'll put it on my shopping list."

Baffled by Ruby's train of thought, Kay said, "Hippie vibes or not, we can't ignore the fact that Rick was killed."

"I suppose not," Lee agreed.

"You should be happy. It's giving you and the funeral home a reprieve," Kay reminded him.

"You can't—" he started, but she held up her hand.

"Remember, we're putting that talk—"

"You mean fight!"

"It's only a fight if you want it to be. We agreed to put it off until after Rick is buried and we've turned his killer over to the police."

Lee huffed, but accepted the fact that he was better off letting the decision ride for the moment. He looked over at Lester, who was shoveling cake into his mouth and clearly hoping that they wouldn't get back around to his pot-smoking.

Kay caught Ruby silently mouthing *Don't worry* to Lee. Kay frowned at her, but let it go.

"Come on. You can help me scrub down the embalming room," Lee said to Lester as he carried his plate to the sink.

"Man, it's after five," Lester grumbled.

"Where are you staying tonight?" Lee asked, knowing full well that Lester planned to sleep on a cot in a small closet off the casket room.

"You know my car crapped out on me again," Lester grumbled.

"I pay you a salary. Room and board is extra, paid for with overtime."

Lester sighed. "Can we have the TV on?"

"Sure," Lee said. "But I pick the channel."

"Maybe…"

They headed to the embalming room, leaving Kay and Ruby in the kitchen.

"Were you really a hippie?" Kay asked.

"Thirty years old and they called me Mother," Ruby said, filling the sink up with soapy water.

"I'll dry."

"Were you really in Vietnam?"

"Got the scars to prove it."

"You were wounded?"

Kay pulled her collar down and showed Ruby the scar on her neck. Kay was quiet for a moment as she took a sunflower-print dishtowel from a drawer.

"The war was worse than anything I'd imagined. I felt like we were just thrown in and asked to make sense out of chaos. Focusing on my job was the only thing that kept me from going insane. We worked so hard to save the wounded and dying that I didn't have time to surrender to my own fears."

"You're a brave woman."

"I felt like a fool for getting myself stuck in that maelstrom of horrors. When we had time, I talked a Green Beret lieutenant into teaching me how to defend myself."

"Really?"

Kay grinned. "Yep. From 1911 handguns to the M14s and M16s, knives and chokeholds. I told him I wanted to learn it all. I was in the middle of a war and didn't want to be dependent on anyone else to defend me. I was scared sometimes after that, but never fearful."

"I'm impressed. Was he cute?"

"Very. Tall and lanky with red hair, all the way from the hills of Kentucky."

"What happened to him?"

"He made it through three tours of duty. I met him when he was on his second. He'd taken an AK round through his arm that had gotten infected. I only saw him twice on his third tour. I still write to him. To quote him, he has a bonnie lass and a house full of lil' hillbillies."

They finished the dishes in silence, except for the sounds of *Magnum P.I.* issuing from the embalming room.

CHAPTER THIRTEEN

What is that noise! Lee's brain screamed early Thursday morning. His hand flailed for the snooze button on the clock radio as it pounded out "Another One Bites the Dust." After twenty seconds of thumping music, he managed to find the right button and brought his hand down hard. Blessed silence returned. For a moment he longed for a few minutes of additional sleep, but he rallied and dropped his feet to the floor.

He found the bathroom and went through his morning routine robotically, trying hard not to be fully awake. Finally dressed, he opened the door, but before he reached the stairs he was faced with a mischievous smile from his sister.

"You never were a morning person," she said cheerily, bumping him out of the way and beating him to the staircase.

"Is Lester going with us?" Kay asked over her shoulder as she headed into the kitchen.

"I hope not," Lee mumbled, yawning.

"We'll take my car." Kay opened the refrigerator and grabbed a jug of orange juice.

"We're going to Skeeter's. You don't need any breakfast," Lee told her.

"Yeah, I meant to ask about that. What's a Skeeter's?"

"Breakfast. Big time. Huge biscuits and pancakes. They cater to the after-one-in-the-morning-drunk crowd, Gator football fans and just about anyone else who wants mega-plates of breakfast food."

She poured a glass of orange juice. "You buying?"

"Knowing Jerome, we'll be stuck paying for him *and* his friend."

"Guess we're the ones looking for information."

"Let's just go before I fall asleep."

Outside, the air was cool and damp. April in North Central Florida could be cold and wet, warm and windy, or any combination of all of it in a single day.

Kay's Nova growled with a rough and unhappy sound as she accelerated out of the driveway. The road to Gainesville held a few early commuters, but nothing to slow them down.

Lee directed her through town, past the university and up Thirteenth Street to the shopping center where the home of Skeeter's Big Biscuits anchored the west corner of the plaza.

"Smoking or non-smoking?" the overall-wearing hostess asked. Before Lee or Kay could answer, they heard Jerome yell to them over the noise of the breakfast crowd.

"I guess we'll take smoking," Kay said unhappily, seeing Jerome's friend sitting at a booth with a six-inch cigar snugly held in the right side of his mouth.

Jerome stood up as they came to the table. "This is Milton Towers," he said, waving his hand in the big man's direction.

Milton took up fully half of his side of the booth.

Dressed in a jacket and pants from Sears, his stomach pressed against the table. His face was pale and pockmarked from what must have been a brutal case of teenage acne. Kay judged him to be at least fifty, maybe older. Only the light in his eyes and his upturned mouth softened his appearance.

"Glad to meetcha," he said. "I'd get up, but these cramped booths make it more work than I feel up to after a night on call."

"I heard about the demolition derby." Jerome smiled and shook his head.

"It was a damn mess! I'm goin' to charge them both if the State Attorney will go along with it." Milton turned to Lee and Kay, who'd slid into the booth across the table from him and Jerome. "Boyfriend and girlfriend get into a fight at a party. She takes off in his car, so he steals his friend's pickup and goes after her. Both of them drunker than skunks. The two idiots managed to bang up a dozen cars and knock down a telephone pole before they were done. Both cars totaled and them in the hospital. I got paperwork up my ass." He shook his head.

The waitress came over with a big smile. "Y'all ready to order?"

"Cindy, you know I am," Milton said eagerly.

"And I know what you want," she said, making notes on her pad.

Kay, Lee and Jerome gave Cindy their orders, then turned back to Milton as the waitress hurried away.

"They want to know about a suicide six months ago. Clint Peters," Jerome said.

"Yeah, that's what you said on the phone. I wasn't the primary, Kendricks was, but I did most of the interviews. Kendricks is the laziest cracker this side of the Mississippi. Tell me what y'all are looking for."

"Was it a suicide?" Kay jumped in.

"You family? Family never wants to believe that their kinfolk killed themselves."

"No, we're… just interested." Lee didn't think they should complicate the issue by bringing up Rick's death and he'd said as much to Kay on the drive to Gainesville.

Milton rubbed his chin. "Everything I saw looked like suicide. He was lying in the tub with his wrists slashed. And don't believe all that stuff about how, if someone was going to commit suicide, they wouldn't make plans to go to Hawaii on vacation the next month, or that they always write a suicide note. Most don't write a note, and almost everyone has some sort of long- or short-term plans. I can't say I understand suicide. I don't. Homicides make more sense to me. But from what I've seen, most people who commit suicide are just overwhelmed by something… sadness, work, finances, relationships, something. My mammaw would tell you that it's a devil got ahold of them. That makes as much sense as anything."

"But this looked like suicide?" Kay pressed.

"More to the point, I don't see how it could be anything else. I went and talked to the doc who did the autopsy. I knew Kendricks wouldn't bother," Milton said with a grim shake of his head. "Anyway, the doc couldn't find any other marks on the body. The cuts were classic wrist slits with hesitation marks all correctly angled to be self-inflicted. I even asked him to do an extensive toxicology, 'cause the victim was a lawyer with friends who were connected. Nothing in his system but a little alcohol, which matched up to the bottle of wine we found open on the kitchen counter."

"Who'd you interview?" Jerome asked.

"Neighbors, friends. I got real interested when I learned that the wife was goin' to get a million dollars in life insurance. That is one very green motive."

"I met her yesterday," Kay said.

"You go down to that nudie place?" Milton sounded like a twelve-year-old kid. "I talked to some of the folks down there. I don't know why anyone would want to walk around like that. Bugs and sand. They're plumb crazy."

"What did you learn when you talked to folks?" Lee asked.

"Everyone said the husband and wife loved each other. They also said he'd been kinda odd the last few weeks before his death. On top of that, there were multiple witnesses who confirmed that Mrs. Peters had been working that afternoon. So if it was murder and if she was involved, then there had to be a third party to the crime. Never found any evidence that she'd been having an affair or even been doing anything but working and spending time with her husband."

"She seemed… nice. Honest," Kay agreed.

"And a million dollars richer. Still… it just feels like I didn't get to the bottom of what happened." The big man shrugged. "It's usually that way with suicides. Why does one man suffer the trials of Job and come out the other side smiling, but another might have something happen that most people could laugh off, but he goes and kills himself? I tell you, some folks are just susceptible to the darkness."

Cindy returned to their table and they paused their discussion while plates piled high with food were distributed among them. Kay couldn't believe the size of the pancake she'd ordered.

"You know I'm not stupid, Jerome. This has to do with that drowning over your way, doesn't it?" Milton said as he cut up his eggs.

"I dated Rick Bruhn in high school," Kay admitted.

Milton grunted and shook his head. "You won't learn nothin' if you come at it from your heart. You need heart for a whole bunch of things, but a murder investigation ain't one of 'em."

"I'd think that would make you a *better* investigator," Kay challenged him.

"Nope. 'Cause you know what follows your heart? Your emotions. Nothing will get you in trouble quicker on an investigation than your emotions. I've seen cops fall in love with everything—the victim, the murderer, their own theory, even the crime itself. Goes the other way too. A man gets to hating everything. Emotions stop the brain from working." Milton tapped his head with his knife for emphasis. "You sure your old boyfriend was murdered?"

"I'm the undertaker and I found the marks on the body," Lee spoke up.

"I know who you are. I came to a friend's funeral over there a year ago. Your daddy did a nice job giving him a proper sendoff. Thad Thompson. The best highway patrolman I ever met. Saved my life when I was a rookie cop."

"You remember me? Just from that service?"

"God blessed me with both the body and the memory of an elephant," Milton said with half a smile before taking a bite of his fist-sized biscuit.

"He didn't drown by accident," Jerome confirmed.

"That how your boss sees it?"

"Not *my* boss. But the dead man's boss who owns the insurance company he worked for made the sheriff take a second look at the case."

"Sounds to me like you're playing with fire. All I can tell you about Clint Peters is that there wasn't anything pointing away from suicide." Milton looked at them all and grinned. "Hope that doesn't spoil the party."

"Would have been interesting if the suicide had been suspicious. Though it doesn't change our opinion of Rick's death," Kay said, looking at Jerome and Lee to see if they were in agreement.

They finished breakfast while talking about mutual friends and the upcoming baseball season, then Kay and Lee thanked Milton for taking the time to meet with them.

"So we can at least bypass *that* hornet's nest," Lee said as Kay drove home.

"I guess," Kay said, sounding reluctant. Lee looked over at her and saw her chewing her lip in deep thought.

"You can't keep kicking Clint Peters's suicide around. You heard Milton. I think we can file that one under done-deal."

"I know you're right. I just got it in my head that there was a connection." She glanced at him. "I'll let it go."

"We have enough to investigate with Rick's murder," Lee reminded her.

"You still think we're right?"

"Sounds like Jerome does too. Maybe the autopsy will settle that question and the sheriff will get on it."

"I'm not sure that would be a good thing."

"Why not?"

"If the investigation becomes official, then the sheriff's not going to want us sniffing around the bushes looking for clues."

"So then we let them handle it," Lee said.

"The whole reason we started looking into this was because of their incompetence. I don't think they've gotten any better in the last twenty-four hours."

"Doesn't matter what we think right now. Now that the sheriff has ordered an autopsy, the ball's in their court."

"That's exactly why I need to talk to as many people as I can before the sheriff gets the autopsy report and makes it official," Kay said with determination.

"I see your point." Lee mulled it over. "We'll certainly be pushed out if they become involved. And you aren't wrong about their competence." He sighed.

"I've got a lunch date with Catherine Ritter," Kay said, then groaned. "What was I thinking when I ate all that food at Skeeter's? Anyway, with luck she'll give me some good suggestions of other people to talk to."

"I'd feel kind of weird questioning them. I didn't know Rick that well."

"You can follow up with his uncle. Find out when his parents are getting into town. Talking with Todd Bruhn will also give you a chance to get him to give his okay to us handling the funeral. We *need* to be the funeral home that holds the service for him. If we have that, we'll at least be close to the family and the suspects, regardless of what the sheriff decides to do. He can't make us stay away from a funeral that we're running."

"I'll give Bruhn a call when we get home," Lee said, not mentioning the other reason he wanted to make sure they held the funeral. It would give him an opportunity to show his sister that he could handle it. And it wouldn't hurt that the funeral would be high-profile, which would also show the whole county that he was capable. *It's a win-win-win situation*, he thought.

CHAPTER FOURTEEN

When they got back to the funeral home, Lester was sweeping the front porch and Ruby was scrubbing the kitchen floor. Kay headed upstairs. So far, all she'd unpacked was her duffel bag, but since it was starting to look like she was going to be in Lang longer than she'd planned, it was time to organize the rest of her stuff.

Hanging up her adult clothes in her childhood room caused her to reminisce about the days when her biggest problems had been an annoying little brother and a father whose business was embarrassing and who didn't understand anything about being a teenager in the sixties. *How could I have been so silly and self-centered?* she wondered.

For her lunch with Catherine Ritter, Kay slipped on the only dress she'd brought with her. Catherine had been a maven of fashion in high school… and she'd also reminded Kay a bit of one of the kids on the island in *Lord of the Flies*. For a brief moment Kay almost chickened out of the meeting. *I could probably just ask Tracy for contact numbers*, she thought, sighing as she brushed her hair. *But Catherine is a first-class gossip and talking to her will give me much more than addresses and phone numbers.* Resigned, she slipped on a pair of low heels and tried to feel beautiful.

Kay made the drive to Gainesville for the second time that day and found the Brown Derby on the southwest side of town. The stone building tried hard to inspire images of Hollywood without much success. Entering the darkened restaurant, Kay informed the hostess that she was meeting someone.

"Miss Ritter is waiting for you at one of our window tables." The young woman, menu in hand, led the way past other diners. As she walked between the tables, Kay pulled at her skirt, feeling like a kid going to her first fancy party.

"Why, look at you!" Catherine enthused as Kay walked up to the table.

"How are you?" Kay asked, sitting down across from her.

"I'm just all roses and kittens since getting rid of my awful husband." Catherine's blonde hair was feathered and sprayed heavily into place, and her neck, wrists and fingers were adorned with expensive, flashy jewelry. She picked up her wine glass and took a deep drink. "Now, tell me all about you. I remember you went into the Army or some such."

"I was a nurse," Kay answered, not wanting to go into details.

"Fascinating. I wish I could do something useful, but my daddy always said I was just made for looking pretty. Go on, have some wine and look over the menu."

After they had placed their orders, Kay decided to plunge into the purpose of her visit before the food distracted them. "I wanted to ask you about the gang that used to hang around with Rick Bruhn."

"Why would you be asking after all these years?" Catherine asked, draining another glass of wine.

Kay shrugged. "I guess, what with Rick's death, that I just got to thinking about old classmates."

"Liar, liar. I shouldn't tell you a thing until you come clean. But I won't press the point. Let's see, who used to hang out with Rick?" She said his name with a thoughtful air and tapped her fingernails on her wine glass. "There was you, of course. And Millie. That girl was a piece of work… The only girl at school who could hold a candle to me." Catherine's eyes grew wide. "I remember now, y'all had a slap-down at the prom! I was so mad that I wasn't there to see it."

"And now she's a famous author," Kay muttered.

"It's utter drivel if you ask me. But she's sold millions, so who am I to judge? The tart whizzed through town a few months ago when… Oh, that's right, Clint Peters was part of the group too." Catherine gulped more wine. "I do hope there's not a curse."

"You saw Millie at Clint's funeral?" Kay asked.

"She was there, but I didn't go. Suicides make for awful funerals. There's all that guilt flowing through the crowd. All the friends and family thinking that they should have done something. Too depressing." She waved her hand, dismissive of the very idea that she'd attend a funeral for a suicide.

"But you saw her?" Kay pressed, trying to keep the conversation on track.

"Millie spent a couple of days hanging out in Lang, acting like she was the chief mourner for Clint. She always did think she owned those boys, including Vince and Burt. I wasn't the least bit surprised when she came between you and Rick. Don't you think for one minute that it was an accident."

The waiter brought their food, so they dropped the discussion while he sorted out the plates. Kay was impressed at the large steak and baked potato that Catherine had ordered.

"You're eating like a bird," Catherine chastised, pointing at the salad the waiter had placed in front of Kay.

"I had a big breakfast," she admitted. "So do you ever hear from Vince or Burt?"

"Vince is a professor here at UF, and Burt is an investment manager or something like that. Makes a fortune investing other people's money. Has a whopper of a home down in West Palm Beach. Millie sure whipped them all into shape. During their junior year in high school, I wouldn't have given you ten cents for their chances of graduating college."

"You think *she's* the reason they're all successful?" Kay asked, surprised.

"Her and Mr. Watts." There was an odd inflection in her tone that Kay couldn't quite decipher.

"Who?"

"You know, Mr. Watts, the guidance counselor. His first name is Lewis or something."

"Lewis Watts," Kay said, remembering the man with a blush of anger. "He tried to derail my plans for nursing school when I made the mistake of mentioning that I might want to join the nursing corps in Vietnam. Actually called me stupid the afternoon I came to get my transcripts."

"Well, I mean, it was Vietnam. Who'd want to go there? I'm sure he thought he was trying to help you."

Kay choked back a rush of fury which had as much to do with long-forgotten memories than with anything the silly woman had said. Kay could still feel the burning in her cheeks that day in Lewis Watts's office. "I almost hit him with my chemistry book. The big jerk. The only reason I didn't was that I needed those transcripts. If I'd caused a scene, he would have called Dad and then all hell would have broken loose."

"He may not have thought much of your decisions, but he sure took a real interest in Millie and the boys," Catherine said.

"I'm trying to think." Kay let her mind drift back to the days when she'd been dating Rick. It was so hard to remember what other people were doing. *I was so… all about me.* "Rick did go to some SAT study sessions. I talked about going to one, but he kind of brushed me off. Odd that I remember that."

"We always remember the slights, right?"

"You have a point. I think I was jealous that he was going to be spending time with Millie. Even though I knew that the other guys would be there too."

"I don't think you had to worry about that," Catherine said, again with that odd note in her voice.

"What exactly are you saying?"

"Mr. Watts had a real thing for Millie." Catherine raised her eyebrows and smiled. "Is that plain enough?"

"Mr. Watts?" Kay found it hard to imagine. "How old was he?"

"Old enough that he should have known better. I always suspected that it was Millie leading him on."

"Surely not…" But the more Kay thought about Millie, the less farfetched the idea seemed. "I hated her after what she did with Rick, but was she that much of a manipulator?"

"Honey, you just don't know. I forget how naïve you were. She had the right stuff and she'd use it whenever she thought it could give her an advantage."

"You don't think she… you know. That Millie and Mr. Watts really did anything?"

"Hard to say. Millie was known for pumping more gas than her tank would hold, if you know what I mean. Then again, Mr. Watts was in his mid-twenties and not bad looking."

Kay knew that she shouldn't have been as shocked as she was.

"Millie was seen with him when she was in town for Clint's funeral," Catherine added.

"He still lives around here?"

"He got his doctorate while he was working in Lang. He's teaching at Santa Fe Community College now."

Kay added Lewis Watts to her list of people to contact.

"Speaking of the funeral, I talked to Tracy Peters yesterday."

"Tracy, now there's an interesting wildflower if ever there was one. Where'd you see her?"

"I went out to… her house."

"At the nudie place!" Catherine had lowered her voice and leaned in across the table. "I just about died when I learned that she and Clint were into that sort of thing. I bet all kinds of scandalous stuff goes on out there." Her eyes were positively glowing.

"I didn't see anything… crazy." *Except for a naked woman on her front porch*, Kay thought. "Tracy seemed nice."

"Oh, she's nice enough. All natural grain. Probably doesn't shave her armpits."

Kay didn't share the fact that she knew without a doubt that Tracy shaved most of her body, though thank goodness not all of it.

"When did you see Clint last?" Kay asked.

"My dreary husband thought he was a patron of the arts and dragged us to every arty-farty event around. I saw Clint and Tracy at the grand opening when the Hippodrome moved its theatre into the old federal building in downtown Gainesville. They were as gaga over the place as my husband."

"Did you notice any tension between them?"

"Tracy and Clint?" Catherine guffawed between bites of

baked potato. "Love birds." She paused and looked thoughtful. "You know, looking back, I thought they *were* laying it on a little thick."

"Like an act?"

"I've seen couples who were… affectionate, but Clint and Tracy positively clung to each other. Maybe I'm not the best judge. My husband said I was as cold as an ice cube in a freezer in the Arctic. And that was in the official court documents." Catherine smiled and Kay had to admit that the grin was frosty.

"Where does Vince live now?"

"He lives just north of the campus. A confirmed bachelor, if you get my drift," Catherine said with a wink.

"Is that a problem?" Kay knew exactly what Catherine was implying.

"Not with me. I knew it in high school when I flirted with him and couldn't get a rise out of him." She shook her head as though Vince had passed up on the chance of a lifetime.

"He was always very sweet." Kay remembered liking Vince.

"Of course he was. Still is. I saw him at a dinner party hosted by the dean of the engineering school. Honestly, he was the only one I could talk to. The rest were only interested in circuits and pocket calculators. I'd have died of boredom if it wasn't for him."

"He's an engineer?"

"No! His friend, if you know what I mean, is. Vince is a history professor. He's written a couple of books and thinks he has a good chance at becoming dean of the liberal arts college or something. He was all bubbly at the prospect of becoming a dean at his young age."

"Was that before or after Clint's death?"

"Just before."

"Have you heard from Burt Sedgewick lately?"

"Now there is a strange duck. He and Millie should have gotten married, except they'd never have found a house big enough to contain their massive egos."

Kay smiled. "Burt always did think a lot of himself."

"He once told me that he thought he might be the smartest man in Florida."

"Just Florida?"

"Well, he *was* including all those rocket scientists over at Cape Canaveral." Catherine laughed. "Of course, the joke's on me. I've got him investing half the money I got from my ex."

"Maybe I should have stuck with the group a little longer," Kay said. "Everyone in Rick's group managed to be successful."

"Except now two of them are dead," Catherine pointed out.

"Maybe it's like the Kennedys and there's a curse on all of that success," Kay said, only half joking. "Though it's probably just a coincidence that Rick and Clint died within six months of each other."

"Enough with this King-Tut's-curse stuff." Catherine pushed her plate away. "I know you're here to get information out of me. So ask away."

"I want to get in touch with all the old group," Kay said, a little taken aback by Catherine's candor.

"I've got their contact information in my purse." She picked up a bag covered in rhinestones and took out a well-worn, brown leather address book. "You'll need a pen." She saw the look on Kay's face and pulled a pen out of her purse. "You're going to need a notepad, too, if you're going to play detective."

"I'm not… I'm just looking into things." Kay's words sounded lame even to her ears.

"You don't fool me. You want to discover what happened to Rick 'cause, deep in your heart, you were still in love with him. Don't let Millie find out; she'll write a novel about it."

Under Catherine's watchful eye, Kay copied down all of the addresses and phone numbers on the back of an envelope Catherine had pulled from her purse.

"Thank you," Kay said, handing the address book back.

"If you need anything else, just ask. I'm rather bored right now."

Kay was glad when she finally got back to her car. Catherine's cynicism was depressing.

Do I go back to Lang now or just drop by Vince's house and hope he's home? she asked herself as she started the car. *He probably won't be home in the middle of the day, but at least I'll get a look at his house.* Kay drove out of the parking lot and headed north back toward the university.

CHAPTER FIFTEEN

While his sister was making her second trip of the day to Gainesville, Lee was sitting in his office at the funeral home considering his options. Kay had suggested that he follow up with Rick's uncle, but how exactly was he supposed to do that? It seemed a little forward to just call him up and ask him when Rick's parents would be getting into town. And he might not be able to call Bruhn at all if the man hadn't taken Lee's advice and checked in at the Howard Johnson's.

It would be easy enough to find that out. An old classmate of Lee's worked as the night manager at the motel. He'd helped Lee get one of the few funerals he'd handled since his father had died. Two months earlier, an elderly man had passed away in one of the motel rooms and, after Lee had picked up the body, it hadn't taken much convincing to get the man's disinterested adult children to agree to let Lee handle the burial. The service had only entailed a burial since the children didn't see any reason to have a funeral, claiming their father had pushed any friends and family he had out of his life. The whole episode had been depressing and not very lucrative, but it had put a little change in the bank.

Lee dialed the phone. "Petey! How's it going?"

"You know I work the nightshift," Pete Owens groaned from the other end of the phone line.

"I wouldn't wake you up if it wasn't important. Did a man named Todd Bruhn check in to the motel yesterday?"

"Second floor double. It was on the books when I came in. Good guest. He didn't make a peep all night." Pete sounded like he was trying to stay half-asleep.

"You never saw him?"

"I told you, he never called the desk or left his room."

After getting Todd's room number, Lee thanked Pete and let him go back to sleep, but he didn't take his hand off the phone after he hung up. *Should I call Todd Bruhn or just go on out to the motel? It would seem less odd if I called, but if I see him in person I might get more information out of him.* Finally, he took his hand off the receiver and left the office.

On the drive out to the interstate, Lee worked out what he would say. His goal was to sound more concerned for the family than about who would get the job of burying Rick. *Finesse is the key*, he told himself.

Lee bypassed the office and parked next to Todd's car before walking up the stairs that were located at the corner of the building. On the second floor, Lee took a deep breath and walked quickly to Todd's door before he could chicken out.

"Come back later!" a groggy-sounding voice yelled through the door in response to his knock.

"It's me, Lee Lamberton," he said, trying his best to be self-assured.

"Who?"

"The mortician."

"Oh."

Two minutes later the door opened. Todd Bruhn stood staring at Lee with bloodshot eyes. He was barefoot, his hair was a mess and he wore wrinkled dress pants and an unbuttoned shirt.

"Sorry, I figured it was housekeeping. My head is killing me." Todd stepped back from the door to let Lee in.

As Lee's eyes adjusted to the dark room, he saw a half-empty whiskey bottle on the floor near the bed along with a crumpled bag of Fritos.

"My dinner last night." Todd dropped down on the bed and waved to the two chairs by the window. "Sit. God, I want a drink." He picked up the bottle of whiskey, but instead of taking a drink, he put the cap on and set the bottle on the nightstand.

"I'm sorry to bother you," Lee apologized.

"Forget it. I'm wallowing in self-pity, which is unfair to my brother and sister-in-law. This is their tragedy."

"Rick *was* your nephew."

"And a good man. I… he was a good man." Todd gave the bottle another look. "I'm better than this. Sorry." He paused. "Maybe I just need to get my grieving done before my brother shows up."

"Have you heard from him?"

"Another thing to feel guilty about. Yes. He called my house and my son answered. I'd figured on that. What I hadn't figured on was my brother getting it out of my son what had happened."

"How old is your boy?"

"Chris is twenty. He handled it pretty well. Still, it shouldn't have been left to him. I just didn't have any choice. I had to get down here, and someone had to be at the house when Edgar called." He rubbed his face. "Now I'm telling you a bunch of crap you don't want to listen to."

"I'm a mortician. I see a lot of anguish. Grief is an

emotion that renders most people vulnerable and creates turmoil in families. Listening to people as they struggle through the process is more than half of my job," Lee assured him.

Todd took a harder look at Lee. "Thanks. I just want to do this right."

"You want to help your family get through this without suffering any more than necessary."

"Suffering. My brother's going to live with that for a long time." He took a deep breath and stood up. "Any idea when the autopsy will be performed?"

"I'll find out."

"My brother called me after my son told him about Rick. He told me that Pearl was hysterical and couldn't deal with anything. He wasn't sure how he was going to get her on a plane so they could fly back to the States. No matter what, they won't be here any before tomorrow. In the meantime, he told me to make whatever arrangements I thought best." He sighed deeply.

"Mr. Bruhn, if you want, you can come by the funeral home and we can go through all the necessary decisions."

"I don't know much about funerals. I've attended a few, but…"

"I'll help you through it. We'll make sure that it's respectful to Rick's memory. There's something else I should tell you. My sister knew Rick in high school. They dated for a while."

"Really?"

"For my sister it was… serious."

"I'd like to talk to her."

"I'll let her know. You can meet her this afternoon."

"Okay, let me get cleaned up and I'll meet you at the funeral home around three."

"I'll see if I can learn when the autopsy will be. That will determine when the body will be released for burial."

Todd put his hand out. "I appreciate the help."

Lee shook the offered hand with as much manly reassurance as he could put into it.

Heading back to his car, Lee hoped that Kay wouldn't mind him mentioning her relationship with Rick. At least he was confident that he'd sealed the deal for the funeral.

Kay found Vince Edwards's house easily enough. It was nestled in an upscale, older residential area north of University Avenue. His place was smaller than most of the other homes in the neighborhood—a cute Florida cottage that looked like it had been built in the 1920s. The yard was shaded by four arching live oak trees that had been standing back when the city had been nothing more than a small settlement called Hogtown.

In the driveway was a blue Ford Pinto with a bumper sticker for a local rock radio station. Kay parked behind it and tried to figure out what she would say if Vince answered the door. *I'll just tell him that I ran into Catherine and she mentioned him, so I thought I'd stop in and say hello.* She didn't think it was a very convincing excuse, but she couldn't think of anything else.

After a third round of knocking, she was about to give up and leave when she heard someone walking across a hardwood floor toward the front door. When the door opened, Vince stood there with a slight frown on his face. He looked younger than she knew he was.

"Hi!" Kay said with raised eyebrows. "You probably don't remember me. I'm Kay Lamberton."

"Who?" His frown changed to a puzzled look that quickly grew into a wide smile. "Kay! Rick's girlfriend. Of course I remember you." His smile disappeared as fast as it had appeared. "Oh, no. Rick. Come in." He walked away, leaving the door open.

Kay followed him into a house that looked like it was waiting for a photographer from *Southern Living.* The interior was all hardwoods, books and overstuffed furniture. Vince's outfit of sweater and jeans on his small frame made him look like he belonged in Riverdale with Archie and Veronica.

"You don't look a day older than when we were high school," Kay said, still astonished at Vince's youthful appearance.

"Micah jokes that I'm a vampire. He's been known to call me Lestat."

"I hope you don't mind me dropping in on you like this."

"No. I had my teaching assistant take over my classes for a couple of days. I just couldn't face going in and lecturing after what happened to Rick. And just six months ago we lost Clint. It's so… depressing." As if to illustrate the point, Vince dropped down onto the couch and buried his face in his hands.

"My brother picked up his body." Kay knew this was probably not the right thing to say, but she couldn't think of anything else.

Vince looked up at her with a blank expression as he tried to process what she'd said, then slowly nodded.

"Of course. Your family owns the funeral home. I didn't even think about that. Must be hard on you. Or are you kind of used to it?" He said this carefully as though he wasn't sure if it was something he should ask.

"No. Not me. I think my Dad was. He buried a lot of people that he knew."

"I heard your father had passed away too. Wow, I'm sorry. This has been a bad time for everyone."

"Did you go to Clint's funeral?"

"It was awful. I guess this one won't be any better. At

least Rick wasn't married. Tracy is so nice. Broke my heart to see her at Clint's funeral. And the awful way he died didn't help." Vince looked down at the floor, lost in thought.

"Did you all stay close after graduation?"

"You know how it is," he said cryptically. "I remember that you joined the Army. That must have been wild. I got a few updates from Rick."

This was news to Kay. "Rick? I didn't talk to him for years after high school."

"Rick used to talk to your dad about you."

"Really?" Her father had never mentioned that.

"Rick felt bad about the breakup. He was afraid that if anything happened to you when you were in Vietnam, that it would be his fault."

"I didn't blame him. Not really. Okay, maybe at first, but I was glad I enlisted."

"I bet you helped a lot of guys over there." Vince seemed to think better of his words. "I don't mean like… I mean as a nurse."

"I know what you mean. And you're right. I *was* able to do some good in the middle of what was a horrible situation. Now enough about me and Rick; what's your life been like since high school? I heard you've written some books."

"That's nothing really. Though my book on the War of 1812 and Florida's role in it did garner some national attention." He paused, then added, "From historians, of course."

"That's great."

"Helped me get tenure. I'm the youngest tenured history professor at the university." There was pride in his voice, something she didn't remember Vince having much of back in high school.

"I guess you've got a good life here."

"Clint's and Rick's deaths have been hard." Vince

frowned, then said, "But my life is good."

"Did you see much of Clint before… his death?"

"I'm ashamed about that. He wanted to talk to me. Left messages on my phone, but I was really busy. Fall semester is crazy around here. I kept meaning to call him back… and didn't."

"That must be tough. He didn't give any hints about why he wanted to talk to you?"

Vince hesitated for a moment. "Nothing. I've tried to work it out, but…" He shrugged, then he narrowed his eyes at Kay. "Why all the interest in Clint's death?"

"Not having been at the funeral, I just wondered about it. Clint never seemed the type to commit suicide."

"People can keep all kinds of secrets bottled up inside them," Vince said in a manner that suggested that he was talking about more people than just Clint.

"You never answered my question."

"Which one?"

"Did you all stay close after high school?"

Vince gave her a crooked smile. "Millie wouldn't let us do anything else. She is the glue that binds us together. I guess you don't have a very high opinion of her."

"That kiss was a long time ago. Rick was a free agent so I can't place all the blame on her."

"She's a force of nature. Rick might not have been able to stop it. What I know is that he regretted it for… I guess the rest of his life."

"What's Millie like these days?"

"Millie never changes. When she enters a room, all the players start revolving around her. She's got the gravitational pull of a black hole."

"I can't tell if you love her or hate her," Kay said jokingly.

"None of us would be where we are today if it wasn't for Millie."

"Is that an answer?"

"It depends on whether I like where I am today or not."

"So?"

"I like being a professor on the road to being a dean. If it doesn't happen here in the next year, I know I can apply at another university and get what I want. I am who I am because of Millie. So, yes, on some level I love her."

"I expect she'll be here for Rick's funeral."

"She's already made arrangements to fly in tomorrow. I'm taking her car and picking her up in the afternoon."

"Her car? I thought she lives in North Carolina?"

"She does, but she still owns her parents' house and keeps her Mustang there."

"I'd like to see her."

"I'm sure she'll want to see you too," Vince said in a neutral tone.

"Will you call me?"

"At the funeral home?"

"Yes."

Vince agreed and Kay stood up, ready to head for the door. Then she stopped and asked, "Do you remember Lewis Watts?"

"What?"

She could tell that he was startled by the question. It also didn't escape her notice that he'd asked *what*, not *who*, as though he knew the who but just wasn't sure why she was asking about him.

"Watts. The counselor at Melon High."

"Oh, him. What about him?"

"Nothing really. He's just one of the people I've been thinking about now that so many memories have been dredged up." Kay tried to keep her answer vague.

"I think Millie knew him better than me," Vince said, looking wary. She had obviously touched a nerve, but what kind of nerve?

"I'll try to remember to ask Millie about him when I see her," Kay said as she walked out the door to her car. As she drove away, she saw that Vince was watching her from the front porch, wearing an enigmatic expression.

"Glad you're here," Lee greeted her as Kay walked into the kitchen.

"That's different," she told him as she poured herself a glass of iced tea.

Lee filled her in on his conversation with Todd Bruhn.

"I wish you hadn't used my relationship with Rick as a lure," Kay groused.

"I just kind of mentioned it. You wanted me to work harder at selling funerals," he argued.

"What's done is done."

"Will you be here when Bruhn comes in?" Lee looked up at the clock. "He should be here around three."

Kay looked at the mixture of anxiety and hope on Lee's face and nodded. "Sure. I'm going to do some of my laundry. Just call me when he gets here."

Less than an hour later, Lee ushered Todd into the office.

"My sister is out back. I'll just go and get her. Would you like something to drink?"

"A glass of water would be great," Todd said, and Lee thought he saw the lingering effects of a hangover in his furrowed brow.

On the way to the laundry room, Lee found Ruby in the kitchen working on dinner.

"Would you please take a glass of water to Mr. Bruhn waiting in the office?" he asked her. "And no crazy talk. We need to sell this funeral."

Ruby smiled and nodded, seeming to take no offense at

the crazy-talk comment.

Lee rounded up Kay and they got to the office just in time to hear Ruby telling Todd Bruhn about her psychic cats.

"Cats know more than most of us," Todd said with a nod and a bemused smile.

"I think the oven is preheated," Lee told Ruby with a hard stare and she left the office.

"Reminds me of my favorite aunt. A little crazy, but generous to a fault." Todd looked at Kay. "After your brother told me you'd gone out with Rick, I remembered him talking about you."

"I liked your nephew a great deal."

"He was a good man. I…" He started to choke up, but cleared his throat. "Let's do what we need to do."

"Sadly, there are a lot of decisions to be made for a funeral to do justice to a deceased loved one," Lee said with the proper tone of respect.

"I understand. I may have to postpone some decisions if I feel that my brother and his wife need to be consulted."

"Of course. First, is the funeral going to be held in Lang?"

"Yes, his parents want him buried in the Old City Cemetery. They own eight plots."

"Fine, I know the sexton. I talked to my contact at the morgue and they expect to perform the autopsy this afternoon and the body should be released in the morning. When do you think Rick's parents would like to have the service and burial?"

"I heard back from Edgar about an hour ago. They're flying in tomorrow morning. Would Monday be too soon?"

"Do you expect his friends and other family members to come from out of town?"

"I don't know. Possibly."

"Why don't we have a viewing on Monday and hold the

funeral on Wednesday? That will give your brother time to get here and allow for any changes if he's not satisfied with the arrangements."

"You'll probably want to publish an obituary in the paper here, in Gainesville and in Atlanta," Kay added.

"I hadn't thought about that. Yes, of course. And some of his colleagues and friends might want to send flowers. Yes, Wednesday seems reasonable. I'm not much of a writer." Todd was sounding overwhelmed and they'd only gotten started.

"I'll be glad to help you with the obituary," Kay told him and he looked at her with grateful eyes.

Lee led Todd through the list of questions that had to be answered and the numerous options that were available while Kay gently made suggestions when appropriate.

An hour later, an exhausted Todd stood up. "We didn't leave my brother and sister-in-law too many decisions to make."

"I think they'll be comfortable with the funeral," Lee agreed.

"I want you to bill me," he told them.

"If that's what you want."

"Rick's parents have enough to worry about."

As Lee closed the door behind Todd, he sighed and looked at Kay.

"Don't give me that look. This was just one funeral. A couple of them a week. That's what you need to stay afloat."

"One a week to stay afloat. Two would bring in a decent profit."

"Not by the time you factor in all the depreciation on equipment, cars and other overhead."

"I bet you could get us on solid footing," Lee said archly.

"No."

"We work well together."

"I liked being able to help him through the process. Honestly, I'd forgotten all the things that have to be worked out. Location of the service, who'll preside, getting the grave dug, clothing, memorial cards… all of it."

"It's important work. You know how Dad felt about the funeral business," Lee reminded her.

"He felt that it was a calling, like being a minister or a priest."

"We spend most of our time comforting people."

"And selling them a lot of crap… Okay, okay, it's not all crap, but a bunch of stuff and services."

"Dad explained it to me one day when I was making fun of all the items we can include in a service. He told me that you let people make their own decisions about what they can and can't afford. For most grieving families, it's the last time they can feel like they're doing something for their lost loved one."

"It's like they're trying to make up for all the Christmas and birthday presents they'll never buy. Dad gave me the same spiel. I guess I understand it a little more these days." Kay thought about all the soldiers she'd seen zipped up in body bags for their final flights home and felt a better appreciation for the work her father had done.

CHAPTER SIXTEEN

The sky was grey and overcast when Kay woke up on Friday. She made it down to the kitchen for breakfast before Lee or Lester showed up. Ruby was making biscuits while reading the horoscope in the *Gainesville Sun.*

"They got Cancer all wrong today." Ruby shook her head as she kneaded the biscuit dough.

"Go figure," Kay said noncommittally, not wanting to engage in a discussion on the merits of the syndicated predictions.

"Yes, and it's just not that hard. Oh, a lot of math, but even Yin can do it."

Kay looked up from pouring her orange juice and stared at Ruby, wondering just how far off her rocker the woman was. Suggesting that her cat could calculate even silly computations seemed a stretch.

"Did you finish the obituary?" Ruby was off on another subject.

"I did. I'll let Mr. and Mrs. Bruhn read it when they get

here." Kay had outlined a few key points with Todd Bruhn the day before and then had spent the evening in the kitchen working on the draft.

"I thought what you had last night was very good."

"Thank you."

"The Bruhns are going to be here today?"

"After Todd picks them up at the airport in Gainesville." Kay remembered that Vince was planning to pick up Millie too.

"You and your brother seem to work well together."

"Don't start," Kay said and got a pouty face from Ruby. The upside was that Kay got to finish her breakfast in peace.

She surprised herself by putting on her best casual clothes after breakfast. *Why am I trying to impress his parents?* she wondered. Was it a sense of unfinished business? Rick's mother had never seemed impressed with her. Kay tried to understand why it was important to her, but finally just gave up. She was confused by her own emotions.

"I'm leaving to go pick up Rick," Lee told her around ten after he'd talked with the morgue attendant on the phone. "Do you want to come along?"

"Sounds like fun." Kay regretted the sarcasm as soon as it was out of her mouth and tried to make amends. "I'd better wait here in case his folks arrive before you get back."

"I'll take Lester and be back as soon as I can. Hopefully the doctors didn't make a mess of it."

Kay waited until the hearse had pulled out of the driveway before going into Lee's office and pulling out the financial journals. A part of her thought that she shouldn't be digging into the records without telling Lee. *The business was left to both of us*, she reminded herself. *What I should feel bad about is not taking a greater interest in the home before now.*

She was a little surprised to find that Lee had continued to keep the financial records in the same way that their father had. Kay felt a pain in her heart when she saw the handwriting change during the month that her father died. Her father's large, round cursive letters and numbers changed to Lee's smaller and less confident hand.

Lee's entries showed an obvious determination to do things right. Unfortunately, no matter how sincerely he put the numbers down, the sums still added up to a business that was slowly sinking. Kay sighed and returned the journals to the file cabinet where she'd found them.

As she was leaving the office, there was a knock on the front door.

"I'll get it," she told Ruby, who had appeared from the kitchen. Ruby nodded and ducked back out of sight.

"Hello?" a high sweet voice sounded from the front hallway.

Kay was struck by the figure of the woman standing in the middle of the entryway. Tall in four-inch heels, she was wearing a pant suit and jewelry that fit her so well that her outfit looked carved out of her skin. As soon as the woman caught sight of Kay, a huge, man-eating smile spread across her face.

"Kay!"

The woman that Kay now realized was Millie Jessup propelled herself across the gap between them so fast that Kay had only two choices—to spread her arms and catch her or be knocked to the ground. She chose the involuntary hug.

Behind Millie, standing at the doorway and looking embarrassed, was Vince Edwards. Their eyes met and Vince shrugged.

"When Vince said he'd talked to you, I just had to come and see you. I know we've had our trials and tribulations, but now we must put all of that behind us," Millie enthused. Kay thought she sounded just like the high-strung heroines in her books.

"Of course," Kay found herself saying.

"Rick… I'm just speechless," Millie said, quickly proving it to be a lie. "Losing Clint and Rick in only six months. I know what people think of me, but I have a heart and they were family." Kay heard a surprising level of sincerity in Millie's voice.

Millie finally broke the hug and stepped back. Her mascara was smeared and tears dampened the corners of her eyes.

"I'm sorry that I didn't make it down for Clint's funeral. I didn't find out about his death until this week," Kay explained.

"I blame myself for losing touch with you," Millie said, though that didn't make a lot of sense in light of how they'd last parted.

"I'm sure hearing about Rick's death was a shock for you."

"Shock is hardly the word for it. I was at my retreat, finishing up my new book, when Vince called. I would have been here sooner, but I was so shaken up, I didn't trust myself to drive home. I had to get a friend to drive me so I could catch a flight down here."

"When I picked her up at the airport, I mentioned that you had come by the house," Vince said apologetically.

"I'm glad you did." Kay meant it too. She had a few questions for Millie. "Why don't we sit down in the parlor?"

"This ol' place hasn't changed a bit. I remember my grandmother's viewing being here," Millie remarked as Kay opened the doors into the parlor.

"Even before Rick's death, I was hoping to look up some old friends and classmates from high school," Kay lied as they sat down in a trio of chairs by the window.

"I'm glad we're getting this chance to meet, but the circumstances are just too awful."

"You're right. I hadn't seen Rick in years and now…" Kay could feel her grief rising to the surface and she pushed it down. "Which is why I'm even more determined to renew old acquaintances. And make some new friends. I didn't know her before, but I got a chance to talk to Clint's widow the other day."

Millie gave the smallest hint of a frown. "Wherever did you run into Tracy?"

"I wanted to pay my respects after I learned that Clint had died, so I drove out to her place."

"Bought with Clint's insurance money." Anger, or maybe jealously, flashed in Millie's eyes.

"Millie, we talked about this," Vince said sternly, earning him an irritated glare from Millie. Even so, Kay could see the anger leave her face.

"You're right. I just can't help but blame Tracy for Clint's death. If she'd let any of us know that he was… suffering, we'd have done something to help him."

"It's not always obvious." Vince's voice was softer now. "I'm sure Tracy would have done anything to help Clint."

The look Kay saw on Millie's face was full of disbelief.

"Maybe," Millie said. "So how *was* Tracy?"

"Hurt, but moving on."

"As we all are." Millie let out a dramatic sigh. "And now there's Rick. How could he have drowned?"

"They took his body to Gainesville for an autopsy," Kay said and watched them both for a reaction.

"Autopsy? You didn't mention that yesterday." Vince sounded hurt that she hadn't confided in him.

"I figured it would be obvious. A young man found dead alone in a swimming pool… they have to rule out foul play." Kay wasn't sure why she was baiting them. Maybe it was Millie's cloying personality.

"But surely it was just a horrible accident." Millie's

eyebrows were raised and her voice had gone up an octave.

"I guess we'll find out when the results come in," Kay said with false innocence.

"I… never considered." Vince sounded baffled and looked concerned, causing Kay to regret her approach.

"There were some unusual signs," she admitted.

"Signs?" Millie asked. "You saw the body? Or did you hear something?"

"Rick's body was here and, when Lee was cleaning it, he saw some odd marks on the inside of Rick's mouth and on his face."

"Really?" Vince said, looking from Kay to Millie and back again.

"Probably shouldn't have said anything."

"No, I'm glad you did," Millie said.

"Would you all like something to drink?" Ruby's interjection from the doorway caused all three of them to turn and look at her. "Water, Coca-Cola… or something stronger?" Either Yin or Yang walked into the room behind her, then turned to rub against Ruby's legs.

"I could use a little pick-me-up. The airplane flight and all," Millie said. "A gin and something sparkly would be fine."

"I'm good," Vince told Ruby.

"I could use a beer," Kay said, getting a look from Vince and Millie.

"Are you all handling the funeral?" Millie asked once Ruby had left.

"Yes. We met with Rick's uncle yesterday."

"His parents were in Europe somewhere," Millie said, standing up and starting to pace the room.

"Todd, Rick's uncle, is going to pick them up from the airport today." Kay watched Millie, who was feigning interest in the books and brochures that lined the walls.

"Please let them know that we're heartbroken and will do anything we can to see them through these trying times."

"Of course."

"We'll see them at the funeral," Vince said with a glance at Millie.

"I guess you'll be seeing all of the old gang while you're here." Kay looked directly at Millie.

"We're meeting up tonight at that seedy little bar on the county line. What's it called, Vince?"

"The Forty-eight Bar. They call it that because it's at the forty-eight-mile marker on the highway."

"That's the one. I don't know why you and Burt like it so much."

"Will Lewis Watts be there?" Kay asked Millie, who didn't bat an eye. Kay assumed that Vince had told her that Kay had mentioned Watts yesterday.

"I left a message for him on his answering machine."

"I was surprised to find out how well you all knew him."

"He was a great counselor and helped us get into good schools when we were just stupid kids. Isn't that right, Vince?"

"His was a big help to me." Vince sounded like he'd practiced the words.

"I'd like to thank him for all the great advice he gave me," Kay said, managing to contain her sarcasm.

"Just give him a call. I'm sure he'd love to hear from an… old student." Millie's tone was becoming edgy.

Kay heard the front door open. She glanced out into the hall and saw Todd Bruhn looking around.

"We're in here," Kay said through the doorway.

"My brother and sister-in-law wanted to come by before I took them home," Todd explained, looking surprised when he saw Vince and Millie behind Kay. "I asked Edgar and Pearl to wait in the car. I wanted to see where things were before… bringing them in. They're having a hard time with… it all."

"Of course they are!" Dramatically, Millie pushed past Kay and embraced a surprised Todd Bruhn. "I'm Millie, a dear friend of Rick's."

"Rick talked about you often," Todd said, giving her a sad smile and an awkward pat on the back.

Meanwhile, a different sort of drama was playing out in front of the funeral home.

"Crap!" Lee said as he pulled up.

"What?" Lester asked.

Todd Bruhn's car was in the driveway and Lee could see an older couple in the backseat, comforting each other. They hadn't noticed the hearse yet.

"That must be Rick Bruhn's parents." Lee threw the hearse into reverse and backed up before they could see him. "Nothing worse than pulling up with the body straight from the morgue and the family standing around."

"Gotcha. I remember the Thibodeau body before your dad died. They sure were upset."

"We didn't have any choice then. We'd just pulled in and they parked behind us. Our only choices were to leave the body baking in the hearse, or take the body bag out with the family standing around to see their loved one being carted like sack of potatoes."

"They have to know that you don't pick them up from the morgue or hospital in a coffin."

"Sure, if they think about it, but who wants to see it?" Lee parked the hearse by the curb where he could watch the driveway without being noticed.

He saw Todd Bruhn come out of the house and walk down to the car. After he talked with Rick's parents for a second, they all went into the house.

Lee sighed and pulled into the driveway.

"Let's be quick," he told Lester as they got out and went to the back of the hearse.

Inside, Todd introduced his brother and sister-in-law to Kay.

"We've met before," Kay reminded him. "Edgar, Pearl, you might not remember me. I dated Rick…"

"I remember you very well," Pearl said. She looked exhausted, with dark circles under eyes that were red from crying. Her dyed black hair had barely been brushed. "Rick thought a lot of you," she said without emotion.

"I liked him a great deal."

"He said you entered the Army as a nurse," Edgar said in a voice that seemed determined to stay strong.

"I did."

"A couple tours in Vietnam, from what he said."

Kay was surprised that Rick knew so much and that he'd bothered to tell his parents. "That's right."

"Brave girl. I'm glad you're here for him."

"Momma Bruhn, I'm so sorry." Millie came forward and hugged Mrs. Bruhn.

"I know," Pearl said, returning the hug. It was obvious to Kay that they knew each other well.

"He'd want you to be here too," Edgar told Millie. "He always said he didn't know what he'd have done without your help."

"We were there for each other," Millie said, with more humility than Kay had ever seen her exhibit before.

More general hugging went on while Kay stood back, feeling out of place. She didn't want to hug everyone and, besides that, there was an odd quality to the scene. What stood out was the genuine gratitude that Mr. and Mrs. Bruhn seemed to feel toward Millie. Kay had spent the last fifteen years since graduation thinking that Millie was nothing more than a conceited witch who'd seduced her boyfriend. But the reality was that Millie meant something to the Bruhn family and Kay wondered why. Had she been part of a support group that had helped him to succeed in life? Maybe. And maybe Kay had just been a silly, jealous girl who'd let her own emotions get in the way of a possible long-term relationship with Rick.

"Is my boy here?" Pearl asked Kay, who was about to say no when she caught a glimpse of Lee coming in the back door from the kitchen.

"I… let me check with my brother. He went to pick Rick up from the… hospital."

Kay hurried into the kitchen where Lee was getting a glass of water and Lester was rummaging through the refrigerator.

"Is he here?"

Lee nodded. "I take it that's the Bruhns?"

"Mrs. Bruhn asked if he was here."

"The autopsy left him in a pretty sorry state. We'd need an hour to get him even reasonably presentable. Really, it would be better if they come back tomorrow."

"They're not in a fit state to see him anyway."

Kay turned and headed back to the foyer, where everyone was standing around silently looking at each other, having run out of platitudes. Kay tried to convince herself that a white lie was the best course of action, but then mentally kicked herself when her mouth spat out the truth.

"I'm sorry. His body is here, but we need a little time to make him… presentable."

Pearl began to cry. Edgar tried to comfort her, half-looking like he wanted to demand to see his son.

"I think we should listen to Kay," Todd said, seeing the

look on his brother's face.

"Why was an autopsy necessary?" Edgar asked.

"There were marks on him that looked suspicious," Kay answered.

"I don't understand?"

"Chester Madison saw the marks and called the sheriff," Todd said. Kay was thankful that he'd intervened and put some of the onus on Madison.

"Rick's boss? What does he have to do with it?" Edgar asked with a confused expression.

"There is a considerable insurance policy at stake," Todd reminded his brother.

"Of course there is. That was Rick's business. I don't care about any of that."

"Mr. Madison is just looking after the company. Rick would want it that way," Todd reasoned with Edgar.

"I guess I can see that, but what's this about marks on Rick?"

"Probably nothing. They just needed to be sure."

"I don't understand any of this," Pearl sobbed.

Lee came into the room and Kay introduced him to everyone.

"Could I speak with you in private for a moment?" he asked Kay before turning to the others. "If you'll excuse us?"

Kay followed Lee into the kitchen, where Jerome was talking to Lester and drinking a beer.

"What is it?" She didn't like leaving the family alone without someone there to calm things down and answer questions.

"I did a little credit check on Mr. Todd Bruhn," Jerome said, setting the empty bottle in the sink. "He's got himself in some serious hot water. In fact, he borrowed twenty thousand dollars from his brother just to keep the creditors at bay for a couple of months."

Kay sighed. She'd just started to like Rick's uncle.

"Maybe that's why he's trying to calm things down," she said, thinking out loud.

"His brother getting a million dollars of insurance money could be his golden ticket," Jerome said.

"Why's he in debt?" Kay asked.

"'Cause he spends more than he makes," Jerome quipped. "It's that simple. He owns a hardware store that is sucking up money like a vacuum cleaner. A big-name lumber store opened a block away and took most of his customers. I'd like to ask him a few questions."

"I don't think that's a good idea," Lee said before Kay had a chance. "Do you know what's in the autopsy report?"

"Man, you think they tell me top-secret info like that? I won't hear about it until it's my case."

"Which it isn't."

"You got a point," Jerome admitted. "Just a few questions…" He frowned. "Okay, but I'm going to be on him like white on rice as soon as the autopsy report comes back."

"We'll see where we are then. What if the sheriff assigns the case to someone else?" Lee asked.

"No matter what the autopsy says, the sheriff's not going to see any sense in putting a bunch of manpower into the investigation. At best, he'll drop it on the desk of one of the investigators in CID who will be more than glad to let me look into it."

"So why not wait? And you'll have Madison to back your play," Kay said.

"Yeah, that's a point." Jerome seemed convinced to let it ride for a while longer.

"We should get back to the party," Kay said, looking toward the foyer where Vince, Millie and the family were trying to make small talk.

"We'll come by in the morning," Todd told Kay and Lee when they rejoined them.

"That will be fine. If you like, we can go back over the funeral details then so you can all be sure that the arrangements are to your satisfaction." Lee looked at Edgar, who nodded grimly, then they escorted the family down to Todd's car.

Kay pulled Millie aside.

"What's the best way to get a hold of Lewis Watts?"

"Why…" Millie started to protest, but gave in. "I've got his number in my address book."

They stepped over to Vince's car, where Millie took her address book out of her purse and wrote down the number. She gave the piece of paper to Kay with an irritated gesture.

"Thanks," Kay said, ignoring Millie's annoyance. "So you're all getting together at the Forty-eight Bar tonight?"

"That's right."

Kay let a pregnant pause play out, angling for Millie to suggest that she meet them there. It didn't happen. Finally Kay said, "Have a good time."

"Thanks," Millie said, then she left with Vince as soon as the Bruhns pulled away.

"So do you think Jerome is on to something?" Lee asked as they walked up the driveway to the house.

"I don't have a clue what I think," Kay said honestly. "Money is a big motivator, but to destroy your family?"

"People have done worse for less."

"I wish Millie was going to inherit the money. I could get down with her being the killer."

"Old jealousies should be buried."

Kay looked at Lee. "You're my younger brother. Don't go being all wise and comforting."

"Never fear, I'm still your annoying little brother."

"I'm going to call Lewis Watts." She held up the paper as

she walked through the door that Lee held open for her.

CHAPTER SEVENTEEN

Lewis Watts picked up on the second ring.

"Who is this?"

Kay was taken aback by the abrupt answer, but she stuck to her planned script. "It's Kay Lamberton, I was a student at Melon County High School when you were a counselor."

"Kay… yes. You wanted to be a nurse in the Army." He sounded hesitant.

"That's right. And you tried to talk me out of it."

"I remember. What can I do for you?"

"I wanted to come by and say hi."

"You do?" He sounded suspicious.

"If you don't mind?"

"Why would I mind?" Watts sounded like he minded a great deal.

"Good. How about tomorrow?"

"I don't know…"

"Or I can be there in an hour," Kay said, throwing him off guard and adding, "That would be great."

"Today?"

"I'll see you then. Thanks."

"I guess…"

Kay recited the address that Millie had given her without telling him where she'd gotten it, and assured him she wouldn't stay long. She hung up before he could say no.

"You railroaded him." Jerome's voice was filled with admiration. He and Lester had been hanging in the kitchen, listening to her conversation.

"It wasn't easy," Kay said.

"I've got work tonight," Jerome told Lester when he offered him another beer. Lester held one out to Kay.

"And I've got to drive to Gainesville… again." But she took the beer, then put it back in the refrigerator. "You don't need to drink two more."

"Hey, I don't have to work or go anywhere," Lester protested.

"Aren't you on the clock?" Kay asked him.

"I'm on call if we have to pick up a body. And later I'm going to help Lee with Rick Bruhn's embalming."

"Then you've had enough."

"You're a drag," he told her as Jerome laughed and headed out to his motorcycle.

The air was cool and damp when Kay got out of her car at Lewis Watts's house. It was a ranch-style house sitting on a couple of acres on the north side of Alachua County, not far from Santa Fe Community College where Catherine had told her he was now teaching.

The yard looked unkempt, though the blooming azaleas made up for the tall grass and untended flowerbeds.

The door opened as Kay reached the porch. Lewis Watts looked younger than Kay had expected from the sound of his voice on the phone. He was wearing an Izod polo shirt and jeans.

"Hello." He gave her a wide grin that showed a set of movie-star white teeth.

"I'm Kay."

"And you're lovely," he said, backing away from the door.

Said the spider to the fly, Kay thought. His attitude on the phone hadn't led her to expect him to be this welcoming and she was suspicious.

She looked around as she followed him into the house. She didn't know what she had expected, but it wasn't the Spartan interior she found. Lewis waved her into the front room where there was a couch, a coffee table, a chair, a lamp and a couple of bookcases neatly filled with psychology books.

"Since my wife left me, I've gone for the uncluttered look. She was a collector and the amount of junk she accumulated in five years was insane."

"Were you married when you were the counselor at Melon?"

"I'd just finished college. That was my first job. I didn't marry Denise until I started teaching at Santa Fe about six years ago."

"I thought you were young."

"I'm surprised you looked me up," Lewis said. "I remember advising you against using nursing school as a jump-off point for the Army. I really thought you should have gone to college."

"It's the deaths of Clint Peters and Rick Bruhn that made me want to look you up." Kay watched him grow noticeably tense as she mentioned their names.

"I don't understand." His tone was far from the easygoing manner he'd affected so far.

"I needed to talk to someone and I thought that, since you knew all of us, it would make it easier for me to talk to you about their deaths." The psychology books had given her the idea to go this route and she was pleased to see him relax immediately.

"I'm not a clinical psychologist."

"I wasn't looking for anything… formal. I just wanted to talk with someone who wasn't a friend or a member of my family." She peddled the lie with a downcast look.

"Of course. I'm glad you came to me. Have a seat. Can I get you something to drink?" Lewis slipped easily into the role of congenial host now that he thought he knew her motivations.

"I'd take a Coke or a water."

Lewis left her and headed for the kitchen, giving her time to look more closely at the books in the bookcases. Most of them were college course books on psychology, mixed in with a few of the latest self-help books.

"I wouldn't recommend most of those." Lewis came in carrying a tray with two glasses and a plate of Girl Scout Cookies. "I end up buying boxes of Thin Mints and Samoas from all the staff at the college. Occupational hazard. I'll give you a couple of boxes to take home." He smiled and set the tray down on the coffee table.

Kay sat down in a chair and Lewis perched on the edge of the couch, sliding a glass of Coke over to her across the coffee table.

"I didn't expect to lose my high school friends like this," Kay said.

"No one expected Clint to take his own life." Lewis took a drink from his glass. Kay could smell the rum that was mixed into his Coke.

"I saw Millie Jessup today and didn't really know what to say to her."

Kay watched him closely, but Lewis showed no reaction to her mentioning Millie. *Does he already know that I've seen Millie?* she wondered.

"Death can build barriers between people. The loss of a friend or loved one doesn't just separate us from them. It often separates us from our other friends and family who are grieving too." Lewis slipped into the dulcet tones of a counselor comforting a client.

"If they'd died by accident or health issues, I could accept it more easily. But Clint committing suicide and now the possibility that Rick was killed…" Kay didn't finish the thought. She didn't need to. The look on Lewis's face told her that this was the first he'd heard about the questions surrounding Rick's death.

"What do you mean, killed?" He was leaning so far forward now that Kay expected him to fall off the couch at any second.

"The county took his body from our funeral home so they could do an autopsy on it."

"I heard that it was an accident. He drowned in his parents' pool," Lewis said, as if he needed her to verify his belief.

"All I heard was that there were marks on his face and throat that looked like… maybe it wasn't an accident."

Lewis's face was flushed and he was breathing heavily. "They can't think that someone killed him."

Kay shrugged.

Lewis stood up and started pacing the room.

"I didn't mean to upset you. I assumed Millie might have mentioned it to you." Kay couldn't decide if she was enjoying playing the coy Miss Marple or if she felt a little guilty about it. If Lewis hadn't looked so stricken by the news, she would have been more at ease with the role.

"Why would you think Millie would tell me?"

"I understood that you two were… close." Kay watched him intently. His face went from puzzled to irritated in a flash.

"Close?" For a moment she thought Lewis was going to deny it, but then his face relaxed as little. "We do socialize some since my wife and I separated. I'm a fan of her writing." This seemed like a lame add-on.

"That's what I'd heard." Kay decided to have pity on him and give him an out, though the devil in her wanted to go for the jugular and tell him that she'd heard he was interested in Millie back when he was a counselor. But the odd look of fear on his face stopped her. *What is he scared of? Discovery of some sordid affair while he was married? Inappropriate behavior with Millie when she was seventeen and he was a twenty-three-year-old counselor? Or is it something to do with Clint's and Rick's deaths?*

"I've got some work I need to do." Lewis still seemed to be working hard to catch his breath.

Kay stood up. "I didn't mean to upset you." Which was a lie, though she could honestly say she hadn't meant to get him *this* upset.

"I… Has the autopsy been completed?" Lewis asked.

"My brother picked Rick's body up this morning," she answered.

Lewis nodded and Kay started toward the door, then she stopped and turned back to face him. "I did want to ask if you saw Clint in the days leading up to his suicide?"

Lewis held up his hand in the universal stop gesture. "I know what you're thinking. I'm a psychologist and should have seen clinical signs of depression. Unfortunately, I only saw him in a couple of social situations in the last weeks of his life. We didn't speak privately. On the surface he seemed fine. Preoccupied, but that was understandable considering the large workload he'd accumulated."

"Thanks for taking the time to speak with me. I didn't

mean to bother you," Kay said and walked out the door. She felt his eyes follow her all the way to her car.

On the drive back to Lang, Kay wrestled with the idea of how to crash the get-together planned for that night at the Forty-eight Bar.

"You can just drop in on their little party," Lee told her when they were all sitting around the dinner table.

Ruby put a ceramic bowl overflowing with spaghetti down in the middle of the table. The aroma of tomato sauce thick with mushrooms, ground beef and green peppers filled the room.

"I know. But if I do that, I might lose the chance of talking to them later." Kay had gone over all sorts of scenarios on her drive back home. "I just want to be a fly on the wall."

"You need to get some spy equipment," Lester suggested, piling a mound of pasta on his plate.

"Where's Jerome?" Ruby asked, sounding a little hurt that someone would miss one of her dinners.

"He got called in early. A cookout got out of hand and they needed all hands on deck. He said to save him a plateful and two pieces of garlic bread," Lee told her.

"How did the… did Rick turn out?" Kay asked. Discussing dead bodies had never been out of bounds at dinner.

"We had to do a lot of filling in. They carved up his skull and left some pieces out when they sent him back to us. And his chest was a mess. I don't know who they have sewing up the bodies at the morgue, but they damn sure better not ever attempt to close up a living person."

"But he'll be ready for his mother and father to see him tomorrow?"

"He looks real good," Lester assured her.

"We did all right," Lee allowed. "What do you think

you'd learn if you went to this night out at the pub?"

"I don't know. I'd like to watch Millie and Lewis interact. He almost went into shock when I told him about the autopsy."

"What could he have to do with Rick's death? What motive could he have?" Lee asked.

"Good question. If you just go by motive, you have to follow the million dollars to the Bruhns."

"Uncle Todd sure needs the money."

"Murder is a crime of passion," Ruby mused as she took her seat at the table.

"Agreed. The question is: What is the passion? Is it for money? Love? Ambition?" Kay said.

"Who's going to be at the Forty-eight tonight?" Lee asked.

"Millie, Vince and Lewis. I don't know who else."

"You could at least go and watch the place. That's what they do on all the detective shows on TV." Lester grinned.

Kay looked at him like a teacher taken by surprise when the dullard in class comes up with the right answer.

"I can do that."

"What?" Lee asked.

"Go and watch to see who comes and goes."

"You aren't a private detective."

"Maybe not." She smiled.

"You're going to get yourself in trouble," Lee grumbled.

"Go with her," Ruby said, and everyone looked at her. "Yin caught a mouse last night."

"I might have a body to pick up," Lee said evasively.

"I'll be here," Lester reminded him.

"Yeah, but…" Lee rolled his eyes. "Fine, I'll go. What time are they going to meet?"

"I'm not sure. We should be there by eight."

"This is crazy."

"Now that I think about it, it might have been Yang that caught the mouse. He sometimes gives Yin toys to play with," Ruby told them.

Everyone nodded as if they understood what the hell she was talking about and finished their spaghetti so they would be eligible for a slice of Ruby's red velvet cake.

CHAPTER EIGHTEEN

"Where are we going to park?" Kay mused as she drove out toward the county line with Lee looking uncomfortable in the passenger seat. "We don't want them to see us."

"*Now* you're worried about the details," Lee sighed. "There's an old service station across the road. The lot's pretty grown up and there are some old cars parked there. We might be able to blend in."

"But will we be able to see anything?"

Lee held up a pair of binoculars. "Dad always took these when we went to the beach."

"I remember."

"I think he liked to look at the boats on the water."

"I hope that's what he was using them for. Thanks for thinking of them," Kay said.

"I guess we're in this together."

"We never did much together when we were younger," Kay said, glancing over at Lee before turning her eyes back to the glow of the headlights leading them down the back country roads of Melon County.

"Age difference. Plus, I *wanted* to hang out at the funeral home and you just wanted to get away."

"Nail on the head. After I turned twelve, I wanted nothing more than to be far away from the family business. Looking back, I don't really know why I wanted to escape so bad."

"Dad could be a little overbearing."

"A little? Ha!"

"Okay, a lot. As much as I love the work, even I found him a little hard to take sometimes."

Kay smiled. "But now when I think back, I realize that all of that watching and hovering and directing came from his love of the business."

"And he really loved us too."

"Yeah."

"Do you remember when I was nine and you took me to the Alachua County Fair?"

"Dad got a call that night."

"He'd been promising me all week that he'd take me to the fair, then Mrs. Gray's aunt died while she was visiting from Alabama, so he had to go pick up the body and get it ready to ship home."

"I'd forgotten the reason. Seemed like Dad was always having to change plans."

"I cried and you said you'd take me."

"Funny. I can remember how nice the weather was. The first really cool weather we had that fall."

"Dad let you drive the Impala."

"1960 convertible. I loved that car. No wonder I offered to take you. I think he only let me drive it like five times."

"He knew how much you liked that car. I think that's why he sold it after you left."

"We had fun that night."

"One of the best memories I have. Funnel cakes and corndogs."

"The stuffed bear you won is still in my room."

"Hey, we're getting close. The Forty-eight is just up ahead on the right." Lee was leaning forward, peering out the windshield.

"I see the lights."

"The old gas station is almost directly across the street."

With no traffic coming from the other direction, Kay turned her lights off for the last hundred yards before pulling into the abandoned station.

Lee could see people milling around the front door of the bar across the street. "Good idea turning the lights off."

"Everyone has probably had a couple of drinks already and, with the lights around the bar, I doubt they saw us." Kay backed into a spot by the side of the old stucco building. "Do you think we'll be able to see anything from here?"

Lee put the binoculars up to his eyes. "Not bad. I can recognize a couple of the people standing around the door." He handed her the binoculars.

"Yeah, that works. I'm not sure what we're going to learn from our little stakeout."

"I brought snacks." Lee held up a bag of Ruffles and a can of dip. "I got some drinks too."

"How can you think of eating after that meal Ruby fixed?"

"In an hour you'll be begging me for some of these chips."

They waited and watched. At a quarter to nine, Millie and Vince showed up.

"Interesting how those two are sticking together," Kay said, staring through the binoculars.

Five minutes later, Kay sat up and stared hard at the bar.

"Look who else is in town."

"Who is it?"

"Burt Sedgwick. He was part of the crowd. Never met anyone with a larger ego. Considering some of the jackasses I met in the Army, that's saying something." Kay hadn't taken the binoculars away from her eyes.

"Let me see."

Kay handed the binoculars across to Lee.

"Sorry, too late. That was him going in the door," she told him.

"I saw enough to say that he could skip a few meals." Lee chuckled and handed her the binoculars again.

Kay soon sat up again. "This is interesting. Tracy, Clint's wife, is here and there's Lewis Watts coming up behind her."

"Did they come together?"

"No, two separate cars. They're being friendly, though." She watched as both figures walked into the bar.

"I'm cold." Kay started the car and let the heater run for a while. For the next thirty minutes, people came and went, but they saw no more of Kay's high-school crowd.

"You know, if we sell the funeral home, you'll find another job. I'll help you. You could even move up to Huntsville with me," Kay told Lee.

Lee hadn't heard anything after "if we sell the funeral home." "I thought we weren't going to talk about it." He'd become pretty skilled at pretending that doom wasn't lurking around the corner over the last couple of days and he certainly didn't want to start thinking about it now.

"You're right," Kay said, resigned.

"Do you know why they call it the Forty-eight?" Lee was looking at the old barn-like structure that housed the bar.

"Vince said it was because it's at the forty-eight-mile marker."

"Right. Which on this road measures the distance down

to Cedar Key on the coast. During Prohibition, booze would come in from Cuba and the other islands in the Caribbean. They'd tell the smugglers to stop at mile marker forty-eight and drop some of it off. This was an illegal juke joint. The sheriff got a cut of the money so no one bothered them."

Kay was impressed with her brother's knowledge of the local booze lore. "Didn't the upright folks in the county get upset about it?"

"Half of them frequented the place. Besides, the sheriff swore he thought the marker was across the line in Alachua County. If anyone ever dropped a dime on them with the Alachua County sheriff, it didn't do any good 'cause he knew where the line really was."

After another half hour, Tracy Peters left the bar alone. Twenty minutes later Vince, Millie and Burt all came out together.

"That's all of them except Lewis," Kay said.

"I guess the party's over."

Kay watched as both Vince and Burt drove out of the parking lot and headed back toward Lang.

After a few more minutes, she said, "I'm going inside to talk to Lewis." Kay pursed her lips. "It might be the wrong move, but with a few drinks in him, this might be a good time to ask him a few more questions."

"I guess we can pretend we're bar hopping." Lee didn't sound sure.

"I want to go in alone. I'll tell him a half truth. I heard they were going to meet here tonight and I thought I might catch them."

"Makes sense. Though I'm not sure you should go in there by yourself."

Kay laughed. "Brother, you don't know your big sister very well. This isn't some biker hangout. It's almost a family bar. You forget I've been in dive bars in Saigon."

She started the car and drove across the street to the bar. The few people hanging out in the parking lot didn't seem to notice that she'd just come from the abandoned gas station.

"Eat your chips and wait here for me," Kay said, getting out of the car.

The bar would have been quaint, or at least picturesque, if it had been better maintained. The rust was real and the windows covered in actual grime. When she opened the door, the smell of cigarette smoke and stale beer reminded her of her days in the Army. The jukebox was playing Willie Nelson's "Blue Eyes Crying in the Rain." The hazy atmosphere inside was illuminated by neon signs hung around the walls.

Kay stood at the door for a minute, letting her eyes adjust to the dim lighting.

"Hey, pretty lady," a drunken lout wearing a crooked smile called to her from a stool by the door.

"Careful someone doesn't knock that stool out from under your ass," she told him.

When she stepped farther into the bar, she caught sight of two tables pushed together with a dozen empty glasses and beer bottles scattered across them. At one end sat Lewis Watts. He was staring down at the table, one hand clutching a glass while the other stretched out in front of him, flexing open then closed.

Kay walked over to him. With a pained expression on his face, Lewis looked up. She thought she saw a look of recognition as he started to stand, then she saw how unsteady he was and realized something was wrong. At first she thought he must have been drunk and was about to pass out, but then she saw the grimace on his face as his hand clutched his chest. She managed to half catch him as he fell to the floor, kicking his chair away and into a man who turned around in anger.

"Call for an ambulance!" Kay yelled, dropping to her knees beside Lewis as he threw up and his muscles started to seize. His eyes were wide open and glazing over.

By the time Kay began to perform CPR, she knew that Lewis was dead and no amount of effort would bring him back.

The Forty-eight's parking lot was awash in strobing lights of blue and red.

"What were you all doing here?" Jerome asked Lee and Kay.

Kay gave him a brief explanation.

"And y'all didn't think to give me a call and ask if that sounded like a blue-ribbon plan? To be clear, that was a go-to-the-principal's-office plan."

"We were just going to watch and see who showed up," Lee said.

"Until she went in and a man keeled over," Jerome said.

"Something like that," Lee admitted.

"Lewis was acting odd when I went by his place earlier today," Kay told Jerome.

"So?"

"And now he's dead after Millie, Burt and Vince met with him."

"You're saying they had something to do with him dropping dead?"

"Seems pretty suspicious," Kay pushed.

"You said they left about half an hour before he collapsed."

"Maybe they poisoned him." Kay took a deep breath. "I know that sounds crazy, but this can't be a coincidence."

"I saved what was left in his glass, though most of it spilled when he fell over," Jerome said.

"There has to be something going on," Kay insisted.

"I called for our photographer to come take some pictures and I'll collect any other evidence I see."

"Are they going to send out a detective?" Lee asked.

"No. Fletcher is on call. He took some notes over the phone, but was unimpressed. A man dropping dead in a bar isn't exactly headline news. You should be glad that I talked him into letting me handle this. If you started giving him all your paranoid murder theories, you'd be getting a psych evaluation at Alachua General. We have nothing until the autopsy report."

"Will there be an autopsy?" Kay asked with more than a trace of scorn for the way the sheriff's office operated.

"Without a doctor on the scene, they won't have much of a choice. The ambulance is getting ready to take him to the hospital. I'm going back in to collect what I can before the bar staff starts cleaning up."

"This is a joke." Kay stared down at her feet and kicked the pavement as Jerome stalked away.

"Jerome is doing what he can. You have to admit it's not obvious how someone could have killed him," Lee said reasonably.

"One word—poison."

"Then the autopsy will find it."

Lee left Kay sitting in her car while he went over to the ambulance to talk to one of the EMTs that he knew.

"Mike, what's the word?"

"Dead. We're taking him to the hospital to be pronounced. Nobody trusts us anymore."

"Heart attack?"

"Most likely."

"Any chance it could be poison?"

Mike shrugged. "Anything's possible, but it sure looks like a heart attack to me. I didn't smell or see any clinical signs that would point in another direction."

Lee thanked him and started back toward Kay when he saw a car parked on the edge of the lot with a man sitting inside. It was hard to tell with the ambulance lights flashing behind him, but Lee thought he recognized the man. He edged close enough to be sure, then hurried back to Kay's car.

"You won't believe who's sitting in that car over there," Lee said, pointing to the Chevrolet Monte Carlo. "Todd Bruhn."

"What?"

"You heard me."

"What's he doing here?" Kay got out of her car and started over toward Todd.

"Maybe you should tell Jerome," Lee suggested warily.

"I will after I talk to Bruhn." Kay picked up speed as she became more determined to find out why he was at the Forty-eight Bar. Lee had to hustle to keep up with her.

Todd got out of the car when he saw them approaching.

"What are you doing here?" Kay asked without preamble.

"I'd assume the same thing that you are," Todd said, his jaw pushed out. "Keeping an eye on Rick's friends. I managed to get inside without them seeing me and just sat in a corner and watched.

"You followed them?"

"Didn't have to. I heard Millie and Vince mention that they were coming out here when we were all at the funeral home today."

Kay tried to think through all of the implications. This revelation meant that if Lewis had been killed, then Todd Bruhn could be added to the list of suspects. On the other hand, if he wasn't guilty and was in fact on their side, then it would give them another perspective on what had taken place.

"What'd you see?" Lee asked before Kay could get the words out.

"Not much. They each had a couple of drinks. Lots of talking and hugging. The other woman—Tracy, I think they called her—seemed like the proverbial fish out of water, and it was only about an hour after she arrived that Millie said something to her that pissed her off. I couldn't hear what they were saying, but from the look of them, it got nasty quick. Tracy stood up and for a minute I thought she was going to slap Millie, then Vince intervened and he walked Tracy to the door."

"We saw her leave. Did you see anything strange with Lewis?" Kay asked.

"The guy that died? No. He was sitting at the end of the table where you found him the whole evening, looking depressed. A couple of the others tried to engage him in conversation, but he didn't look interested."

"What did he eat or drink?"

"Just a couple of mixed drinks. Eat? Maybe some of the pretzels they had on the table."

"What did he do when everyone left?"

"He stood up and they all shook hands and hugged before he sat back down again. He still had a drink. He finished it, then just sat there until you came in."

"That's it? No one argued with him?" Kay had been expecting something more.

"Just the opposite. Everyone seemed solicitous of him. Honestly, I didn't think he looked very good the whole time."

"I understand you owe your brother a lot of money." This came from Jerome, who'd walked up behind them without anyone noticing.

Todd wheeled to face him. "What's that got to do with anything?"

"You tell me." Jerome stared back at him.

"Are you suggesting that I killed my nephew so my brother would get the insurance money?"

"Folks have killed for less." Jerome smirked. "A lot less."

"That's crazy. I loved my nephew and would never do anything to hurt my brother and his wife. If I ever hear you repeat that lie, I'll make a complaint to the sheriff." Todd was sputtering with indignation.

"Are you telling me that it's a lie that you're broke and have borrowed thousands of dollars from your brother?" Jerome taunted him.

It was too dark to tell for sure, but Kay was sure that Todd's face had gone beet red.

"I may be financially bankrupt, but I'm not morally bankrupt," Todd said through clenched teeth.

"I just wanted you to know that we're going to turn over every stone to find out who killed Rick Bruhn," Jerome told him. "No matter what types of worms we might uncover."

Todd's mouth was opening and closing as he tried to think of the best way to express his outrage.

"That's enough, Jerome," Kay said, coming to Todd's rescue. "I think he gets the point. I'm also sure that he wants you to conduct the type of investigation that doesn't spare anyone's feelings."

"I want to find out what happened to Rick," Todd said, his anger still close to the surface.

"I'm glad you feel that way," Jerome told him.

Todd turned to Lee, who'd been standing to the side and cringing at the thought that Jerome was going to get Todd so mad that he'd take Rick's funeral somewhere else.

"Mr. Lamberton, I hope that Rick's body will be ready for his parents to see him tomorrow."

"We cleaned him up this afternoon. They left him in… We were able to make him presentable. I know this has been a terrible blow to your family. I promise you that I'll do everything I can to help your brother and his wife through this ordeal."

"I hope that this man won't be there throwing accusations around when my family comes to view the body."

"I guarantee that no one will be asking questions tomorrow." Lee gave Jerome a hard look.

"I give you my word as well," Jerome told Todd grudgingly.

"Try and think about what you saw tonight," Kay said to Todd. "If someone killed Lewis, then they were probably involved in Rick's death too."

Todd nodded. "I'll try, but I really didn't see anything unusual. We'll be at the funeral home at eleven o'clock tomorrow."

He got back into his car and drove away with Jerome watching him closely.

"Way to almost scare away a paying customer," Lee said angrily.

"Follow the money, man. That's all I'm sayin'."

"You have a point," Kay admitted. A million dollars for the Bruhns. A million for Tracy. "I wonder if there was an insurance policy on Lewis?"

"Good question," Lee said.

"Now you're talking." Jerome smiled.

"If he was a friend of Rick's, then he probably had a policy. That man seemed to sell one to everyone he knew. We can ask Chester Madison. He'll know," Lee said.

"If there was a policy on Lewis Watts, Madison is going to be more than interested." Kay watched as the ambulance took off toward Gainesville with its lights flashing but no siren.

Lee and Kay rode back to the funeral home in silence,

both lost in their own thoughts and tired of speculating on mysteries that they weren't going to solve without more evidence. When they got out of the car, they were greeted by Yin and Yang. The two tubby tabbies rubbed against their legs, looking up at the humans hopefully. Kay saw that the lights in Ruby's apartment were off.

"Your momma's asleep so you're begging treats from us," Kay said, reaching down to pet each of the cats. "Missing a meal wouldn't kill either one of you," she told them before going into the kitchen and bringing out some tuna.

"They're ungrateful moochers," Lee told her with a smile and a shake of his head, then he headed up to bed.

Kay sat down on the back stoop and watched the two cats change bowls, hoping the other had something better.

"You each got tuna out of the same can," she told them.

After the bowls were empty, Yin gave himself a cursory bath before coming over and clambering into Kay's lap. Yang performed his cleaning yoga ritual while keeping one eye on Yin and Kay. "You can get some scratchies after your bath if you want," she told him.

Kay enjoyed the cool night air and the quiet companionship of the two well-fed felines.

"Your momma says you all have psychic skills. Now would be a great time to demonstrate them. Who killed Rick?" Yin purred as she petted him. "You can spell it out in the sand or something. Or maybe just send me the answers telepathically," she told him. "Anything?"

Yang finished his bath and waddled over to slap Yin on the back with his paw. Yin groused a bit, but got off of Kay's lap. Yang hopped up and replaced him.

"You two are a trip." Kay smiled, feeling more at home than she had in a long time. She listened to the quiet hum of the town which was mostly shut down by this time of night, even on a Friday. All she heard were a few cars moving about.

Can we really solve Rick's murder? she wondered. She knew there were murders every year that went unsolved. Even some where the killer had left more clues than in this case. If it hadn't been for Lee, Rick would have been buried and no one would have been the wiser.

"You haven't been any help at all," she told the two cats as she nudged Yang off of her lap. She got a beer out of the refrigerator in the kitchen, then wandered up to bed.

CHAPTER NINETEEN

Lee had a plan for Saturday morning. It involved getting everyone to hit the decks running so the place would be clean and showing its best side when the Bruhns arrived. He didn't want to give them any excuse for changing funeral homes.

"I want you to spray down the driveway, then sweep the sidewalk and path up to the door," Lee told Lester at breakfast as the other man forked pancakes onto his plate.

"Sure thing, boss."

His answer was a little too flippant for Lee. "I'm serious. As soon as you've stuffed those pancakes down your throat, I want you to get busy."

Lester held up his fork and nodded.

Lee moved on to his next collaborator. "Ruby, would you give the bathrooms a good scrubbing?"

"Of course. We don't want the Bruhns taking their son somewhere else."

Lee cringed a bit at her on-the-nose assessment of his

motives.

"I can do some vacuuming if you want," Kay offered.

"That would be great," Lee said and meant it. "And, Lester, as soon as you get done outside, I'll need you to help me get the body set up in the viewing room."

Lee had no intention of making the Bruhns go into the embalming room to see their son. Besides, if they did a good job of showcasing the coffin and their work, it would serve as proof to the Bruhns that they had chosen the right funeral home for the service.

Everything got off to a good start, with even Lester throwing himself into the preparations. But then events soon took their own unguided course.

The front door opened as Kay was running the vacuum over the area rugs in the entry hall. A grim-faced Millie Jessup plowed across the threshold, hauling Vince Edwards and Burt Sedgewick in her wake.

"Are you happy now?" Millie yelled at Kay.

"What—" Kay started to ask when Millie charged toward her. Kay had to backpedal to avoid being knocked over.

Vince grabbed onto Millie, who struggled against him.

"You killed Lewis!" she shouted.

"You're crazy," Kay said, still keeping her distance.

"What's going on?" Lee came running into the hall in response to the shouting.

"She killed Lewis with her stupid questions." Millie was a little calmer as she tried to explain.

"What are you talking about?" Kay sputtered in complete confusion.

"He had a bad heart. Everyone knew that. Why do you think I hadn't told him about the possibility of Rick's death being something other than an accident?" Millie's voice was rising again.

"I didn't know anything about it," Kay said.

"He's had issues since we were in high school. He carried pills."

"I didn't know," Kay repeated.

"He was all upset after you left his house yesterday," Millie said, shaking Vince off of her.

"How was I supposed to know?"

"What were you doing over there in the first place?"

"We all need to calm down," Lee said. He wanted to step between the two women, but the glares he got from both of them changed his mind. "I just think we can discuss this in a more rational way."

"I'm sorry if anything I did contributed to his death," Kay said, her emotions in turmoil. *Did I really upset him that badly?*

"What good is it to say you're sorry?" Millie demanded.

"You say he had heart problems?"

"Yes!" Millie shouted.

Kay looked at Vince and Burt, who solemnly nodded their heads in agreement.

"You didn't need to go barging around town like a bull in a china shop," Millie said petulantly.

"You're probably right. I just want to know what happened to Rick."

"We all do. Until you told me, I thought it was just an accident," Millie said. Vince and Burt stayed silent, still nodding their heads like bobble-head dolls.

"Maybe I shouldn't have gone to Lewis and surprised him with the news," Kay admitted.

"You couldn't have known it would affect him like that," Lee said, coming to her side.

"What was wrong with his heart?" Kay asked.

"He had an atrial fibrillation. At least that's what he was diagnosed with when he was younger. I think it had developed into a more serious condition. I just know he took digitalis and some other medications regularly," Burt said.

"I might have been too hard on you. I can't blame you if you didn't know about his heart problems." Millie seemed to deflate in front of their eyes. "I could really use a drink."

"What would you like?" Lee asked.

"A triple anything." She paused. "Gin and something clear."

"We can go into the parlor," Kay said as Lee hurried off to fetch Millie's drink. She pointed the way for the others, then hung back so she could speak with Burt. "It's good to see you."

"It's been a long time," he said, giving her a little hug. He had been six feet tall and a solid hundred-and-ninety pounds in high school. While he was still six feet tall, Kay guessed that he'd tip the scales at nothing less than two-fifty now. *Lucky for him he can afford a tailor-made suit*, she thought as they joined the others.

"Is Rick here?" Vince asked.

"Lee has spent the morning getting the viewing room set up for Rick's parents," Kay said as Lee came back with Millie's drink.

"Thank you," she said, taking a big gulp.

"You've all done so well since high school," Kay said, looking around at the three of them.

"It's all thanks to Millie." Vince nodded toward the woman who had already downed half of her gin fizz.

"Now I don't know about you, but I've got a few talents of my own," Burt said jokingly.

"We all have talents, but Millie and… Lewis helped us reach our full potential." Vince's demeanor was somber as he spoke of Lewis.

"You got me there. Lewis was a good guy. Helped us a lot," Burt said, looking down at his feet. Millie drained the rest of her glass.

"I can't believe that we've lost Rick and Lewis," Vince said.

"Don't forget about Clint," Burt added.

"That one never made sense to me. Why would he kill himself?" Vince shook his head.

"Pressure. Every day, I go to work and spend twelve, fifteen hours playing with other people's money. Big responsibility. I'm lucky. I don't sweat anything. But that wasn't Clint. He let things get under his skin. Being a big-time lawyer with people's lives on the line…"

Kay and Millie silently observed the men's discussion.

"He wasn't a criminal lawyer. Wasn't like he was saving people from the gallows," Vince pointed out.

"Hell, for a lot of people, their professional lives are more important to them than their personal lives," Burt said. "That's the kind of shit he was dealing with. He'd lost a couple of cases the last few months before he died."

"Did he say something to you?" Millie asked suddenly, causing Burt to stare at her.

"We were at some grand opening. Afterward, we had a few drinks. Yeah, he said some stuff." As Burt spoke, Kay noticed an interesting exchange of looks between him and Millie.

"His suicide is water under the bridge at this point. We should be thinking about poor Rick," Millie said.

"Someone killed him? Is that what the police are saying?" Burt directed this question to Kay.

She glanced around to see if she'd have any support, but Lee had snuck back out after delivering Millie's drink.

"There were signs that he was killed," she said evasively.

"Signs?" Burt asked, pushing her for more.

"Marks on his face and his throat."

"Who'd want to kill Rick?" Vince said.

"I don't know," Kay said. "That's why I've been asking

so many questions."

"Of us?" Vince sounded astonished.

"Everyone I can. Someone has to know something."

"Aren't you supposed to go over the three elements of a murder: means, motive and opportunity?" Burt seemed eager to explore the topic.

"That's right."

"Motive is always the go-to on those detective shows," Burt said.

"That's my point. Who would want to kill Rick?" Vince asked again.

Kay wanted to add that they should be applying the same questions to the deaths of Clint and Lewis, but she held her tongue. The three friends were stirred up enough.

"This is crazy. I just can't imagine anyone wanting to harm Rick," Millie said.

"Money," Burt responded. "Always follow the money."

"You're just saying that 'cause money is your god," Vince said with a smirk.

"Eff you, buddy." Burt smiled. "Okay, there might be a little truth in what you're saying, but you got to admit that money and love are the two reasons most murders are committed. Isn't that right?" he asked Kay.

"You aren't wrong."

"So who benefits from Rick's death?" Burt asked.

Kay hesitated to answer.

"Come on," Burt prodded. "You've been asking all the questions, so you must know. Who inherits Rick's money?"

"It's the insurance!" Millie said suddenly. "Rick made all of us buy his silly old insurance. He must have had a policy on himself."

Millie, Burt and Vince all turned their eyes on Kay, who squirmed a little.

"There was an insurance policy on Rick's life," she

admitted.

"So who benefits?" Vince asked.

"His parents," Kay said softly.

The other three exchanged looks.

"That seems a bit rough. We all know his folks. They don't seem like the Hitchcock, knife-in-the-back type," Vince said, and the others pursed their lips.

Kay wasn't going to tell them about Todd's financial troubles and the fact that Edgar had been willing to loan him money in the past.

"What about his job? Would any of his co-workers benefit from his death?" Burt continued to lead the discussion.

"From what Chester Madison said, the company will be in worse shape with Rick gone," Kay said.

"You know that's true," Millie piped up. "That man could sell a fish a bikini."

"Maybe it's love," Vince said. "Was he dating the wrong person's wife? Or did he ditch the wrong woman?"

"No women in his life." Millie shook her head. "He and I talked about that the last time I heard from him. We were just kidding around, but I gave him a hard time about the sorry state of his love life."

"He never was one…" Burt stopped and looked at Kay, then snapped his fingers. "That's right. You two were a real thing."

"You're stepping on toes, Burty," Millie said with a frown.

"Oh, the prom. Stupid of me. That was years ago."

"He never forgot you. You can take comfort in that," Millie told Kay with a sad smile.

"Like Burt said, it's water under the bridge," Kay said, embarrassed.

"Anyway, I think that's why he didn't do much skirt-chasing. Once bitten and all that stuff," Millie said.

"So not love," Burt said. "Are you *sure* he was killed?"

"We'll know more when the autopsy report comes out."

"Even then, will they tell you?" Millie asked.

"We have a few connections," Lee answered, coming back into the room.

"I guess knowing people at the morgue would be a perk of the job," Millie said with just a hint of sarcasm in her tone.

"Kay, can I speak with you?" Lee asked, pointing his head toward the kitchen.

"Thanks. It's a little uncomfortable being outnumbered," Kay said when they were alone.

"Todd called and they're headed this way. I don't think Rick's mom and dad should have to share this time with others."

Kay and Lee went back to the parlor and explained the situation. Somewhat to Kay's surprise, the others agreed to leave. It wasn't like they hadn't had their chance to see the Bruhns the day before, and would see them again at the public viewing and funeral.

Millie led the others out the front door with a few goodbyes and promises to renew the discussion of Rick's death at a later time. "Let us know when you find out about the autopsy," were her parting words.

"What did you learn?" Lee asked as soon as they were gone.

"That Millie is the boss, though I already knew that. I think Burt's right about following the money. Of course, they couldn't see his parents being involved in anything."

"Which leaves us with Todd."

"I haven't taken his parents off the list completely. I told you that I didn't like them that much when I was dating Rick. So we'll see what I think of them now. I'm not ruling anything out. Tracy got a huge chunk of money too. We could go back to the old crisscross."

"*Strangers on a Train.*"

"Where either Todd or Rick's parents killed Clint and then Tracy killed Rick."

"This reminds me of one of those Parker Family mysteries," Lee said, shaking his head.

"You read those?" Kay was surprised.

"Right after you left. I was bored one Sunday and decided to read the first one."

"*Elements of Death.*"

"I thought they were girly books since they were yours, but I got hooked when the first person died. The image of someone opening a can containing white phosphorus stuck with me."

"The books were brutal."

"Looking back, I'm surprised they were marketed as kids' books. It's funny that we both read them, and now here we are solving a real-life murder."

"Real life will only be imitating art if we actually *solve* the murder," Kay said.

"The Parker Family had a hundred-percent success rate."

"You said Rick is ready for his parents?"

"I think we covered everything. Want to look?"

Kay entered the viewing room and was struck by how well Lee and Lester had prepared the room.

"Where'd you get the flowers?" Kay asked, admiring the floral arrangement beside the coffin.

"I have some delivered every week and keep them in the cooler." He held up his hand. "I know it's an expense. I just like having some fresh flowers on hand if someone's viewing a body before anyone has sent any."

"That was Dad."

"Guilty as charged."

"Is this the coffin they wanted?" Kay didn't think it looked like the one that Todd had picked out.

"No. His won't be here until later today."

Kay looked down at Rick's body.

"You did a wonderful job." She reached out and brushed some lint from Rick's lapel. The makeup that Lee had used was lifelike, with a depth that most embalmers couldn't achieve.

"It's what I do."

Kay felt her eyes moisten. She had seen Rick in the cooler when he was stretched out on the steel trolley. That had been hard to take, but now to see him dressed and lying in a coffin for his final days above ground was a different kind of hard.

The sound of the front door opening pulled Kay out of her dark thoughts. She wiped at her eyes, then went with Lee to meet the family.

CHAPTER TWENTY

The Bruhns didn't look any more rested than they had the day before. Pearl was supported on either side by Edgar and Todd. Their hands hovered near her elbows, ready to steady her if necessary as she walked slowly into the funeral home.

Lee stepped forward and greeted them with a solemn look of sympathy.

"I want to see my son." Pearl looked directly at Lee as though she thought he might deny her request.

"This way."

Lee walked to the viewing room with the three mourners following close behind him.

Kay watched and found it hard to imagine that this woman was faking her grief. Her acting skills would've had to be on par with Vivien Leigh and Bette Davis. Edgar was more stoic, making his complicity possible. But likely? Kay couldn't say. Finally, she focused on Todd. His appearance at the Forty-eight Bar had added to her misgivings over his motives. Considering his money problems, she felt that he had to occupy the top spot on her list of suspects.

Todd and Edgar had to hold Pearl up as she broke down sobbing at the sight of Rick. Finally, she settled into a chair that Lee has placed discreetly near the head of the casket and spent an hour with her son. Kay noticed that Lee had set the height of the bier so that Pearl could sit in the chair with her hand on Rick's chest, crying softly.

"Would you like some water or something stronger?" Lee whispered to Edgar and Todd.

"I would," Edgar said. "Would you stay with her?" he asked Todd, who nodded.

Edgar followed Lee into the kitchen.

"I'll just have a glass of water, but I wanted to talk to you without Pearl hearing our conversation. I think it would just make things worse for her."

"What's on your mind?" Lee took down one of his mom's fancy dinner glasses and filled it with ice and water.

"This business about Rick being murdered. I can't wrap my head around it."

Lee carefully recounted the marks he'd found on Rick and the reaction of his boss, Chester Madison, that had spurred the sheriff into action.

"I get all that. My problem is with who could do such a thing."

"I wanted to ask you about that," Lee said. "Tell me about this trip to Europe you took with your wife. Rick paid for it?"

"We were surprised. I mean, I had mentioned to Rick at Christmas that I wanted to do something special for Pearl, it being our fortieth wedding anniversary, but I didn't know what I could afford. About a month ago, he called me up and said he wanted to send us to Italy and France for our anniversary. I didn't know what to say at first, but then I thought about Pearl and how much she'd love a trip like that. I also knew that Rick had the money. I guess I didn't think much beyond that."

"It's none of my business, but have you had money problems?"

Edgar looked down at his feet. Lee waited and, just when he thought Edgar wasn't going to tell him anything, he looked up. "I guess it's no big secret. Three years ago we had to move Pearl's mother into a nursing home. She didn't have very good insurance or any money in the bank. Paying for her care drained our savings down, and then, last year, my brother hit a rocky spot so I loaned him most of what was left. Not everything, but it hasn't left us with a lot of reserve. Certainly not enough for a trip to Europe or anything like that."

"And Rick knew about this?"

"I didn't go into details, but he'd helped out some with his grandmother's bills, so he was aware we were a little tight." As soon as the words were out of his mouth, Lee could see Edgar's expression change to one of horror. "Oh, no. He wouldn't. No."

"Wouldn't what?" Lee asked, though he was sure he knew where Edgar's train of thought had taken him.

"No, that's crazy."

"What?"

"He wouldn't kill himself so we'd get his insurance money. That's insane. He made good money and we weren't in that bad a shape. It's just money." Edgar looked lost and Lee knew that the thought, however crazy, was going to eat at him. "Whatever you do, don't suggest that to Pearl. If she thought for one minute that Rick had hurt himself out of some misguided notion that he was going to help us, it would kill her."

"You have my word. Other than paying for the trip, did you notice Rick acting any differently in the last couple of weeks?"

"I don't know. He was in Atlanta and we live here. We talked a couple of times a week, but what can you tell from a phone call? With money being tight, I'd been getting pretty stingy with the phone calls. Long-distance calls add up fast, and I wouldn't call him collect. My stupid pride." Edgar's hands were shaking.

"We don't have to talk about this anymore."

"No, I want to hash this out," Edgar insisted.

"Can I get you something a little stronger to drink?"

"You could pour a little whiskey in here." Edgar held out the now half full glass of water.

Lee took the glass and pulled a bottle of whiskey out of a cabinet. Lee had always joked that his father had kept a little liquor in every room, though it wasn't stretching the truth by much. And in times like this, it came in handy.

"I think that someone killed your son," Lee told Edgar bluntly as he handed him the glass.

The older man took it and downed half the drink. "I can't think of any reason someone would do that."

"Rick never mentioned anyone who was mad at him or had threatened him?"

"There were a few customers of the insurance company that were upset about the payouts on their policies. That sort of thing, but nothing serious or… I guess I should say, nothing that Rick seemed to take very seriously."

"Rick came down to Lang for Clint Peters's funeral, right?" Lee asked.

"Yes. He stayed with us."

"Can you remember anything unusual about the visit?"

"He was very quiet. I worried about him. Clint's death was close to home. The first time a close friend of his had died."

"Did he say anything about Clint's suicide?"

"What do you mean? He couldn't believe that Clint killed himself, that's for sure. The funeral was held shortly after he arrived. I noticed that he wouldn't accept the death at first, but with the funeral, and after talking to Clint's wife and his friends, Rick resigned himself to the fact that it was a suicide. His reaction seemed pretty natural."

"Most people can't understand when someone they're close to kills themselves," Lee sympathized.

Edgar was quiet for a moment, then he said, "My cousin committed suicide and my uncle told me that he felt like a question mark had been placed over his relationship with his son. He hadn't seen any signs that the boy was suicidal, which left him wondering if they were as close as he'd thought they were. Rick might have felt like that about his friendship with Clint. He told me that he'd never imagined Clint would kill himself."

They talked for another half an hour until Kay came in and told them that Pearl looked exhausted.

"I shouldn't have left her for so long." Edgar finished the last of the whiskey in the glass.

Lee and Kay followed him back to the viewing room where Pearl sat in a chair, far away from the coffin, with a nervous Todd watching over her.

"I think I need to get you all home," Todd told Edgar.

"Yes," Edgar agreed, going over to his wife and helping her up.

Kay and Lee walked them out to Todd's car, then watched as they drove away.

"What did y'all talk about in the kitchen?" Kay asked Lee.

"Money is an issue for the parents as well as Uncle Todd. Still, I can't see Edgar or Pearl killing Rick. There was a moment in the kitchen when Edgar considered the possibility that Rick had killed himself, but he couldn't bring himself to believe it."

"Why would Rick do that?"

"I can think of a few reasons, but the biggest is that suicides can be contagious. I read an article about it. After a high-profile suicide, there's often a cluster of suicides. Like the idea spreads or something."

"That's creepy," Kay said with a grim shake of her head. "Though I can remember a dozen suicides while I was in Vietnam, I can't say anyone wondered why they happened. We were always impressed that there weren't more."

They walked back toward the kitchen with Lee taking a detour to close the lid on Rick's casket and reverently shut the doors of the viewing room as he walked out. His father had always been adamant about closing the coffin and the room when no one was present with the deceased. "Common decency," his dad had told him.

"I figured you all would be busy, so I made up some egg salad for lunch. You want one or two sandwiches?" Ruby asked from the kitchen counter when they came into the room.

"One," Lee said, walking to the refrigerator to fetch the pitcher of tea that Ruby always had ready.

"So what's going on? Are we dealing with one suicide, one murder and one natural death?" Kay asked him when he was seated.

"No matter what we think, the cops are convinced that Clint's death was a suicide," Lee said. "But the evidence I saw on Rick was suggestive of something more than an accident."

"Suggestive," Kay mused. "That's not much."

"If someone did cram something down his throat and fill him full of pool water, then we have a very clever killer. They aren't making it easy on investigators," Lee said.

"Point taken." Then an idea occurred to Kay. "Oh, hell."

"What?"

"There's a possibility that we've been ignoring evidence."

"What evidence?"

"When we were at Rick's house, I looked at the pool in the back yard. There were a couple of inflatable rafts back there."

"I saw them. So what?" Lee looked confused.

"When my friends and I go to the beach, we take rafts, but none of us want to blow them up. So last summer I bought a little foot pump."

"I used one when my girlfriend and I went rafting on the Ichetucknee River," Lee said, his eyes growing large. "You can suck water into it and squirt it out."

"If you wanted to, you could take an unconscious person and pump water into their mouth with it."

"Would the murderer be dumb enough to leave it at the house?" Lee questioned.

"Who would be the wiser if they cleaned it off and left it wherever they found it?"

"This is just speculation. The Bruhns might not even have a pump. A lot of people just blow them up with their mouths or a bicycle pump or something."

"We won't know until someone checks."

"Jerome," Lee suggested.

"Seems rough bothering the Bruhns at a time like this."

"You brought it up. Besides, Rick's father seems as interested in finding out what happened to his son as we are." Lee got up and went to the phone. "Jerome should be up by now."

Lee dialed the number and had to leave a message on Jerome's answering machine.

"We'll just have to wait until he gets back with us," Lee said, returning to the table where Ruby had placed a sandwich and a half at his place. Lee didn't argue and ate the sandwiches, along with a pile of Pringles potato chips.

Kay was eating her own sandwich, then she dropped it on the plate with a wide grin on her face. "Wait a minute. Did you say you and a *girlfriend* went to the river?"

"Yeah, last summer."

"This is the first I've heard of a girlfriend."

"Ex-girlfriend. She moved up to Birmingham, so we decided to let it go." Lee didn't look like he was over it.

"Pretty little thing too," Ruby said. "Not too squeamish either."

"Squeamish?" Kay asked.

"Come on, you know the ones that can't take dating a mortician," Lee said.

"I guess that would be a stumbling block for some girls. At least when I was a kid, everyone knew what our family did so it wasn't a surprise to my potential boyfriends."

"Same when I was dating locally," Lee said. "But when I meet a girl in Gainesville, I have to decide how honest to be with her right off the bat."

The phone rang as he stood up to take his plate and glass to the sink, but Kay beat him to it.

"Thought you were going to burn the place down or something. Seems odd you'd be answering the phone," Jerome said, his voice dripping in sarcasm. "Let me talk to Lee."

"After that snarky comment, you can talk to me." Kay went on to explain their idea about the pump.

"I guess it's possible. Of course, I still don't know what the department's going to do. I haven't heard nothin' back about the autopsy."

"Can't you just go over to the house and ask the Bruhns if they have a pump for their rafts?"

"Thin ice. That's what I'd be walking on."

"Fine, I'll go," Kay told him.

"What if they're the killers?"

"I think I can defend myself from Edgar and Pearl. Honestly, there's a possibility that Todd might be involved, but I can't see it with the parents."

"As long as a couple of brilliant detectives like you and Lee have ruled them out, then I'm good. But you can't go there by yourself. If you find something, you'll want a witness and the evidence needs to be collected properly.

"Then go with me. The sheriff can't give you too much grief if you're just there to keep me from messing things up," Kay argued, hearing a very dramatic sigh from the other end of the phone.

"Damn it, girl! Fine, I'll pick you up in ten minutes."

"Good." She hung up before he could change his mind.

"You shouldn't back Jerome into a corner," Lee said, smiling and shaking his head. "I'll drive into the morgue in Gainesville and talk to Glen." He went to the sink to rinse off Kay's plate as she headed up to her room to grab her purse.

"I like her," Ruby said, taking the plate from Lee and giving it a good cleaning.

"She's all right for a sister. Where's Lester?"

"He ate earlier. Said he had to get the cars cleaned for the funeral."

Lee grabbed the keys to Bertha before going outside to find Lester vacuuming the new hearse.

"You scared the hell out of me," Lester complained, turning off the vacuum as Lee came up behind him. "I got all the cars cleaned. How many family cars do we need?"

"I'll check with Todd tomorrow. The funeral isn't until Wednesday."

"I just wanted to get a head start."

"We'll do this right." Lee heard the back door open and looked up to see Kay come out. "And maybe we can convince her not to sell," he half whispered to Lester, who nodded grimly.

Then they all heard a loud roar and turned to look as Jerome skidded into the driveway on his motorcycle.

"I guess we'll take my car," Kay said, frowning as Jerome idled down. He had a backpack strapped over his shoulders and was wearing a black leather jacket and jeans.

"No way, hop on." He reached behind him, grabbed the helmet tied to his seat and held it out to her.

"I don't think so."

"I thought you flew around in helicopters in Vietnam. You can't be afraid to ride on a motorcycle." He gave her a big grin.

"I trusted the helicopter pilots," she shot back.

"If you want me to go to the Bruhns' house, then get on." It was clear to her that Jerome was serious. It was also clear that this was his way of getting back at her for pushing him into this. Kay snatched the helmet out of his hand and strapped it onto her head.

Once Kay was seated behind him, Jerome eased the bike around and took off down the driveway and back out onto the street.

"They seem to be getting along well," Lester joked.

Lee just rolled his eyes and reminded Lester to keep an eye out for the delivery of Rick's casket. Then he hopped into old Bertha and headed for the morgue.

CHAPTER TWENTY-ONE

When Kay and Jerome arrived at the Bruhn home, Kay climbed off the motorcycle and clouted Jerome with her helmet.

"You were purposefully hitting every pothole," she told him.

"And you were digging your claws into my stomach," he responded.

"Cause and effect." She took a deep breath and tried to think of Jerome as a deputy rather than her brother's jerky friend. Visibly letting her irritation go, she asked, "Who does the talking?"

"This is your show." Jerome took off his backpack and pulled out two pairs of latex gloves, a fingerprint kit and a plastic evidence bag. "I did plan for success."

"Let's keep our fingers crossed." She headed for the front door with Jerome walking close behind her.

"I know this is a bad time, but we need to ask you a couple of questions," Kay told Edgar when he answered the door.

"If it's important. But please be quiet, Pearl's sleeping."

"We can talk out back if you want. That's why we're here," Kay offered.

"That might be a good idea. I've disconnected the doorbell. We've had a dozen friends come by bringing food. They're being kind, but…" Edgar let the sentence trail off as he stepped outside and they followed him around the side of the house. "Pearl wants us to have the pool torn out." He shook his head sadly.

Once they were on the pool deck, Edgar asked, "What's this all about?" His eyes shifted from Kay to Jerome and back again.

"Do you have a pump for inflating air mattresses and pool floats?" Jerome asked.

Edgar looked like he didn't understand. "What?"

"Like a foot pump for filling up a raft," Kay explained.

Edgar stared at her. "Are you mad? My son is dead and you want to know if I have an air mattress pump?"

"It might have been used in your son's murder," Jerome said bluntly.

Edgar took a moment to mull this over. "It should be in the wooden box over there." He pointed to a five-foot-long box tucked back in a corner near the pool pump.

The box had a latch, but it wasn't locked. Jerome pulled on a pair of gloves before turning the latch and lifting the lid. He dug past several pool toys and finally, under a Styrofoam boogie board, found a black rubber air pump. It was a simple foot-operated model with a thick rubber bladder that you stepped on to pump air into a toy or mattress. Jerome held the bladder up to his ear and shifted it back in forth.

"There's some kind of liquid in there." He gave Kay a quick smile. "I'm going to fingerprint it before we mess with it anymore."

"What… How could this have been used to kill my son?" Edgar's voice tremored.

"We aren't sure." Jerome looked uncertain. "You understand that you have to keep all of this quiet? If you tell anyone else what we're doing, or repeat what I tell you, it could jeopardize the investigation." Jerome stared at Edgar, who nodded.

"I won't tell a soul." He took a deep breath. "Not even Pearl."

"We think someone crammed something like this—" Jerome held up the pump. "—down your son's throat and pumped pool water into his lungs."

"Dear God," Edgar whispered.

Jerome closed the lid of the box and set the pump on top of it. Taking out his fingerprint kit, he worked for half an hour, dusting sections of the black rubber pump and shifting it this way and that as he looked for prints.

"Three partials. Impossible to say how old they are. Now let's see what kind of water is in this thing." He pulled a small plastic evidence bag out of his pocket and handed it to Kay. "Hold this."

He examined the end of the tube before unscrewing the valve. "There." He put the end of the tube into the bag and gave the bladder a squeeze. "Perfect," he said as water squirted into the bag. He put the pump down and took the bag, holding it up to his nose to take a sniff. "Smells like pool water to me." He let Kay and Edgar smell it before folding the top of the bag over a couple of times and sealing it.

With Kay's help, he placed the pump in a larger evidence bag. Giving Edgar a sideways glance, Jerome said under his breath, "Maybe they can get some skin tissue from the rubber tube."

"What if his brother is involved and he tells him that we

came and got the pump?" Kay asked Jerome after they'd left Edgar standing sadly on the pool deck.

"That might not be a bad thing either. If Todd gets scared we're on his trail, he might make a dumb mistake like running off."

"Makes sense," Kay said as she walked a little faster so she could get ahead of Jerome and grab his backpack. She held it open while he inserted the pump and the other evidence.

"You'll have to wear the backpack on the trip back to your place," he told her.

She saw his point. If he wore it now with the bulky pump inside, there wouldn't be room for her to sit behind him.

"I'll get you for this," she grumbled before donning the pack and climbing on the bike behind him.

Lee parked Bertha in the loading zone at the entrance to the morgue. He wasn't worried about taking up space. The area could accommodate half a dozen hearses. When he was younger and would come with his dad, Lee had always wondered what type of disaster they expected where there would be that many hearses lined up to pick up bodies.

Lee found Glen Doyle at the morgue's reception station. The fifty-six-year-old, partially balding man was reading *The Cellar* by Richard Laymon. He set the paperback down and gave Lee a smile.

"Quiet in here," Lee observed, walking up to the desk.

"If you want to be a doctor and have weekends off, become a pathologist," Glen said, picking up his log and giving it a once-over. "If you're here for a body, it isn't on the list."

"You'll be shocked to learn that I want to talk to you," Lee said, and held up the bottle of halfway decent Scotch he'd bought at the ABC liquor store on the way in. The hearse had received a few odd looks from the store's patrons.

"You're a good man with a nice bottle of booze. What can I do for you?"

"I want to know what they found when they did the autopsy on Rick Bruhn."

Lee knew that Glen had once been a pathologist himself, but that he'd done something bad enough to have his medical license revoked back in New Jersey. No one in Gainesville seemed to know what Glen had done to get stripped of his license, but there was always a steady flow of speculation, which Glen seemed to relish since he would drop various and contradictory hints from time to time.

"Ah now, my boy, you don't want me breakin' the rules, do ya?" Glen asked in his best Irish accent.

"Would I have brought you a bottle if I didn't?"

"And this is the best they had?"

"Do you need better?" They'd developed this game of answering a question with a question years earlier.

"Do you want to know everything in the report?"

"Do you want all the Scotch in the bottle?"

"Touché. You win." Glen stood up and grabbed a ring of keys from the desk. "Dr. Chandler performed the autopsy on Mr. Bruhn. I remember because of all the fuss when they brought him in. Chandler gave the sheriff a hard time for waiting a day before calling for an autopsy. He was particularly unhappy that no one from our office got to look at the scene."

"Dr. Porter examined the body at the scene."

"And that's where the problem lies. Chandler thinks Porter is an idiot. And he's not far wrong, from what I've seen."

Glen unlocked the door to Chandler's office.

"An orderly man, is our Dr. Chandler."

Glen went over to the wall of filing cabinets and opened the drawer marked "B." He flipped quickly through the files before pulling one out, then dropped down into the chair behind Chandler's desk. "Rick Bruhn. Let's see what we have." He scanned the forms, illustrations and pictures.

Lee paced the room as Glen continued to study the file. From the looks of his office, Dr. Chandler was a man with no life except his work. The walls were covered with various diplomas and certificates from institutes around the globe, but there wasn't a single photo of friends or family.

"Interesting. You've got an inventive killer. Not very skilled, but quite imaginative."

"Does Dr. Chandler say that the cause of death was homicide?"

"Not quite. He goes so far as to call it 'death by misadventure, possibly at the hands of another.' As usual, Chandler hasn't stuck his neck out. The man's a professional turtle."

"But *you* think it was murder?"

"It was murder," Glen said decisively. "Someone forced some sort of tube down his throat after he was unconscious. We know that he was unconscious from the lack of defensive wounds and damage to his mouth and throat. I don't think you could do that to a person who was awake. Even if he was tied up, the victim would be able to resist the assault, which would leave bruises and abrasions either from the binding or the perpetrator's hands."

"What knocked him out?"

"Most likely this contusion." Glen held up a photo and pointed to a wound on the back of Rick's head.

Lee remembered having to cosmetically rebuild the back of Rick's head during the embalming.

"No way he could have done it to himself?"

"No. Even if he stuck the tube down his throat, which is possible—you can overcome your own gag reflex—he would have died quickly and then who would have removed the tube? The report says the body was found in the pool. I guess it could have been assisted suicide, but really, does that make any sense?"

Lee would be glad to tell Edgar Bruhn that there was no chance his son had killed himself. He could at least lay that guilt aside.

"What do they think caused the wound to the back of his head?"

"The proverbial blunt object." Glen stood up and pulled an X-ray from Rick's folder. "Here, let me take a closer look."

He attached the X-ray to the shoulder-height lightbox hung on the wall in Dr. Chandler's office. Glen took a diagram from the file and held it up, comparing it with the X-ray. "A baseball bat or a pipe, something like that. Definitely not a crowbar or a fire poker."

Lee watched as Glen returned the X-ray and diagram back to the folder, thinking about what he'd learned. Had he seen any objects at the Bruhn house, either the night he'd picked up the body or the next day when they'd gone back, that would fit that description? He also wondered if the sheriff's office would conduct a proper search of the house now that the coroner's office had confirmed that homicide was at least a possibility.

"Have they sent the report over to the sheriff's office?" Lee asked.

Glen looked at the date on the autopsy. "I doubt it. A copy goes to the chief coroner for review before it's sent out. Probably be dropped in the mail on Monday."

"The process is infuriatingly slow," Lee groused.

"Chandler usually calls law enforcement with his

preliminary findings."

"With the sheriff dragging his feet anyway, he's not likely to have anyone jump into action before the official report is received."

"It's a good excuse to sit on your ass and do nothing," Glen agreed.

"Thanks for taking a look at it for me. I appreciate you taking the risk."

"They aren't going to fire me. If they did, all they'd have left managing the place are a bunch of interns and employees who are greener than a frog's butt."

"When do you think they'll do an autopsy on Lewis Watts?"

"The heart attack that came in last night? Tuesday at the earliest. We have a homicide and a hit-and-run from last night. With today being Saturday, we'll probably have one or two more before the end of the weekend that law enforcement will want to have moved to the head of the line."

"Another favor?"

"Another bottle?"

"Credit?"

"Who do I look like?"

"That's a tough question. I'd like to say a friend and a man who wouldn't want justice to wait."

Glen put his hand over his chest. "You're breaking my heart. But what kind of justice are you talking about? It was a heart attack."

"That's what I want to make sure of."

Rolling his eyes, Glen put the Bruhn file back where it came from, then pushed Lee out the door of Chandler's office. After locking it behind him, he led Lee to the section of the morgue where the wall of drawers was located. Lewis Watts was in the third draw he tried.

"I've asked them to put a label on the outside of the drawers. Anytime I make a suggestion, they look at me like I'm a rutabaga."

After he pulled the drawer all the way out, Glen took the paperwork out of the plastic bag that was sitting on top of the corpse.

"Anything you can tell me would be helpful."

"You're listed as one of the witnesses, along with a woman named Kay Lamberton. A relative of yours?"

"Kay's my sister. We were there when he collapsed."

"I can see why you'd have an interest. Always puzzling when someone drops dead right in front of you." Glen read through all the vitals that were taken by the EMTs and the attending hospital officials. "Everyone on scene seemed comfortable with a diagnosis of heart failure. Did you see anything that would lead you to think anything else?"

"No. But would you be surprised if I told you that this case is related to Rick Bruhn's and a suicide that occurred six months ago?"

"Frankly, no. Friends and family deaths often come in groups. Sometimes there's an obvious cause and effect, like when a couple that's been married for a hundred years has one spouse die and the other follows in less than a week. Is anyone surprised? No. Or a girlfriend is killed in an accident and the boyfriend dives into drugs and six months later is in the morgue. Other times the correlation isn't as clear. Two cousins who hardly know each other commit suicide and their uncle dies in a car accident. Maybe the uncle's mind was tormented by the suicides so he wasn't concentrating on his driving. You get the point."

"Yes. And maybe the three deaths I'm talking about aren't directly linked. But Rick's was a murder, so…"

Glen nodded and started to do an examination of the body. "I can't cut on it, so we'll leave it here on the drawer slide and I'll just see what I can see."

A bell dinged behind them.

"Damn it! Someone just came in. I should have locked the front door." Glen hurried out to see who it was, leaving Lee alone with the body of Lewis Watts.

The body's facial muscles were taunt, with bulging eyes and pale lips. Lee walked up and down beside the drawer, examining the body, and saw evidence of lividity in the buttocks. Nothing else looked out of place.

"A student from U of F wanting to know if we had intern positions open this summer," Glen reported as he returned, rolling his eyes some more. "Now let me see what we have here."

Glen went back to his examination. He spent a long time on the mouth, lips and eyes. "There are signs of vomiting."

"He did throw up right before he died," Lee confirmed.

"Without a more thorough examination, I can't give you a definitive cause of death. But from a cursory look at the deceased, his medical history and the eyewitness testimony, I'd say he died of a cardiac event. He took various medicines for his heart condition, including digitalis as a cardiac glycoside."

"How do you know what drugs he was prescribed?"

"We do our homework around here." Glen held out one of the sheets of paper that had been in the plastic sleeve.

Lee saw that it was a report of a phone call with Watts's mother, in which she'd told them what medicines she was aware he'd been taking. She had also told the caller that Watts's heart issues dated back to when he was a teenager.

"Interesting." Lee handed the paper back to Glen. "Okay, I give up."

"Unless someone slipped him something that caused the heart attack."

Lee raised an eyebrow. "Like what?"

"He was taking digitalis, so an overdose would look like a heart attack. Of course, he might have taken the overdose himself. People *do* accidently overdose on prescription drugs. Especially if they've been drinking. According to the police report, alcohol might have played a role, though the officer on the scene said that the staff reported he'd only had two drinks and had nursed them for a couple of hours."

"If someone did slip him some digitalis, how quickly would it affect him?"

"The final dose would have to be given within a couple of minutes of his death. It would trigger heart attack symptoms almost immediately."

"Kay said that when she entered the bar, there wasn't anyone around him."

"If he was drinking a mixed drink or a beer that he'd gotten earlier, like the report said, and no one was nearby, then I'd say it's your average, run-of-the-mill heart attack. He's young, but with a history of AFib it's not that surprising."

With nothing else to learn, Lee thanked Glen, told him to enjoy his Scotch and headed back out to the parking lot. The sun was falling below the trees as he drove Bertha through the streets of Gainesville, listening to the Doobie Brothers on the tape deck and thinking about murder.

"So where does that leave us?" Kay asked Lee after dinner, as Ruby cleared the plates from the table. Over the meal, Lee had told her what he'd learned during his trip to the morgue.

"I think we just have the one murder," he said, sticking a toothpick in his mouth.

"Maybe. But I want there to be another explanation, otherwise I've got to live with the thought that telling Watts about Rick's murder caused him to get worked up and have a heart attack."

"According to Glen, the only way a heart attack could have been induced would involve slipping him something, but it would have been fast-acting."

"And no one was around him for at least the last fifteen minutes of his life."

"Yep. And he'd been nursing the same drink since before the others left."

"Fine, we'll concentrate on Rick," Kay said in resignation.

"Finding the pump was great. Now we need to go back and look for the blunt object that the murderer used to knock him out."

"I'm sure Mr. Bruhn would let us look around again, but don't you think the killer might have taken that with him?

"True." Lee leaned back in his chair. "I've been trying to think about the attack on Rick. I figure he had to have known his killer."

Kay nodded in agreement. "Probably it was someone he knew well enough that he didn't worry about them being behind him. And if it was a motiveless crime, why would they bother to make it look like an accident?"

"Agreed. There was too much calculation. Someone like the Axeman of New Orleans or the Villisca axe murderer would just hack away and walk off. Someone like that has no reason for subterfuge," Lee said.

"I didn't know you were that well versed in axe murderers."

"I did a report for history class in high school. Mrs. Jenkins was unimpressed."

"I feel like this keeps coming back to high school. I want to know why Millie and the gang were such good friends with Lewis Watts."

"He wasn't that much older than they were. And didn't you say that he and Millie had some sort of weird relationship-thing going on?"

"That's what Catherine implied," Kay said. "I think there's more to it. Millie wouldn't have been nice to him if she wasn't getting something out of it for herself."

"I see your point. But why are we worried about Lewis if we've accepted that he died of a heart attack?"

"Another piece of pie?" Ruby asked as she started to put foil over the pie plate. They both declined and Ruby looked a little disappointed.

"I think that there's something we aren't seeing," Kay insisted.

"Without asking them directly, how are you going to find out what their connection was to Lewis Watts?"

"I don't know yet. But I'm sure it goes back to high school."

"Back to Rick. If we knew what he was running from, that might tell us why he was killed."

"Who would know that? Chester Madison claims he doesn't know why Rick went AWOL from the company. And his father was surprised when Rick sent them on the European trip."

"Lots of dead ends. We know how Rick was killed. Now we just need the why and the who. Solving mysteries always seemed easy in the Parker Family stories." Lee stood up and stretched. "I'm going to let it rest for tonight. Want a beer?"

"Sure."

Kay stood up and decided that Lee was right. Her brain needed a break. They took their beers into the family room and watched an episode of *Love Boat* before saying good night.

Kay went up to her room and pulled the first of the Parker Family mysteries off the shelf. Three hours later she had to force herself to break away from *Elements of Death* and turn off the light.

Instead of heading up to bed, Lee went into the viewing room and opened the lid of Rick's coffin.

"Who did this to you?" Lee asked aloud. Over the years, he'd gotten into the habit of talking to the bodies. Usually he apologized for the indignity of death, but occasionally he questioned the person about their lives… especially the ones he'd known to be assholes.

Rick lay there in repose, not offering any sign that he'd heard Lee.

"The day you all start talking back will be proof I've gone crazy… or that I've slipped into a scene from *Night of the Living Dead*." Lee tucked in the silk dressing and closed the lid of the coffin.

When he was halfway out the door, he heard a loud truck horn honking in the back drive. By the time he got outside, Lester was already there, pointing the driver to the back door. The casket that Rick's parents had ordered had finally arrived. The driver handed Lester a clipboard with the shipping invoice, but Lee took it out of Lester's hands.

"Never sign until you've inspected the coffin," he told Lester.

The wind whipped drops of rain through the trees as they brought the coffin in through the back door. Overhead, unseen by the men, Yin and Yang sprawled on the back of the couch in Ruby's apartment and watched them work through the rain-splattered windows.

With the truck gone and the door locked, Lester turned to Lee. "Do you want to switch him out tonight?"

"No, let him rest where he is. There will be plenty of time tomorrow," Lee said, and turned off the lights in the embalming room.

CHAPTER TWENTY-TWO

Sunday dawned damp and dreary. According to the *Gainesville Sun*, the weather wasn't going to improve for a couple of days.

"It'd be nice if it cleared up for the funeral." Lee looked over at Kay, who was crunching on a piece of toast and looking unsettled. "Would you like to go over to the Bruhns' place again? I want to make sure that we're in agreement about some of the details for the viewing and the funeral."

"Can we look around for the murder weapon?"

"I knew that's what you were thinking about. We should take Jerome if we're going to do that."

Kay frowned, but nodded. "I'll call and wake him up."

"No hurry. Let's wait until noon."

"Spoil my fun," she said with a grin.

Kay spent the rest of the morning in the family room, reading *Elements of Death*. She had just reached the part where Joey and Ellie realized that the killer was using the periodic table to leave clues with the initials of the people he'd killed and the means he used to murder them, when Lee came into the room.

"Jerome said he'd meet us there."

"Golly, you mean he doesn't want all three of us to ride on his motorcycle?" Kay said caustically. In a quieter voice, she asked, "Did you get Rick moved over to his coffin?"

Lee nodded. "I think the Bruhns will like it. It's unpretentious, but doesn't look cheap. Has a very nice interior. Rick looks comfortable."

"Do you ever find it odd talking about the dead like they're alive? Or like it matters one bit whether they're comfortable or not?" Kay knew she was venting and that this was more about her mood than it was about the way Lee thought of his work.

"The family still sees their loved one as a person. And that's how Dad taught me to think of them. If I couldn't see them that way, I don't think I'd be a very good mortician."

Kay gave him a small smile and grabbed her purse.

When they pulled up to the Bruhns' house, Jerome was sitting on his motorcycle in the driveway. The weather hadn't improved and his helmet was covered with water droplets.

"This seemed like a good idea before we got here," Kay told Lee. "Disturbing them again makes me feel like a jerk."

"We didn't know what type of weapon we were looking for before I found out about the autopsy results," Lee reminded her.

Jerome took off his helmet when they got out of the car.

"Great weather," he said, shaking himself and sending water flying off of his oilskin rainsuit. He unbuttoned the jacket and hung it over the back of the motorcycle. "You said you called first?" he asked Lee.

"Right after hanging up with you. Edgar sounded tired,

but accepting."

The door opened before they were even on the porch.

"I told Pearl that you were coming. We both want you to do whatever is necessary to catch the bastard that killed Rick." Edgar had obviously moved on from grief to anger.

"We're just going to take a look around," Jerome told him.

"I'd like to know exactly what the autopsy said." Edgar was looking from Jerome to Lee, with an occasional side glance at Kay.

"I'll tell you what I know." Lee figured it would be best if he kept Edgar occupied so that Jerome could look around.

Kay was torn between her two agendas. Looking for the murder weapon was important, but she figured Jerome was equipped to do that without her help. So she decided to see if she could talk with Pearl.

"How is your wife doing?" she asked.

"She's in the living room if you want to visit with her. I think she'd like that." Edgar's eyes were sad and tired.

Kay found Pearl sitting on the couch, staring at a TV that was turned off. She looked up and gave Kay the smallest of smiles.

"Kay Lamberton. I'm so sorry."

The apology confused Kay. "What for?"

"When you and Rick were dating, I wasn't very nice." Pearl's voice had a melancholy and distant quality that Kay found unsettling.

"You have nothing to apologize for. I was just an immature teenager."

"It was your father's business," Pearl admitted. "I didn't want my son's father-in-law to be a funeral director. Silly, I know. No, not silly. It was stupid."

"I wish your son and I would have had a chance of making it work, but do you know whose fault it was?" Kay paused for a moment. "It was mine. I could have fought for him. I could have listened to what he had to say. Do you know what happened at the prom?"

Pearl nodded. "He kissed Millie. He regretted that kiss more than you'll ever know. I heard him say it a dozen times. More than once, he chastised me for not being nicer to you."

"That's all in the past now." Kay wasn't sure she wanted to say the next bit and she took a deep breath. "I loved your son. He'll always be my first love." She leaned in and took Pearl's hand. "No one can take that away from Rick or me." She felt tears welling up in her eyes as Pearl patted her hand.

"Did Rick ever talk about Lewis Watts?" Kay asked after a few minutes, trying to make the question seem like a natural transition in the conversation. Pearl took it in stride.

"Some. He was always around when the whole group of them got together."

"Didn't that seem a little odd?"

Pearl thought for a second. "No, not really. He tutored Rick and the others. I think he helped them get into good colleges."

"I remember a couple of Saturdays when Rick went to some kind of tutoring session with Millie and the rest of them," Kay said.

"They formed a sort of study group," Pearl said.

One I wasn't invited to join, Kay thought.

She wondered if Pearl knew that Lewis Watts had died. She would hate to be the one to break the news to her if she didn't, especially since the last time she'd told someone explosive information it had probably led to Watts's death. Kay decided the best course was to see if Pearl brought it up.

"Was there any other… relationship between the gang and Lewis that you knew of?"

"Relationship?" Pearl suddenly narrowed her eyes. "Oh, I know what you mean. I caught Millie being… feely with him once at a cookout. That was years ago. After that, I guess I paid more attention. I didn't think it was proper. But I also didn't think it was my place to step in." She waved it all away with her hand. "He's dead. I won't speak ill of him anymore."

"Millie's not dead," Kay couldn't help responding, even after getting the confirmation she'd wanted.

"True enough. I understand how you must feel toward her. I have mixed feelings too. Funny, I wouldn't have said that a week ago." Pearl's eyes returned to the blank TV screen, though her gaze went right through it.

"What would you have said about Millie a week ago?" Kay asked gently.

"She helped to motivate and focus Rick. Before she started herding that group of boys, they were all over the place. They would have been lucky to get into the University of Florida or Florida State." Pearl took a deep breath. "That's too much. They were smart and would have gotten into a state university with no problem, but not Ivy League schools like they did. Millie made that happen. I think they all knew it."

"Could someone have been jealous?" The thought had just occurred to Kay that the whole group could be the target of someone else.

"I know there were people who didn't like them. Thought they were… What's the word? Cliquey or something."

"I was on the outside of it. I just remember being jealous of the amount of time that Rick spent with his friends. I thought it was weird that Millie was always with them. In high school, girls only hung with guys that were their boyfriends or guys they *wanted* to be their boyfriends."

"Why are you worried about all that stuff in the past? You can't think that has anything to do with who… hurt

Rick. Can you?" Pearl looked at her closely.

"With Lewis dead too… I just don't know."

"Didn't he die from a heart attack?"

"He did. I just… First there was Clint Peters's suicide, Rick, and now Lewis. It's like a curse has fallen on that group."

"I see what you mean. Rick took Clint's death pretty hard. Maybe…" Pearl stopped and chewed her lip thoughtfully.

"Maybe what?"

"Just maybe… Clint's death started something…I don't know." Pearl's voice was weaker and Kay could tell that she was getting tired. There was no point in torturing the poor woman for answers she didn't have.

"I'd better go see if Jerome has had any luck." Kay stood up. "Can I get you something?"

"No, dear. I'm fine." The flat monotone of her voice made it clear that she wasn't fine at all. Her eyes went back to the TV and Kay made an awkward exit.

A quick glance told her that Lee was still in the kitchen talking with Edgar, so she hunted up Jerome. She found him looking through the garage, peering behind the hot water heater.

"Find anything?" she asked.

"I've got five things that look like good candidates. My favorite is a piece of pipe just outside that door that looks suspiciously clean." Jerome moved over to a stack of boxes.

"Are you going to take them as evidence?"

"That's the point of us being here."

"Has the sheriff made any decision about investigating the case?"

Jerome glared at her. "You just going to stand there asking questions, or are you going to look around a little?"

"You don't have to be an asshole."

"You know being a deputy is my job, but having you and Lee find extra work for me to do isn't exactly making my day. The sheriff said it's a case, but he isn't going to dedicate a bunch of resources to it 'cause he thinks, quote, 'it's a bunch of bullshit,' unquote. So I've just got to cram this in around my regular duties."

"We aren't doing this for the fun of it." Kay was miffed that Jerome was giving her a hard time. "It's the sheriff you should be pissed off at."

"I'm always pissed at him and the whole department, which gets me exactly nothing."

They both looked out through the open garage door as a car pulled into the driveway.

Todd Bruhn climbed out of the car and headed straight for Kay and Jerome, oblivious to the light rain falling on his head. He wore a determined expression and his eyes locked on them.

"What are you people doing here?" His voice was stern, but subdued so that he wouldn't be heard by anyone in the house.

"We're looking for the weapon that killed your nephew." Jerome moved forward to meet him.

"You couldn't call me first? I could have gotten Edgar and Pearl out of the house. Don't you think this is all very upsetting for them? Their son's viewing is tomorrow, for heaven's sake." The words shot out of his mouth in rapid fire.

"We needed their permission to search the house. Or do you think we should have gotten a warrant?" Jerome wasn't backing down.

"I just think you should have had some respect for their feelings," Todd stammered, his voice losing some of its indignation. "What have you found?"

"A few things," Jerome said cryptically.

"Like what?"

"Things we think might have been used to hit your nephew over the head before his killer drowned him." Jerome spoke every word with his eyes focused on Todd.

Kay watched the exchange and wondered why Todd was so upset. Was he truly angry that they might be disturbing Rick's parents, or was he mad because he hadn't known that they were searching the house?

"Why are you keeping information from me?" Todd asked, his voice wary.

"Our job is not to keep you informed."

"No… but I could help make sure that you don't upset Edgar and Pearl more than necessary." He seemed to be pleading his case, which Kay thought was very odd.

"You want to protect your family. I get that. And we want to find a killer. With a little bit of luck, those two goals won't conflict." Jerome shrugged.

Todd looked like he wanted to say something else, but then he suddenly looked at the door into the house. "I'll be inside," he said, walking past them and through the door.

"Well, well, wasn't that interesting?" Jerome smiled. "Looks like we shook someone's tree."

"He *was* overreacting a bit."

"Wants to know what's going on with the investigation." Jerome didn't have to tell Kay that bad guys often followed investigations into their crimes, hoping to stay one step ahead of the authorities. "Guess that bumps him up the list."

"Money," Kay mused.

"And lots of it."

"Not that it goes straight to him."

"Even better, 'cause then he can act all innocent. 'Money? What money? I don't get no money.'" Jerome's tone was mocking.

"If Lewis was murdered, what possible motive would

Todd have for getting rid of him?" Kay asked.

Jerome gave her an irritated look. "That wasn't a murder. The man just dropped dead." He paused for a moment, then allowed, "*If* he was killed, then maybe Lewis found out something that linked Todd to the murder." He held up his hand. "But Lewis wasn't killed."

"And Clint wasn't killed either," Kay said doubtfully.

"But Rick was," Jerome said. "I'm going to take one more walk around the house, check in the bushes, then I'll collect all the items and we'll be done here."

"Aren't you afraid that Todd might do something with them?"

"I've fingerprinted them already. If he moves any of them, I'll know it, and won't that say something?" Jerome gave her a big smile before they went out into the drizzle to walk around the house.

CHAPTER TWENTY-THREE

On the way home, Kay told Lee about the odd confrontation with Todd.

"He's probably just being protective of his brother," Lee suggested.

"He was pretty intense."

"So we're back to the insurance money being the motive."

"We still need to discover if Lewis had any insurance."

"You're going to get a chance to find out," Lee said, pointing to a car in the funeral home's driveway. Standing next to the car was Chester Madison.

Kay pulled around and parked in the back of the building. By the time Lee and Kay got out of the car, Madison was there to meet them.

"I thought I'd come by and see how the investigation is going. I've heard about the death of Lewis Watts."

"We were just wondering if Watts had an insurance policy with your company," Kay said.

Madison nodded. "He did. However, it had a special exclusion for heart attacks. Since he had a history of heart problems, he had a choice of paying a very high premium or having a policy that exempted heart attacks or other issues arising from his preexisting condition."

"Interesting. So no money will change hands?" Lee asked.

"Not unless the death is attributed to something other than his long-term health issue. From what I understand, that's unlikely."

"I learned what was in Rick's autopsy." Lee tried not to look too proud of his sleuthing.

"I've already received a copy," Madison said, popping Lee's ego bubble. Lee was pretty sure he knew who'd sold Madison a copy of the autopsy. He'd have to give Glen Doyle a hard time the next time he saw him. "I also heard that you guys have been over at the Bruhns' house collecting evidence. Twice."

"We found the pump used to fill Rick's lungs with pool water," Kay chipped in.

"And several objects that might have been used to knock him over the head." Lee looked over at Kay, realizing that he probably could have worded that a bit more delicately. She didn't seem bothered.

"You've had time to search for clues and question witnesses. What conclusions have you come to?"

Lee and Kay looked at each other.

"None," Kay said bluntly. "No conclusions. We *do* have suspicions and avenues to investigate."

"Good," Madison declared.

"Todd has the best motive—money," Lee said, then laid out what they knew about Todd's financial problems and his relationship with his brother.

"You're excluding the parents from the suspect list?"

"Yes," Kay stated.

"Agreed. I've met them both in the past and twice in the last couple of days. Their grief is real."

"Have you met Todd Bruhn?" Lee asked.

"He contacted me after you told him that I'd insisted on the autopsy."

"What do you think of him as a suspect?"

"He can't be ruled out." Madison didn't elaborate.

"The sheriff isn't going to actively investigate the case," Kay said, thinking of what Jerome had told her.

"I knew that would be the case when I had to force him to do an autopsy. On the other hand, he will not interfere with Deputy Jerome Carter, and he's agreed to commit the resources needed to evaluate and catalog any evidence collected by Deputy Carter."

"How did you get him to agree to those terms?" Lee was surprised, knowing how hardnosed the sheriff was.

"All it took was a phone call from the head of the Florida Department of Law Enforcement to vouch for me."

"But sheriffs are elected and independent. They don't work for—" Lee started to argue.

Madison held up his hand like a teacher disappointed in a student's answer. "True. However, when sheriffs have cases that are politically sticky, they often call in the state agency to give them cover. Sheriff Pratt does not want any future calls to the FDLE to go unanswered."

"Got it." Lee smiled.

"What other lines of inquiry are you pursuing?" Madison asked.

"There's something odd about the relationship that Lewis Watts had with Rick and the others in the group," Kay said.

"I think you're right. And I'm troubled by three deaths so close together. Three people from the same high school clique dead in just six months. That's too much of a coincidence."

"I'm going to talk to Tracy Peters again tomorrow night at the viewing," Kay blurted, learning about her own plan as her mouth spoke the words. "What I really want is to find out more about the relationship between Lewis Watts and the group."

"He was a counselor at Melon County High School, right?"

"Yes. At the time that we were all in high school, he was in his early twenties and just out of college."

"His notes and files on the students would still be at the school," Madison said.

"I could go by and see if anyone will talk to me." Kay tried to think of anyone at the school that she might know.

"Not this week. Spring break starts tomorrow," Lee informed them.

"Longshot anyway. Gives me a week to think of someone I can ask." But in the back of Kay's mind, a nagging voice was telling her she *already* knew someone.

It started to rain hard. Madison looked up at the sky, pulling his coat in closer to his body. "I'll let you all get to work."

"You'll be at the viewing tomorrow?" Lee asked.

Madison nodded, then turned and walked back to his car.

"He's a queer duck," Lee said.

"I know there's someone at the school I can ask," Kay said thoughtfully. "But I just can't remember…"

"I know a dozen people who work there, but none of them are going to let us look through the school records just 'cause we want to."

"I understand that. Still, there's someone…" Kay said, trying to pull the name out of her memory.

She was inside and halfway to her room when she finally remembered. *Oh hell*, she thought.

How low will I go? she asked herself as she sat on the edge of her bed and thought of her next move. *School is out for the week. Will that make it easier or harder? Will he even go for it? Do I have the guts to use him like that?*

The questions whirled in her head as she felt herself rise from the bed, grab a piece of notepaper from her purse and head toward the phone in the hall. She stood by the small end-table for another minute, then squared her shoulders and dialed the phone. A small shiver of regret for what she was about to do ran through her. *This is for Rick*, she told herself.

"Hello?" Zach Terrill sounded surprised that his phone had rung.

"Zach, this is Kay."

"Kay! I'm glad you called. I figured I'd see you tomorrow at… the viewing." His voice changed quickly from excited to awkward.

"I know. I'm feeling a little overwhelmed by it all." *You are disgusting*, her inner angel told her. *It's all for Rick*, the demon on her other shoulder whispered. "I was wondering if you'd like to go out to a movie or something." *Shameless.* The angel hung its head.

Zach took a minute to process his good luck. "Yeah, sure, that'd be great." He paused, then asked, "You want me to pick you up? What movie were you thinking about?"

"Whatever you'd like to see. I just feel like getting out of the house for a little bit."

"Sure, of course. I've got the paper here. I'll see what's playing," he said eagerly.

"Pick me up around six."

"Do you want me to look at the paper now?"

"No. Decide what you want to see and we'll work it out." She didn't want to get into a big discussion over the phone about a movie that she didn't really care about.

"Yeah, all right, we can go to dinner beforehand if the movie is later."

"I'll see you at six."

"Great," he said as Kay hung up, feeling like a heel. *Catching a murderer is worth exploiting a friend's emotions*, the demon whispered in her ear.

At a quarter to six, Kay came downstairs dressed for deceit.

"Where are you going all dressed up?" Ruby asked her as she stirred a pot of beef stew.

"You don't want to know." Kay's ambivalence to her own plan hadn't gone away while she'd dressed and applied more makeup than she normally wore.

"A date is nice. Yang brought me a lizard this afternoon. He's getting to be a better hunter all the time. The trick is to have patience and keep your eye glued to the prize." Ruby kept stirring as she talked.

"Trust me, this is *all* about patience and keeping my eye on the prize," Kay said, adjusting her skirt.

There was a knock at the front door.

"Here I go."

Kay took one last look in the hall mirror before opening the front door.

"Wow! You look great," Zach said. "Are you ready?"

"Let's do this." She managed to give him her best almost-genuine smile.

"Cool! I thought we could go see *Excalibur*. It just opened on Friday, but being Sunday night it shouldn't be too crowded. It starts at seven-thirty, so we'll have time to get there and grab something from the snack bar." He paused. "I mean, if that sounds good to you?"

He had to take long strides to beat her to the car, where he opened the door for her. Kay noticed that the blue Blazer looked spotless inside and out, making her suspect that Zach had spent part of the afternoon cleaning it for the date. *Pile on the guilt*, she thought.

"I was surprised when you called. The way you left it the other day…" Zach said, backing out of the driveway.

"I appreciate the company," was all that Kay could think to say without being more of a hypocrite than she was.

"The movie is at the Oaks Mall."

"Sounds good."

Now she had to decide when to bring up his mother and her job at the school. Should she do it *after* sitting in the theatre with him for two hours, letting him believe that she wanted to spend time with him, or before? If she did it now, he could just turn around, dump her at home and be done with her. If she waited until after, then he might feel really betrayed and indulge in the pleasure of dumping her on the side of the road somewhere in the thirty miles between the theatre and the funeral home. She was also afraid that waiting until the end of the date would make it too easy for him to say no.

"The film is about the King Arthur legend," Zach said to make conversation. Like a door swinging open, Kay saw her opportunity.

"I did a book report on *The Once and Future King* for my senior English class." She gave a calculated pause. "Does your mother still teach English?" *You know damn well that his mother is a guidance counselor now*, her inner angel scolded.

"She's a counselor at the school." Zach turned and looked at her as he drove. "Speaking of which, I heard that Lewis Watts died."

"I was there." Kay wasn't sure how he'd receive this news.

"What?" His head kept swiveling back and forth from the road to her.

"I had just gone into the Forty-eight when I saw him collapse."

"That's a coincidence." Zach sounded more than a bit confused.

"Not so much. I knew he was there."

"You were going there to meet him?"

"Not really."

"Oh." In that word was a world of questions, but Kay figured that Zach didn't want to push her less than thirty minutes into a date that he hoped would go well.

"I was watching the Forty-eight because Millie, Vince and Burt were meeting a couple of other people there," she said, taking mercy on him. Besides, she figured she'd have to explain some of this when she finally asked him for help gaining access to old records at the school.

"I guess this all has to do with Rick's murder."

"I just wanted to keep an eye on them. I didn't know that someone else was going to die," Kay said, trying hard not to sound defensive.

"I heard that Watts died of a heart attack?"

"It looks that way."

They rode in silence the rest of the way to the mall, where Zach parked near the theatres. He reached out and put his hand on Kay's arm when she started to get out of the car.

"What's this all about?" he asked.

"What?" Kay had a sinking feeling that the jig was up.

"This date?"

"I…" She started to feign innocence, but quickly gave up the pretense. "I'm sorry. I need your help with something."

"Anything," Zach said reflexively.

"You might want to hear what the favor is first," she warned. "I want to get a look at any records the school still has on the old gang."

"Why?"

"I think that there was something strange going on between them and Lewis Watts."

"Strange how?"

"For one thing, I heard that he was friendly with Millie."

"Friendly?" Zach seemed confused for a minute before it dawned on him what she was talking about. "Oh, like *really* friendly?"

"That's what Catherine Ritter told me."

"If she said it, then it's probably true. She should have been a gossip columnist. I still don't understand, though. What does that have to do with anything now?"

"The only thing I know is that, as soon as I started getting interested in what might be going on, Lewis Watts dropped dead."

"That would be hard to ignore." Zach was quiet for a moment before asking, "But how can *I* help you?"

"Your mother works at the school."

"She's not going to hand me a bunch of school records. Besides, this week is spring break and she went down to Cedar Key with some of her friends."

Kay didn't know how far she could push him. She already felt awful for having used his feelings for her to get this far.

When she didn't say anything, Zach said in a voice that sounded hurt, "You want me to go into the school and get them."

"This was a bad idea." Kay couldn't look him in the face. "You can take me home."

"You don't want to see the movie?"

"I guess we can if you want to." She didn't know which would be worse—a long, silent drive home now or sitting through a movie and *then* having the long, silent drive home.

"We're here now," he said curtly.

"I'm really sorry. Rick's murder has me going a little

crazy." Kay was still looking down at her hands.

"Let's go see the movie," Zach said, opening his door and climbing out of the car.

At first she thought he was going to keep walking, but instead he stopped and waited for her to catch up. As they headed toward the mall, the air was still and the sun was sinking below the trees, giving the western sky an orange glow.

Excalibur was full of mud, clanking armor and slashing swords. Kay felt uncomfortable at the sex scenes, not for any prudish reasons, but because they reminded her that she wasn't on a real date. Instead it was a cruel trick that she'd played on a good guy who didn't deserve it.

"That was a little weird," Zach commented as they left the theatre.

"I kinda liked it, actually." Kay was being truthful. The idea of a quest taken up and hardships overcome spoke to her.

Zach smiled at her. *Was that forgiveness*? she wondered. She was surprised to realize that a part of her wouldn't have minded if he'd taken her hand.

"Would you like to go somewhere for a drink?"

"I wouldn't mind stopping at the Forty-eight." She didn't know why she said it.

"Okay," he said to her surprise.

Once they were in the car, Zach put the key in the ignition, but didn't turn it. Instead he looked back at her. "Tell me one thing before we go any further. Is there a chance for there to be something between us, or was this all really about getting access to those files?"

Kay didn't answer right away. She wanted to be as honest with him as possible. Considering him for a moment, she thought that nothing about him was a deal-breaker.

"Maybe. But until I get the… situation with Rick settled

in my mind, I can't think about starting a relationship."

"Guess that makes sense," he said and started the car.

The Forty-eight was quiet on a Sunday night. Inside, less than half the tables had anyone sitting at them and the barstools were mostly unoccupied. They took a booth against the back wall, about thirty feet from where Lewis Watts had died. The tables had been rearranged from the night before. Kay wondered which of the chairs Lewis had been sitting in and managed to creep herself out.

"What do you think you'll find in the school files?" Zach asked.

"I don't know. I'm just running out of things to check." She stood up. "I'm going to the bar, see if I can get anyone who was here Friday night to talk to me."

"Do you want me to go with you?"

"No, I'll be okay."

Zach took out his wallet and handed her a couple of twenties. "Ordering drinks and leaving a tip might help. I'll take whatever they have on draft. And spend those wisely. That's my lunch money for the week." Kay wasn't sure if he was kidding or not.

A beer and a tequila sunrise, plus a twenty-dollar tip, brought a waitress over to sit down at their table.

"Hank said you wanted to talk to me about Friday night." The tall, dark-haired woman didn't look comfortable sitting with them. Kay figured she was only in her late twenties, but bar life had already added a few extra years to her face.

"Who waited on him?"

"The dead guy? I did. Well, there were two of us working the table when the whole party was here. After everyone but the guy left, Nancy went to cover a couple of other tables. I wasn't happy about it. He had nursed the same drink for over half an hour, and he sure didn't look like a big tipper." She paused and swept a strand of hair back behind her ear.

"I would have been a lot nicer to him if I'd known he was going to die. I guess that sounds stupid, but you know what I mean."

"Did anyone talk to him before he collapsed?"

"After the others left? No, I was watching him 'cause I wanted to clear the table and get in a paying customer. I make all my money on tips, and from the looks of… well, I guess I said that already."

"Did he look sick or anything?"

"Just the usual—crying-in-his-beer, down-in-the-dumps. There are only three kinds of customers in here: loud and obnoxious, weeper-creepers or the rare ones that are nice and tip well."

"How long did he sit there alone?"

"I had just delivered drinks to the table about ten minutes before everyone else got up and left. He spent a good twenty minutes drinking one crummy vodka on the rocks."

"Did you notice anything else odd about him or the people he was with?"

The waitress thought for a minute. "They were kind of… I don't know, happy but not happy. Funny group. But there were lots of weirdos in that night. One woman claimed that she saw another woman's purse smoking."

"She thought the purse was, what, like on fire?" Zach asked.

"I don't know. The woman tried to point it out to me, but I couldn't see it. Hey, I think she was one of that group."

"The woman who said someone's purse was smoking?" Kay asked.

"No, the purse belonged to one of the women in the group. But I think the woman who told me about it was just drunk. We get everything short of pink elephants around here. One of our regulars claims we sell bootleg."

Kay gave her another ten dollars for talking with them

and let the woman go back to work.

"I can vouch for the fact that he died about twenty minutes after the rest left." Kay finished her own drink and spun the ice around in the glass as she thought about the little she'd learned.

"You act like you want this to be a murder." Zach smiled.

"No. I just can't get the look he gave me out of my mind. I came in that door and got about halfway across the room when Lewis half stood up, looked me in the eyes, then collapsed onto the floor, vomiting and dying."

"What a horrible experience." Zach reached his hand out. Kay hesitated for a moment before putting her own hand in his.

"I've seen people die. The thing that gets me is that there was a look of recognition in his eyes and… something else. Maybe a plea. I don't know how to describe it."

"Sounds natural to me. He suddenly felt his heart constrict, saw you coming toward him and wanted you to help him. He probably *did* recognize you. You did go by his house the other day."

"You're right." Kay sat back in the booth.

"What's the plan for tomorrow?" Zach asked with the grave air of one who has accepted a dangerous mission and wants to know exactly what he's facing.

"You're going to help me?" She squeezed his hand.

"Against my better judgment."

"Can you get a key to get into the counselor's office?"

"Mom left her keys with me when she headed out for Cedar Key." He shook his head. "It's like I was meant to be thrown in jail for stealing public records."

"No one's going to get thrown in jail," Kay said. "Will there be anyone there tomorrow?"

"The janitors usually do a serious scrub-down while the students are gone. And there might be a few people who just drop in to pick up something, or do a little work while the place is quiet."

"We don't have to do this if you think it's too risky." Kay knew she was acting crazy and really wouldn't have been mad if he'd put his foot down and refused to help her.

"No. I can just fake my way through this. Anyone stops us, I'll just tell them that I'm picking up something for my mom. Of course, if there's anyone actually in the office then we'll have to call it off."

"I understand. I just want to look through the files..." Kay squinted. "And maybe copy anything that seems really important."

Zach sighed. "Then bring some dimes. There's a copy machine in the office, but you have to feed it."

They made plans to meet at ten in the morning. As he drove her home, they talked about the movie and pretended that they weren't going to commit a felony the next day.

At the funeral home, Zach got out and came around to her side of the car, but Kay was out before he could open her door. She stood and faced him. He reached out and took her hand.

"You're crazy," he said with a smile.

"I actually knew that." She smiled back and found herself wanting him to lean forward and kiss her. He must have seen it in her eyes. He put his other hand on the small of her back and drew her close, kissing her gently if a little reservedly. Kay thought it was just right for a first date and gave him a second kiss.

"See you in the morning," he said before getting in his car and backing out of the driveway.

"I must be crazy," Kay told one of Ruby's tabby cats, who was sitting in the driveway watching her. By the time she'd gone into the kitchen and returned with a small snack for him, he'd been joined by his brother.

Yin and Yang finished their tuna just as Ruby called to them from the door of her apartment.

"They're down here," Kay yelled up to her. "And I just gave them a treat."

"That's all right then," Ruby shouted back. Both cats looked at Kay as if she'd betrayed them.

"Go on upstairs. You know she'll give you more anyway."

As if they understood, both cats rubbed against her legs before chasing each other up the stairs.

Kay heard the sound of the TV coming from the embalming room as she quietly went through the house and up to her room. She didn't want to rehash the details of her date with Lee. Besides, she wasn't sure that he'd approve of her plan to look at the school records.

Once in her room, Kay opened her windows. The air was cool and fresh and she could hear Ruby's voice coming through her own open windows. A glance across to the apartment showed her that Ruby was sitting in an old recliner with Yin in her lap and Yang on an arm of the chair.

"Don't worry. If we have to move, we'll find a place. Kay's a nice young lady and Lee works hard. I think we'll be fine. No matter what happens, you two have nothing to worry about. You're family now and I'll take care of you."

Kay felt more than a twinge of guilt. Where would this rather strange old lady and her two overweight cats find a place to live? *I have to do what I have to do*, Kay told herself, closing the window. Then she settled down on the bed with *Elements of Death*. A flip through the book told her that she only had thirty pages to go.

CHAPTER TWENTY-FOUR

Kay heard vehicles coming and going even before she was out of bed. Downstairs the air held the sweetly cloying smell of cut flowers that she remembered so well from her childhood. As she came down the stairs, Lester walked into the hallway carrying a bouquet of gladiolas four feet high.

"I guess a lot of people remember him," Lester said, taking the arrangement into the viewing room to set it beside the many others the florist had already delivered.

Kay looked into the room. *Rick touched so many people's lives*, she thought. Even if many of them were sending flowers more for his parents than for Rick, she knew that they remembered and had liked Rick.

"Where's Lee?" she asked Lester as he hurried to answer another knock at the door.

"We picked up a woman from the nursing home last night. Her family is burying her in Tennessee, so we prepped her for the trip and Lee headed out for the airport first thing this morning."

Kay nodded and went into the kitchen. Ruby turned away from the sink and smiled at her.

"There are biscuits warming in the oven and gravy on the stove."

Kay helped herself to coffee and a couple of biscuits spread liberally with strawberry jam, then sat at the table to think over her plans for the morning. She'd chosen a pair of slacks, a dark blouse and a pair of loafers for her spy adventure. The idea was to look nice enough to be a teacher, a parent or someone from the county, but to have clothes that she could take off running in if she had to.

She left early enough so that she could stop by the bank and pick up a couple of rolls of dimes. When she arrived at Zach's, he came out of the house before she reached the porch.

"Did you have to take the day off?" she asked, knowing it was a dumb question.

"I've got lots of vacation time. We'll take my car."

"I see we both dressed up." She took a second to admire him in his tie and jacket as they got into the Blazer.

"These are my work clothes. I figured the more I looked like an authority figure, the better my chances will be of talking us out of any trouble we run into."

"You can still back out. Or let me have the keys. If I'm caught, I'll swear I stole them from your house."

"Don't tempt me. Who knows, maybe I need some adventure in my life," Zach said, looking over at her as he drove.

"I need to be honest with you. My plan is to go back to Huntsville when we're done working out the details of the funeral home."

"The funeral home?"

"We're going to sell it. The business hasn't made money since Dad died."

"Lang's a small town. You have to give people a chance to adjust to change."

Not you too, she thought. Aloud she said, "Maybe. I think the trouble is that Lee isn't a salesman."

"I don't remember your dad being much of a salesman," Zach said frankly.

"No, but he was… social. He had a large network of friends and spent a lot of time just talking to people."

"You mean he was a glad-hander," Zach said, then pointed out the windshield toward the school. "There it is."

As if I'm not well aware of where the high school is, Kay thought, but then realized it was a sign of his nervousness.

"The worst part is I feel like I'm betraying my mother's trust."

Kay looked down at her lap. "I can understand that. We haven't done anything yet."

Zach took a deep breath. "Mom's tough. I think she'd tell us to do it if she knew what was at stake." He pulled into a visitor's spot in the school parking lot. There were only two other cars in the lot.

"Looks pretty deserted," he observed.

"Have you thought of what you'll say if someone asks what we're doing here?"

"Mom wants me to pick up some assessments she needs to review before next Monday."

They got out of the car and walked to the back of the school.

"This is the entrance the faculty uses after hours," Zach said. The padlock was already unlatched.

Kay felt a strange mix of emotions being back at her old high school. It didn't look any different than the day she'd graduated. That day, she'd been thrilled at the thought of leaving both the school and the town behind her. Now she felt like she was being pulled into a nostalgic vortex of emotions and experiences.

"It even smells the same," Kay said, entering the main hallway as Zach held the door for her.

"All schools smell like this. A mix of sweat, hormones, chalk and whatever cheap cleaner they use."

They didn't see anyone as they made their way down the dim corridor to the main administration office. Zach took his mom's key ring out of his pocket and searched through the keys. The first two he tried didn't work, but "Third time's the charm," he said as the door finally opened.

They entered into the reception area where a chest-high counter ran half the length of the room. On the far side of the counter were the school's PA system and a couple of desks. One side of the reception area held the doors to the principal's and vice principal's offices, as well as the nurse's room. The two counselors' offices were on the other side. Zach headed to the door stenciled with his mother's name.

"Only took me two tries this time," he said, opening the door and hustling Kay inside. "We shouldn't have to worry in here."

Kay looked around the room. There were a desk and a couple of chairs in the middle of the room, while the walls were covered with filing cabinets and three bookcases filled with books on psychology and education and lots of college brochures. She went over to the filing cabinets and started opening drawers.

"I didn't think about there being another counselor. What if the files aren't in this office?" she asked.

"You're in luck. All the filing cabinets are in Mom's office. The other office has all the information about college entrance exams and small tables for letting a student take the practice tests. If the files are still at the school, they should be in one of these cabinets."

Five minutes later, Kay had found the files from the

1960s, organized by the year that the students had graduated. She pulled the files for Millie, Clint, Rick, Burt, Vince and, after a moment's hesitation, her own. Zach paced up and down the room, occasionally listening at the door or peering carefully out the window.

The first thing Kay noticed was that her file was about an inch thick while the others were only about half that size.

"Mostly 'Just the facts, ma'am,'" Kay mumbled as she flipped through each file in turn. "Except mine."

While the files of the Golden Five, as she was starting to think of them, had held only a few notes, all glowing and complimentary, Kay's file was full of notes that had been made by her various teachers, all the way back to first grade. Her teacher that year, Mrs. Elroy, had commented on her spirit and good nature and noted that she was bright and a quick learner. However, Mrs. Fisher, her second-grade teacher, must have had a different Kay in her classroom, because she wrote that the girl was willful and could be disrespectful when confronted about her ill behavior. Fisher had gone on to say that Kay's intelligence was undisciplined, causing her to guess as often as to do the work.

"That bitch," Kay grumbled.

There was a clear pattern where the teachers she'd liked had obviously liked her in return, but the ones she didn't get along with had some pretty harsh things to say about her.

"Quit looking at your own file," Zach said, looking over her shoulder. "That's not why we're here and we can't stay all day."

"You're right. Here, put mine back." She handed him her folder, then opened Clint's and Rick's files on the desk and laid them side by side to compare, looking closely at each year starting with ninth grade.

"I don't remember Rick being this good of a student." He had graduated with honors, she remembered that, but she was surprised to see that he had an overall grade point average of 3.98. "Maybe," she muttered. Clint's was even better, but she wasn't surprised by that. Clint had been one of the smartest guys in their class, graduating as valedictorian.

"Learning anything?"

"They were all pretty smart. Smarter than me, apparently."

She had just spread out Millie's, Vince's and Burt's files when they heard a sound out in the main office.

"Crap!" Zach whispered.

"They don't have any reason to come in here," Kay reassured him while her own panicked inner voice wondered how the hell she could know such a thing.

"Unless they're the janitors," Zach said, helping to spike her anxiety.

For no real reason, they crouched down on the floor behind the desk.

"This will give us an extra second before they see us," Kay said and almost giggled. Zach jabbed her in the ribs with his elbow.

After five minutes they heard the footsteps of whoever had been in the outer office walking away. The sound of the outer door opening and closing released the tension in the room. Quietly, Kay and Zach stood up, and she went back to work comparing files.

"This is interesting." Kay was looking back and forth between the five files.

"What?" Zach stepped over and stood beside her.

"They all took their SATs twice."

"A lot of students do. That way you can submit the higher of your two scores."

"They took the second one after spending several months attending study classes on the weekends."

"So?"

"They took the first test in January of their junior year. That's the same test I took. We went to Gainesville where they gave it in one of the big lecture halls at the university."

"Yeah, so?"

"They took the second test ten months later in October of their senior year."

"Again, so what?"

"Rick and I were going hot and heavy at that point. Taking a second test is one thing, but those tutoring classes are quite another. Rick worked at Lang Farm and Feed that summer and Saturdays were their busiest days. He'd spend almost all day loading pickups with feed and hay and be too tired for anything else by the end of the day. He made it up to me by taking me out on Sunday. I know that he went to a *couple* of meeting with Lewis Watts and the other kids, because I remember he brushed me off when I suggested I could go along. But he certainly didn't spend half a day at study sessions every Saturday for months."

"Yeah, okay. Maybe he just signed up because he thought he'd do it, or believed it would look good on his record."

"You don't get it. Look at his test scores!" Kay held Rick's first scores up next to his second set of scores.

Zach whistled. "Whatever he did made a hell of a difference. No wonder he got into a great school."

"His score was 1150 the first time—550 in math and 600 in English. That's close to what I got. So how the hell did he get 1510 on his second test?"

"Obviously he studied. Maybe he didn't want you to know how hard he was trying. Maybe the others went to the study sessions and he got their notes."

"Fine, maybe that's possible. Now why didn't he ever tell me that he nearly aced the SATs?"

"You *would* think that would be worth bragging about,"

Zach said thoughtfully.

"Now look at the others." She arranged all of the test sheets together.

Zach read them out. "Clint: 1230 first test, 1560 second test. Burt: 1080 first test, 1500 second test. Vince: 1120 first test, 1530 second test. Millie: 1110 first test, 1550 the second *and* she aced the English portion. That's one great tutoring program."

"*None* of them bragged about these test results." Kay tapped the sheets with her finger. "Look, the results went out two weeks after the test. Early November. Why wouldn't Burt and Millie have shouted it to the world?"

"Maybe you just don't remember. You did say that you and Rick were going hot and heavy, which is what I remember. You know, I was there too. Though Rick had sort of pushed me out as a friend at the start of the year."

"I want a copy of these tests."

Once in the main office again, Zach looked over his shoulder nervously. "This is where we're most likely to get caught."

Kay was already taking out her dimes and putting the test results on the copy machine. Fifteen minutes later they were done and leaving the office with the copies securely folded in Kay's purse. Once they were safely in Zach's car, they both relaxed and gave each other a big smile.

"What do you think is going on?" Zach asked as they headed back to his place.

"These test scores are hinky."

"I have to agree with you."

"Stop!" Her voice loud and commanding, Kay was pointing at a Majik Market store.

"What?" Zach said, confused.

"The phone. I want to call Jerome."

Zach pulled into the lot and parked on the side of the

store near the four payphones. A young man was leaning on his bike by the phone farthest from the store's door.

"I'm waiting on a call," he said, moving toward the phone possessively as Kay approached.

Another phone's receiver was ripped off. The third had a quarter stuck in it. The last phone seemed to work, but Kay growled to herself when she realized she didn't have Jerome's number and the phone books were all torn up. Muttering curse words, she used a quarter to call home so she could get Jerome's number.

"When are you coming back?" Lee asked.

Kay gave him a rundown of her morning's activities. "I want to see if Jerome can help me find out more about the tests."

"You're dogging it, I'll give you that," Lee said admiringly. "Any chance you'd be willing to help out with the viewing tonight?"

"I guess."

"I think we're going to have a big crowd. Having you here would be a huge help," Lee said.

She agreed to be back by five and Lee gave her Jerome's number. After a quick explanation of what she'd been up to, Jerome told her to come on by.

"Would you mind making one more stop?" Kay asked Zach as she got back into his car.

Jerome lived in the older, historically black section of Lang. His house was made of cinderblock and painted dark green with yellow shutters. The garage door was open and Kay could see an old Plymouth parked next to Jerome's motorcycle.

Jerome came out and met them on the stoop.

"Some paint job, ain't it? Grandma loved green and yellow. I'm too lazy to repaint it."

"Zachary Terrill," Zach said, sticking out his hand.

"Your parents must have thought you were going to be a movie star with a name like that," Jerome said, shaking his hand. "Hey, I know you. You play on the county's baseball team. We beat the crap out of you all last year."

"I remember. I was sore for two days."

Kay explained why they were there.

"And you want me to do what, exactly?" Jerome asked.

"Call the testing center and see what you can find out about the day of the second test. Like maybe who the proctors were?"

"Proctors?"

"The people who hand out the tests and make sure no one is cheating."

"The odds of that…" Jerome shook his head. "You really think someone cheated?"

"Yes. Or at least I think something weird went on with the test." She took the results out of her purse. "See? These are their first tests and these are the second set."

"They did better. So what?"

"These are the types of scores that get you into Ivy League schools." She paused and added, "That *did* get them into Ivy League schools."

"Okay, I kinda see where you're going with this."

"I think this is what ties them all together."

Jerome sighed. "I need to go to the office to make the call."

"I'll pay for the long-distance charges," Kay told him.

"If the testing center isn't run by idiots, they're gonna want to call me back to make sure I'm really a deputy."

"Oh."

"Follow me over there."

At the sheriff's office, they followed Jerome into the building. The department only had twenty full-time officers, including six investigators. Not being one of the investigators, the only personal space Jerome had in the office was a locker in the back.

"Martin won't mind if I use his desk," Jerome said, leading them back to the small space where the investigators worked. There was only one deputy sitting at a desk and he gave Jerome a nod as they walked over to a surprisingly neat desk.

"We have to log all long-distance calls," Jerome said, pulling out a notebook. It took a call to a long-distance operator to get the number of the testing center. When he finally got through and explained what he wanted, the woman on the other end told him she'd have a supervisor call him back. "It could be later this afternoon," she warned.

"You heard the lady," Jerome said, hanging up the phone. "I'll let you know if I hear anything before tonight."

"Tonight?"

"I told your brother I'd work the front drive. I traded shifts with one of the other deputies."

Feeling let down, Kay let Zach drive her back to his house.

"You did great," Zach told her as they got out of the car.

"Who would kill Rick just because he cheated on a test?" she asked.

"Someone he beat out of a job. Maybe that's who he was running from," Zach suggested. Kay had filled him in on most of what they knew so far.

"I hadn't thought about that." Kay began to see a couple of directions this new information about the tests could take the investigation. "Maybe someone has been after them. That's why Clint killed himself, and the person might have put enough pressure on Lewis that he had a heart attack." Kay was warming to the idea. "But who?"

"I don't know, but I think you're on the right track for solving the why." Zach reached out and touched her hand as they stood beside her car.

"We aren't going to solve it right now. I need to get back to the funeral home." She squeezed his hand and gave him a smile. "Thanks for what you did today."

CHAPTER TWENTY-FIVE

"Which would you like—the viewing room or the front door?" Lee asked Kay, who was looking at him with narrowed eyes.

"If I have a choice, I guess I'll take the viewing room. That will give me a chance to see everyone when they come up to the coffin."

"Don't get so wrapped up in playing detective that you don't work the room."

"What do you mean, 'work the room?'"

"Come on, you have to remember some of this. Keep an eye on everyone in the room. If someone looks like they're going to collapse, or worse, looks like they're going to attack one of the other visitors, intervene. Hand out tissues and let people know where the water and lemonade are. The lemonade is very important in case someone feels like their blood sugar needs a boost. At almost every viewing or funeral, someone starts to fall out."

"Low blood sugar, lemonade, got it. Do I need to remind

you that I'm an RN?"

"Which is a bonus. Remember when Dad had two people die at one funeral?"

Kay smiled in spite of herself. "I'd forgotten about that. Dad was worried that folks would think he was purposefully knocking off old people for his business. One had a heart attack and the other was a stroke, I think." Kay had been mortified that the incident had been newsy enough that even the kids in her middle school class were talking about it.

"Lester and I will split front door duties."

"The place looks nice. You've done a good job for Rick's family."

"Thanks, but it's not all me. For all of her crazy, Ruby is really good at cleaning."

"And cooking," Lester said, coming up behind them with a saucer-size chocolate chip cookie in his hand.

"Don't get crumbs on the floor," Lee told him.

"Jerome said he'd be here too," Kay mentioned.

"He'll be acting as crossing guard. Mitchell, the guy who owns the shopping center across the street, lets us use the parking lot for large viewings and funerals."

"How much does he charge?" Kay asked.

"No money changes hands," Lee said shiftily, avoiding Kay's eyes.

"What are you hiding?"

Lee sighed. "You'll find out when you look at all the receipts anyway. Mitchell has several friends—friends of the female persuasion and friends that his wife doesn't know about. Sometimes he likes to buy them gifts. When the gifts are flowers, I let him call the orders into our account at the florist and he pays me back in cash when the bill comes in. On occasion, I've let him charge other gifts."

"So he can fool around on his wife?" Kay felt her face flush with outrage.

"That's a lot of parking. Without it we'd be in a bind."

"Why don't you do whatever Dad did?"

Lee looked down at the floor. As his silence lingered, Kay understood the truth. "Great! My father was enabling a womanizer."

"They were friends from way back," Lee said in a small voice, knowing it was a feeble excuse.

"Totally unacceptable." Kay paused. "Even if we have no choice."

"So what's that mean?"

"It doesn't matter, 'cause we're selling the place as soon as we get someone arrested for Rick's murder." Her words were clipped and her irritation clear.

Lee wanted to say more in their father's defense. *Let it go*, he told himself. *I don't want to get her even more pissed off.*

Todd, Edgar and Pearl Bruhn arrived at four-thirty for the viewing, which was to start at five. Lee led them into the viewing room where Rick was now laid out in the coffin that Todd had chosen.

"It's nice," Pearl said, putting her hand on the mahogany casket. Her eyes were drawn to her son, who looked comfortable in his repose. She turned to Lee, who had stepped back to allow the parents one last moment alone with their son before the guests began to arrive. "I am grateful for what you've done for my son. The thought that he might have been buried without anyone knowing that he was murdered is mortifying. You've given us a chance to get the evil person who did this." There was grit in her words and her eyes sparkled with tears.

Lee stepped forward. "I just hope that we can make his killer regret the day he decided to harm your son and your family."

Lee made sure they knew where the restroom was and told them to let Kay know if they needed anything, then he headed for his post at the front door. Lester was already there as backup. One of his father's cardinal rules had been to always have someone at the front door during a viewing or funeral to direct people and answer questions. "You never want someone to enter the funeral home and feel lost," he'd told Lee.

Meanwhile, Kay observed the three Bruhns as they waited for the guests to arrive. Todd looked nervous and would occasionally glance over at Kay. She wondered if he was just uncomfortable with funerals, or whether it was knowing that Kay and Lee were aware of his precarious financial situation. He struck Kay as a man with a lot of pride, pride that would be unsustainable under the scrutiny of people who knew he was a failure, at least financially.

Old friends of the Bruhns began to arrive, including the neighbors that Kay had talked to after the murder. She thought about the neighbors and their eyewitness accounts. They'd mentioned a woman in a sports car. Could that have been Millie?

Kay was overwhelmed with all the questions that they still didn't have answers to so, in an effort not think about them, she tried to observe and serve. Women and men needed Kleenex, directions to the restroom or information about the funeral and the graveside service. As more people arrived, Kay became lost in her duties as hostess. And, as a nurse, she kept a close eye on Pearl and Edgar.

At six o'clock, Millie made a grand entrance with Burt and Vince flanking her.

"I can't believe that Rick is lying here in his coffin," she said loudly enough for everyone in the room to hear. A number of guests had turned to watch her anyway since she was a well-known author, their own homegrown celebrity. The Bruhns seemed as enthralled with her as the other mourners.

Maybe she's a good distraction, Kay thought. The Bruhns had hugged and shaken hands with so many people that if Millie could take some of the pressure off of them, that wasn't a bad thing.

"Your brother is good at what he does."

Kay turned to see Chester Madison standing beside her.

"He learned from the best," she said, noticing the pride in her words. Her father had been a very good mortician and people had been comforted by the work that he'd done. She didn't know why it had taken her this long to realize that she was proud of her dad. *Even if he had some suspect practices when it came to womanizing friends*, she couldn't help thinking.

"Men should do what they do best. Rick was a great salesman. I was glad that I could give him a stage on which he could demonstrate his talents." As he spoke, Madison looked at Rick.

Tracy Peters arrived and, after giving her condolences to the Bruhns, went straight to the coffin. Kay was glad to see that she was wearing a full set of clothes. Noticing the tears streaming down Tracy's face, Kay moved over to her and handed her a Kleenex.

"Thank you. I… I didn't know Rick as well as Clint or the others. But being here so soon after standing by Clint's casket… it's a lot to deal with."

"That's understandable," Kay said gently. "Would you like to get a drink?"

"I would." Tracy was trembling as she spoke.

Kay guided her into the kitchen where Ruby was getting coffee ready to refill the pot in the hallway.

"Ruby, would you take over in the viewing room for a bit?" Lee had told Kay that Ruby could spell her off if she needed a break.

"Sure, right after I refresh the coffee." Ruby headed out with the new pot.

Kay poured two fingers of whiskey into a glass for Tracy and handed it to her.

"I should have taken a little toke before coming here," Tracy said, miming a smoke.

"I'm glad you came. I'm sure that the Bruhns appreciate it."

"I met them a few times. When we first got married, Clint and Rick got together any time Rick was in town and we'd make the rounds on holidays. A couple Fourth of Julys, we hung out at their pool and had a cookout. Nice people. Like Rick."

"I know we talked about some of the things that Clint was working on at the time of his death. Did you think of anything else that might have… depressed him?" Kay asked.

"After you came by, I looked into some of his cases. Clint was all about his work. His life consisted of me and his law business. Anyway, I called up some of his clients and just… you know, talked to them. Do you remember the professor I told you about? The one they caught for plagiarizing her master's dissertation?"

"You said Clint lost the case."

"Exactly, so I was nervous about calling her, but I got my nerve up and did it. I thought she might be mad that he'd lost her case. Instead she was so kind. Said that she'd been upset when she heard he'd died. She went on to tell me that, after her case was decided, Clint called her and told her how sorry he was. I didn't even know this, but he told her he wasn't going to charge her for his services. I looked in his records and she's right— he'd made a notation that the case was pro bono."

"Did he ever say anything about the way he got into college?"

"What do you mean?" Tracy looked confused.

"His grades? Tests? That sort of thing."

"Clint was very proud that he went to Yale. Without the partial scholarship, I don't think he would have been able to go."

"You know he did really well on his SAT?"

"That makes sense. I mean, to get into Yale without being a legacy."

"Did you see anything odd the night that Lewis died?"

Kay's change of topic surprised Tracy. "Like what?"

"I don't know. Anything. Like someone you thought was acting funny. Or something out of place. I'm just curious if there was a sign that he was going to have a heart attack."

"I'm not the best person to ask. My anxiety was through the roof that night. I didn't know how I was going to feel, seeing all of them again after Rick's death." Tracy shrugged and looked down at the inch of amber whiskey still in her glass before flipping it up and drinking it.

"Can you describe how they were all acting?"

"I don't know what you're getting at. Was Lewis killed too?"

"He died of a heart attack," Kay said, evading the question.

Tracy thought for a moment. "Nothing unusual. Millie was the center of attention, as always. She wouldn't have it any other way. Maybe she focused a little more on Lewis than normal. Typically, he was the one following her around like a lost lamb."

"I heard that Millie and Lewis used to have a thing between them."

"Millie toyed with him. Look, you probably shouldn't take what I say about Millie too seriously. I didn't like her from the first time I met her, but that's not her fault. If I'm being honest, she's never done anything bad to me. I just always felt like she flirted with Clint, but she flirts with anyone wearing pants. It was a nice gesture on her part, inviting me to meet up with them. It gave me a chance to uncover some feelings I've kept buried since Clint's death."

"What about Vince or Burt?"

"Those two? If Lewis followed Millie around like a lamb, then they followed her around like acolytes. I think they'd do anything for her."

"Did you notice Todd Bruhn at the bar?"

"Who?"

"Rick's uncle."

"I've never met the man," Tracy said.

"Did anyone else come up to the table or approach Lewis?"

"No."

Suddenly the kitchen door opened and Millie stood in the doorway, staring at them accusingly.

"I heard you talking about me. And I've seen the way you've been watching me, Kay. What are you thinking? Are you still upset about Rick kissing me in high school?"

"No. I'm just looking into the murder of my friend," Kay said.

"He was my friend too!" Millie said loudly. She was breathing hard enough that Kay could smell alcohol on Millie's breath.

Before Kay could say anything else, Lee came up behind Millie.

"Ladies," he said, almost pushing Millie into the kitchen so he could close the door. "We can hear you in the viewing room."

"I feel like I'm being accused of something and not being given a chance to defend myself."

"No one is accusing anyone. Yet," Kay said.

"So we can all calm down now." Lee didn't want a full-blown cat fight breaking out during the viewing.

"We can talk after the viewing," Kay offered.

Millie considered this for a moment before nodding. "Good. As soon as everyone leaves, let's get it all out in the open." She pirouetted and left the kitchen.

"You think that's wise?" Lee asked Kay, clearly skeptical.

"What else was I going to say?" Kay said.

Lee shook his head and headed back toward the front door.

Kay looked at Tracy, who had been standing to the side and trying to stay out of the fray. "Can you remember anything else about that night at the Forty-eight?"

"Not really. Like I said, I was in a fog, what with meeting everybody again six months after Clint's funeral. My eyes were even playing tricks on me."

"Your eyes?"

"Seriously, for a moment I thought I saw smoke coming out of Millie's purse. Weird."

"Oh, yeah, the waitress told us you mentioned it to her."

"No, I didn't." Tracy sounded surprised.

Kay shook her head, trying to make sense of the new information. "Okay, that *is* strange. Two people thought that Millie's purse was on fire."

"The smoke or whatever I saw was just fleeting. There one minute, but when I looked more closely it was gone. There were a lot of people smoking in the bar, so I decided it was just a fluke of the air currents."

"Guess that makes sense." Kay wasn't convinced.

"I better go back out front." Tracy moved toward the door. "We don't want Millie storming in here again."

By nine o'clock the visitors had dwindled to a handful and Pearl and Edgar were exhausted. Lee decided to start encouraging the last of the mourners to leave. His father had told him that the bereaved would often find it hard to ask people to leave, even when they'd clearly had enough. Gentle encouragement usually would serve to help bring the event to a dignified and timely end.

When he went to the front door with the Bruhns, he saw Millie waiting in the shadows of the front porch. Kay stepped forward and politely told Pearl and Edgar goodbye. Lee watched as Jerome, his duties as a crossing guard finished, escorted the Bruhns to their car in one of the reserved spots in the funeral home's driveway.

"I want to know what your sister thinks she's doing?" Millie growled at Lee as soon as the Bruhns were out of earshot.

"You know what Kay's doing. She's looking into Rick's murder."

"She's not a cop."

"I am," Jerome said from the bottom of the porch steps.

"I'm going to talk to the sheriff about this."

"Be my guest." Jerome uttered a harsh laugh.

"Let's go inside. No sense in standing on the front porch and arguing," Lee told them.

Kay had just finished closing Rick's casket and turning off the lights in the viewing room when she saw them enter the front hall. Before she got to the door, Jerome came into the viewing room and shut the door behind him.

"I need to talk to you," he said. "I got some information from the testing center."

"Let me guess: Lewis Watts was a proctor that October."

"Bingo, ringo. And the only names I recognized on the test roster were our five friends. Ten other people and none of them are from around here. At least not that I've ever heard of."

"If the test was in Gainesville, they might not be local to Lang."

"The test was given at the school."

"Melon County High?"

"That's what was on the paperwork."

"Surely there was more than one proctor."

"Funny about that too. There are two other people listed and, as far as I can tell, they never existed."

"Damn. They faked the test."

"There was a lot of work involved. Lots of faking with the other proctors sending in paperwork that imaginary people don't usually have."

"Wow. This is all beginning to make—"

There was a knock and Lee opened the door. "You need to come talk to Millie. She's getting hotter by the minute."

"Okay." Kay looked at Jerome.

"Just play it cool," he suggested.

Lee ushered them all into his office, where Kay positioned herself between Lee and Jerome. "Where are Vince and Burt?" she asked.

"We don't need them here." Millie's tone was dismissive.

"Y'all seemed attached at the hip earlier," Kay observed.

Lee watched them both, hoping that this didn't turn into a women's roller derby match.

"There!" Millie pointed at Kay. "That's the snarky, accusatory attitude I'm talking about. Just say it!"

"What?"

"You know what. You have some crazy idea that I killed Rick."

"We're just looking—" Lee started.

"Shut up!" Millie put her hand in his face.

Jerome's smile suggested he was enjoying the fireworks.

"I think you're involved in… something," Kay said, trying to stare Millie down.

"You don't know what you're talking about," Millie told her. "I haven't done anything wrong. If you force me to, I'll get my lawyer in here to prove it to you."

"It's always the guilty person who whips out the lawyer." Kay's blood was beginning to boil, though her boiling point was admittedly low when it came to Millie.

"There we go. Come on, say it!" Millie prodded.

"Did you do it?" Kay snarled

"No! What motive could I have?"

"Cheater."

As soon as the word left her mouth, Kay regretted it. She knew in her heart that the best strategy would have been to keep that information under wraps for the moment. She had a split second to hope that Millie wouldn't know what she was referring to, but the shocked look on the other woman's face told everyone in the room that a nerve had been touched with a red-hot poker.

For a second, Millie was at a loss for words, then her eyes became icy and fierce. "If you think I'm going to back down now… you'll find out just how wrong you are."

Without waiting for a response, she turned on her heel and jerked the door open, stalking out of the office. The other three stood there stunned, listening to the front door open and then slam with such a bang that they expected the glass in the door to shatter. Then there was silence.

CHAPTER TWENTY-SIX

"Not to be overly critical, but you probably should have kept that last bit under wraps." Jerome smiled ruefully.

"What was all that about?" Lee asked.

Kay hadn't had time to fill Lee in on everything she and Zach had found at the school, nor had Jerome told him about the information he'd learned about the exam.

"We have a clear motive for Millie," Kay told him.

"They were doing some serious cheating," Jerome added.

"Cheating?"

"On their SATs," Kay said, and went on to explain the rest.

"No one kills someone 'cause they cheated on a test." Lee frowned.

"They do if it means their whole lives will come tumbling down," Kay said.

"Just because of one test?"

"They all live in a house of cards built on the foundation of those test results. Each of the five got into Ivy League schools on the strength of those scores. I'm pretty sure there was a little fudging of their grades too, which wouldn't have been hard for Lewis Watts."

"Wouldn't someone have found out?"

"They were all good students. Personable and well-liked. The second set of grades were upgraded just enough, and none of them made a big deal about it. No bragging or showing the results around. The only other people who saw those results were the folks at the SAT and the college entrance boards. If any of them had called up the school, they would have been referred to the students' counselor."

"Lewis Watts," Lee said, nodding. "But why would he stick his neck out like that?"

"He was young, Millie was flirting, maybe some money even traded hands," Jerome suggested.

"We've learned he had a heart condition too. That might have made him a little more cavalier."

"Yeah, life is short. I can see that," Lee agreed. "But it's been years. Why now? And why Rick?"

"I've been thinking about that," Kay said. "Clint had a case he was handling for a professor who had plagiarized part of her Master's thesis. Not even her doctoral, just her Master's, but the university was terminating her. He lost the case just before his suicide. I think that seeing her take the fall made him feel guilty for having cheated and gotten away with it. There he was, watching a client go down for something that was no worse than what he did. Clint was a good guy at heart. He was married to a Mother-Earth-type and spent a lot of time with people who literally let it all hang out. Knowing he was a fraud had to have eaten at him."

"I can see how it could isolate a man from his friends and family. I guess he really only had the old gang," Lee said.

"I don't know how he originally got conned into participating in the big cheat. Maybe he was just young. But once he went to Yale, there was no turning back."

"I see it every day, man," Jerome said. "Good people talk themselves into doing bad things by telling themselves that they'll make it right, or that they'll do so much good that it will make up for it. My grandma always told me, 'sin never grows nothin' good.'"

"Wise woman." Kay smiled.

"That still doesn't get us to Rick," Lee argued.

"I'm just guessing, but Rick must have been able to put two and two together and figure out why Clint killed himself. I imagine he'd been stewing on it for the last six months, until finally he decided to do something about it."

"What?"

Kay shrugged. "I don't know. Maybe he was going to come clean. Or he might have wanted to get *everyone* to agree to come clean. Or he might have just decided to give up his life that the lie had bought and start over somewhere else."

"But someone didn't want him to do it," Jerome said. "'Cause if he outed himself, that would have blown down everyone's house of cards."

"Exactly. The neighbors reported people coming by the Bruhn house last week while Rick was staying there. I bet it was the gang trying to reason with Rick," Kay said.

Lee whistled. "I'm beginning to see the implications. That's why he had the gun under the mattress."

"He might have already told one of them, or even all of them, and he was worried what they would do to stop him from destroying their cushy lives," Kay said.

"So the killer is either Millie, Vince or Burt," Lee reasoned.

"Millie." Kay was emphatic. "The other two just follow her lead."

"We'll have a better idea when we bring them in." Jerome didn't look happy. "They'll have some ugly good lawyers.

Arresting rich people isn't nearly as easy as putting poor people in jail."

"What if she skips town?" Lee asked.

"From the look on her face when you mentioned cheating, she's already on the road back to her home in Chapel Hill. No way I can stop her. We don't have a single piece of hard evidence. Maybe we'll get lucky with some of the items we took from the house. All we'll need is a fingerprint on the pump or one of the possible murder weapons."

"She probably wore gloves." Kay frowned. "Lewis's death still bothers me."

"You said that you and Zach didn't get any useful information at the bar," Lee reminded her.

"Unfortunately. Still…"

"Let's try to pin her down for one murder for now, shall we?" Jerome said.

They agreed, then joined Ruby and Lester in the kitchen.

"A woman scorned," Ruby said, putting a platter of cinnamon toast on the table.

"By who?" Kay was more than a little puzzled by the comment.

"Fate, dear. She has been cast aside by fate. The viewing room was done up very nicely," she told Lee with a smile.

"Lester helped arrange the flowers." Lee gave credit where credit was due.

"There were so many, it wasn't easy to make it look right," Lester said, taking several pieces of toast onto his plate. "So when are you going to arrest her?" Even Lester had noticed where their suspicions lay.

"I keep tellin' everyone that I need evidence. We don't even have enough for a search warrant on her car," Jerome complained.

"So we got a killer on the loose." Lester munched away at

his toast.

"Means, motive and opportunity," Jerome said. "We got the motive. I bet if she had an alibi she would have produced it tonight, so I'll click off the opportunity box. He probably would have let her into the house, and she's certainly strong enough to have clouted Rick on the head, so we'll give her the means too. All we're missing is the evidence."

"What's the next step?" Kay asked him.

"I'll bring in the two weak links and see if I can get either one of them to squeal on Millie or each other. Shouldn't be that hard. First one who talks gets the best deal that the State Attorney can offer."

They chatted a little longer, discussing their roles and responsibilities for the funeral on Wednesday. It was scheduled for ten o'clock at the First Baptist Church, the only venue in Lang that was big enough for the expected crowd. The graveside service would be at noon in the Lang City Cemetery.

Once alone in her room, Kay settled down on her bed with the second book in the Parker Family mysteries, *The Corpse in the Laboratory*. She tried to get into the story, but the real life murder mystery she was living preoccupied her mind.

How crazy is Millie? she wondered. Had she killed Rick or had she gotten one of the others to do it for her? All three of them were at risk of having their current lives destroyed by the revelation that their careers had been built on a foundation of lies. It was possible that the universities would revoke their degrees. With Millie, it would be worse. Her books were currently a minor media sensation and, no doubt, a feeding frenzy of talking heads would be willing to devour her.

Kay knew she wasn't going to come up with any answers

tonight. Sighing, she marked her place in the book and set it on the nightstand before turning off the light. She pushed all her cares far away until sleep finally came.

Kay found herself back in a hospital north of Saigon where she had worked for a couple of weeks. A young man from Alabama was lying on a hospital bed that she was trying to adjust. She was frustrated that the crank on the bed wouldn't work, and worried that she would hurt the wounded soldier with her attempts to raise his head. Suddenly, an object came crashing through the window and hit her in the thigh.

"Grenade!" the soldier screamed.

Kay lurched up in bed and let out a shriek. The grenade was beside her in the bed. Frantically, she flung it away from her. Only then did she realize that she was in her own room and that someone was yelling outside.

"Fire! Fire!"

Kay looked over and saw the smashed window and the can on the floor that a frantic Ruby had thrown at her. Kay rushed over to the window and saw Ruby standing in the driveway, smoke billowing around her.

"There's a fire. Get out!" Ruby yelled.

Kay rushed to her door and almost opened it before remembering some of her training. She paused and put her hand against the wood. No heat. She opened it and rushed into the hallway.

"Fire!" she yelled as she ran to Lee's room. She pounded on the door, then flung it open. "Get up! There's a fire."

"What?" Lee said groggily, rolling out of bed. "Where?"

"Back door I think. Let's go," Kay ordered.

Lee got up and slipped on a pair of shoes, then followed her out the door in his pajama bottoms.

"Is Lester here?" she asked, remembering that he occasionally spent the night.

"No. I've got to get Rick's body out," Lee said as they hurried down the stairs. They could smell smoke now.

"Let's get outside and assess the situation first," Kay told him, tugging hard at his arm as he started to veer toward the viewing room.

Before they got to the front door, they could see the glow of flames through the glass panels of the door.

"There's a fire at the front door too. We need to go out a window," Kay said.

"The office window is the easiest," Lee said, heading that way.

"I know. I used to sneak out that way." Kay was on his heels.

They both scrambled out the window, then Kay closed it behind her. "Try to keep the oxygen as low as possible in the house."

They ran around to the back door where Ruby was already using the hose to throw water at the flames as they spread across the back porch.

"I called the fire department," she said at the same time that Kay heard the sound of sirens in the distance. "There's someone in a car across the street. They're up close to the building. I could see them from my apartment."

"This is Millie's work," Kay growled. She looked down to see that she was wearing a long T-shirt that fell to her knees. What surprised her was that she had the leather strap of her purse slung over her arm. She must have grabbed it as she left her bedroom. Reaching into the purse, she pulled out her keys.

"Put the fire out," she said over her shoulder to Lee and Ruby as she jumped into her car.

Without a plan, she started the car and roared down the driveway. Just as she reached the street, she saw a Mustang spin out of the shopping center's parking lot. Kay followed it and, within seconds, both cars were roaring past the fire engines headed toward the funeral home. *This is crazy. You're an idiot*, was the refrain playing over and over in Kay's head as she pushed down harder on the accelerator.

A motorcycle flashed past, following the fire engines. As soon as it went by, she knew it was Jerome. Luckily, it was four in the morning and there was no traffic. Checking her rearview mirror, she saw a single headlight gaining on her as she tried to keep the rear lights of Millie's car in sight. She prayed that Jerome had turned when he saw her.

The sports car slowed for a turn and, in a moment of inspiration, Kay knew where Millie was headed. Kay slowed down and made the turn behind Millie, who roared off as soon as she was clear of the ditch.

Kay checked her rearview mirror to make sure that the motorcycle had followed her, then rolled down her window and waved to Jerome. He came up beside her as she drove, still trying to keep up with Millie.

"She's going to the school!" Kay yelled to the black visor, the wind whipping her words away. "School! School!"

The visor nodded and the motorcycle accelerated around her. At the next opportunity, Jerome turned off the main road and Kay hoped he was taking a shortcut. She pressed on the gas, trying to get close to Millie again.

Soon she could see the school coming up on the left. Millie's Mustang began to slow, but she still took the turn into the driveway too fast. The rear end of the sports car skidded around and Kay had to slam on her brakes as pieces of the school's chain-link gate flew over the back of Millie's car.

Kay saw Jerome standing next to his motorcycle in the middle of the driveway. Kay expected Millie's car to stop, but instead she made a small adjustment and veered away from the main building to squeeze her car down a covered walkway that led to a central courtyard. The pillars of the walkway were too close together for Kay's car, so she slammed on the brakes.

Jerome came up beside her as she jumped out of the car.

"She's insane!" To Kay, it sounded like Jerome had some admiration for Millie's lack of sense.

"She tried to burn down the funeral home."

"I know. I heard it on my scanner."

"You could have brought a patrol car."

"You got to be kidding me. In one of those old things, I'd still be ten blocks away. Stay here." He held his left arm out to bar her way as he started down the walkway. Kay fell back a couple of steps, but continued to follow him.

"I can't hear her car anymore," Kay said.

"Stopped in the courtyard. I told you to stay back! She's probably armed."

"I bet she plans on burning the whole place down."

"So stay back!" Jerome insisted.

"I blew it when I let her know we knew about the cheating. She doesn't care about being charged with murder. It's the humiliation and loss of her status. I pretty much let her know that she hasn't got anything to lose at this point."

"Great." Jerome's sarcastic comment was delivered in a hoarse whisper as they approached the courtyard. "I don't see any flames or smoke yet. If you see smoke there's fire, so does it go the other way? If you don't see smoke, there isn't any fire. Damn it, I always babble when I'm nervous."

Kay felt the handgun in her purse. For a moment she thought about taking it out, but decided to leave it where it was.

"Hello!" Millie yelled. In the glow of the lone security light, they could see that she was standing on the far side of her car. "Good. I hope you get blown to bits when I light this off."

"It's over," Kay called. "We know you killed Rick and we know why."

"Exactly why I want us all to go up in a big ball of flame."

"Clint couldn't take the guilt, could he?"

"Mr. Goody Two-Shoes. Of course not. I should have known back in high school that he didn't belong with the real winners."

"So he killed himself and then Rick grew a conscience."

"Blah, blah, blah. I told Rick to just give it some time. 'I'm feeling guilty,' he whined. I should have let you have him. Men can be such crybabies. I even tried the argument that Clint would have died for nothing if Rick outed all of us. The fool wasn't having any of it. All of us talked to him. In the end, I didn't have a choice. I had to kill him."

"Give yourself up, and I'll work a deal with you," Jerome yelled.

"I'm not some idiot off the streets. Only the State Attorney can work a deal."

"I'll get whatever you need."

"I need a time machine. You can't offer me anything because none of us can put the genie back in the bottle. All I ever wanted was to be a bestselling author. To hang with the big boys. Be on those stupid morning TV shows. Now… I don't want them spending the next year spitting on me while I rot in some jail. They aren't any better than I am."

Kay was thinking about Lewis. If she got the chance, she wanted to ask Millie about him. Something Jerome had said was nagging at her. Fire and smoke.

"Hey, don't they say there's no such thing as bad publicity?" Jerome tried to make it sound like a joke, but yelling across the courtyard wasn't conducive to light jests.

"Kay, I'm not a bad person. I just wanted to be successful and to help my friends. But now I've got fifteen gallons of gas in the back of this car. I've already opened the cans. The windows are closed except for a small crack. When I flick my Bic, car parts are going to go flying. Run while you can."

Smoke, that was the clue. She remembered the title of the fifth book in the Parker Family series, *Ice Cold Death*, and everything fell into place.

"I know how you killed Lewis!" Kay yelled. Jerome frowned at her.

"Bullshit!" Millie yelled back. They could hear the hysteria rising in her voice.

"I bet I do," Kay challenged.

"No way."

"Make a deal."

"What?"

"If I give you the right answer, then you don't do this."

"And if you don't know the answer?"

"Then no matter what happens, we bury the part about you all cheating on the test. You're still a killer, but we'll come up with a different motive."

"How are you going to keep it a secret?"

"Only Jerome, Lee and I know about the cheating," Kay lied.

"How do I know I can believe you?"

"How do I know I can believe *you*?"

"You got a point."

"The nurses I was stationed with in Saigon had an honor code that we lived by. We called it Bitch's Honor. If you declared it, you couldn't break it. No matter what."

"Ha! I never trusted other women."

Kay figured that was true. Millie liked to work with men, the weaker sex. The ones she could control.

"We go way back. I think we can trust each other." *Not for a minute*, Kay thought, but this was the only plan she had.

"Fair enough. If we are going to trust each other, I want this face to face."

"I'll come halfway," Kay offered.

"No. I'm not leaving the car. Mmmm, I can smell the gas fumes," Millie taunted.

"Then Jerome comes with me." Kay looked over at Jerome, who was shaking his head fiercely.

"Sure, we'll make it a party."

"What do you think you're doing?" Jerome asked Kay in a harsh whisper.

"We go out there, you might get an opening."

"That car blows up and we'll all have a lot of openings," he hissed.

Kay stepped out from the corner of the building where she and Jerome had been crouching.

"We're coming over," she said as Jerome reluctantly stood up beside her. He stuffed his .38 Colt Police Positive revolver in the small of his back and they walked halfway to the car. Kay figured they were about twenty feet away.

"That's close enough," Millie said. "Let's hear what you've got, hotshot."

Kay had let Jerome get about a foot ahead of her while she slid over so that she was partly behind him. "You froze digitalis or some other stimulant in an ice cube and slipped it into Lewis's drink."

"Now how would I have gotten the ice cube into the bar and dropped it in Lewis's glass without it melting?" Millie was trying to bluff, but Kay could tell from the tremble in her voice that she was on the right track.

"That was the clever part. But it was too clever. Once I figured out what was smoking in your purse, I knew what you'd done. You used dry ice. That wasn't smoke that Tracy and another woman saw coming from your purse, it was the carbon dioxide vaporizing. All I had to do was ask myself why you would have dry ice in your purse."

"You're too smart for your own good." Millie's voice was frigid with hate.

As soon as Kay heard the tone of her words, she knew what Millie was going to do. So she implemented the crazier part of her plan. Without letting herself think about what she was doing, Kay reached over and pulled Jerome's revolver out of his pants. She pointed it at the car and blasted all the windows out of it while Jerome screamed words she didn't hear and Millie tried to get her lighter lit.

Jerome was still screaming as he ran forward and knocked Millie to the ground. Kay went over and helped him subdue her.

"What was that crazy shit?" Jerome yelled while he held the struggling Millie down.

"I figured I could shoot out the windows and clear out the vapors." Kay was sitting on Millie's legs while Jerome struggled to get his handcuffs out of his back pocket.

"That was my gun! What if it had caused the car to explode?" Jerome was still shouting.

"As long as the bullets just passed through the glass, it would be fine. Besides, I went to school with her and saw her light her cigarettes a million times. Never once did she ever get her lighter lit on the first try," Kay said, not knowing if that was true or not.

"Crazy!" Jerome muttered. To Millie he said, "And you are just…" He ran through a number of curse words in his head and decided to settle for "screwed." He pulled her up off the ground.

"I'll sue you."

"Good luck with that," Jerome told her. "Whatever you're going to do, you're going to do from jail. I will just tell you that you have the right to remain silent…" He went on reciting her Miranda rights while half pulling her toward the front of the school.

"I guess we'll be using my car," Kay said as they approached the car and motorcycle.

"Good guess. I need to get to a phone."

They heard sirens headed their way.

"I don't think you have to worry. Somebody must have reported the gunshots."

"I'm going to report you for being certifiable," Jerome told her.

Kay ignored him and asked Millie, "How much do Vince and Burt know?"

"Talk to my lawyer," was the only thing Millie would say.

CHAPTER TWENTY-SEVEN

At ten o'clock on Wednesday, Kay and Lee were dressed in their best black suits for the funeral of Rick Bruhn. They had gotten to the church an hour early and, with Lester and Jerome's help, set up the casket with Rick's body on a bier and arranged the flowers. When the Bruhns arrived, Kay met them at the door.

"We will always be grateful to you for catching Rick's killer," Edgar told her.

"I never dreamed…" Pearl shook her head and wiped at her eyes with a handkerchief. "Millie seemed like such a good friend to Rick. I can't understand it."

Todd Bruhn stood back and only came forward after Lee had escorted Pearl and Edgar into the church.

"I think Rick's only mistake was not holding on to you in high school," Todd said while shaking her hand.

Chester Madison arrived just before the service began and told Kay and Lee that he wanted to talk to them after the funeral.

After the service in the full church, almost everyone drove to the cemetery for the burial. Kay rode with Lee in the Cadillac hearse. Unlike Bertha, it still had a new-car smell.

"The guy from the insurance company is going to come tomorrow to inspect the damage to the funeral home," Lee said while following Jerome, who was in a patrol car providing an escort for the procession. "I guess you're going to get your way. We'll have to close down for a couple of weeks while the front and back entrances are repaired. If you're determined to sell, there isn't any reason to plan on reopening." Lee could already feel the loss. Closing the funeral home was going to be like losing another member of the family.

"When I took off after Millie in my car, I just wanted to catch her so badly I wasn't thinking about anything else."

"That was insane." Lee looked over at her.

"You're right, it was crazy. But then when Jerome had her handcuffed on the ground, I thought about the funeral home. I prayed that the fire engines had gotten there in time and that you'd been able to contain the fire. There was a pain in my heart when I thought that Lamberton Funeral Home, and all of my memories, might have been turned to ashes."

"I was worried about you chasing after that maniac. I'm grateful that Jerome caught up with you."

"What I'm trying to say is, I've changed my mind. I want us to try and save the funeral home," Kay said.

Lee looked at her. "Are you serious?"

"Eyes on the road." Kay smiled. "There are some conditions, of course. I'm going to run the business side of things."

"You're staying here?"

"Until we get the home running in the black. That means I'll be moving into my room, which is the other condition."

"Of course. When you say you're going to make the business turn a profit, that doesn't mean you're going to fire anyone, does it?"

"That bunch of hangers-on? I wouldn't have the heart. Which reminds me, I need my window fixed. That was a hell of throw Ruby made."

"She told me that Yin…" He thought for a minute. "Or maybe it was Yang… one of those fat cats woke her up. When she saw the place was on fire, she called the fire department. Lucky that Millie didn't know Ruby had her own telephone line when she cut the one to the funeral home. Anyway, Ruby told me she was on some sort of All American girls softball team or some such in high school, and she decided that the quickest way to get your attention was to hurl a can of mushroom soup through your window."

"Glad she didn't hit me on the head," Kay laughed as they pulled into the cemetery.

When the service was over, Chester Madison walked over to the hearse.

"Can we talk here?" he asked.

"Sure, we have to wait around and get the tent down and the chairs out of the way for the backhoe," Lee told him.

"My confidence in you all was warranted. I spoke with the State Attorney, who's been in touch with Deputy Parker. He's confident that they'll be able to bring indictments against Millie for both the murder of Rick and the murder of Lewis Watts."

"We didn't save your company any money," Kay apologized.

"In fact, you cost us an additional quarter of a million. We're going to have to pay out Lewis's policy since he didn't die of a heart attack. At least, not a natural heart attack. But don't worry about that. Millie has plenty of money, and our lawyers are already preparing a lawsuit against her for the cost of paying out the policies when she's proven to be the killer."

"I'm glad. I believe that you were a good friend to Rick." Kay gave him a broad smile.

"I just wish he'd confided in me. I wouldn't have cared about the exam he cheated on. We might have needed to lower his profile in the company, but I never would have abandoned him. I heard a rumor that you're going to sell the funeral home?"

Lee and Kay looked at each other. "We've changed our minds. I'm going to run the business side of things and Lee's going to run the funerary side."

"That sounds very wise, and it brings up an arrangement I'd like to make with you." He looked back and forth between them. "I'd like to make you a loan to get back on your feet."

Stunned, Kay didn't know how to respond. Finally, she said, "We can use the cash, but what type of interest rates are you talking?" She remembered seeing the prime rate at almost fourteen percent in the paper just a day earlier.

"A percentage point."

"What? There must be a catch." Kay looked hard at Madison.

"There is. We have almost a thousand life insurance policies in this area. Law enforcement has proven… inadequate. I would like you all to act as my eyes and ears and watch for suspicious deaths."

"Right now we aren't getting too much of the local business," Lee said regretfully, not believing that Madison really meant to bail them out.

"I'm confident that will change. I'll make sure that this affair will be reported very positively in the local papers. We'll also send out a flyer to everyone within a hundred-and-fifty miles that has a policy with us that we'll offset their funeral costs by twenty percent if they use your funeral home."

"Why are you doing all of this?" Kay asked.

"For the reason I told you… and because Rick was like a son to me. He loved you. You've done him, his family and me a great service. This is a small way for me do one last thing for him. I know he would have wanted me to do this for you."

They talked details for a few more minutes before Madison went on his way, promising to send the paperwork to them.

"With that money, we can make some improvements and have some working capital available." Kay was overwhelmed by the change in plans and the change in their luck.

"You realize that he's lined us up to play detective whenever he needs us," Lee reminded her.

"I'm not worried. How often is someone going to get killed in Melon County, Florida?" Kay asked with a smile.

Kay and Lee return in:

Gambling on death

A Mortician Murder Mystery–Book 2

Coming spring 2022!

ACKNOWLEDGMENTS

The idea for this new series owes a lot to my wife's own upbringing. When I first met my future father-in-law, he was the only funeral director in a small, North Florida town in the 1980s. My wife has vivid memories of playing hide-and-seek in the casket room, being driven to school in a hearse and being fascinated by the mysteries of the embalming room. I hope these memories add a little realism to this series about a challenging and often misunderstood profession.

Cover Design by Melody Barber
www.aurorapublicity.com

ABOUT THE AUTHOR

A. E. Howe lives and writes on a farm in the wilds of north Florida with his wife, horses and more cats than he can count. He received a degree in English Education from the University of Georgia and is a produced screenwriter and playwright. His first published book was *Broken State*. The Larry Macklin Mysteries is his first series and he released a second series, the Baron Blasko Mysteries, in summer 2018. The first book in the Macklin series, *November's Past*, was awarded two silver medals in the 2017 President's Book Awards, presented by the Florida Authors & Publishers Association; the ninth book, *July's Trials*, was awarded two silver medals in 2018. Howe is a member of the Mystery Writers of America, and was co-host of the "Guns of Hollywood" podcast for four years on the Firearms Radio Network. When not writing Howe enjoys riding, competitive shooting and working on the farm.

Made in United States
Troutdale, OR
01/21/2024

17040454R00181